The Dolphin

Susan Clegg

Published by Linen Press, London 2023
8 Maltings Lodge
Corney Reach Way
London W4 2TT
www.linen-press.com
© Susan Clegg 2023

A CIP catalogue record for this book is available from the British Library.

Cover Art: Unsplash
Cover Design: Lynn Michell and Zebedee
Typeset by Zebedee
Printed and bound by Lightning Source
ISBN: 978-1-7391777-4-4

For Lee, Anna and Frances

About the Author

Susan Clegg's varied career has included working in an art gallery, managing a Japanese restaurant, working for a tour operator bringing Japanese tourists to Europe, waitressing in the directors' dining rooms at a city stockbroker, head cashier at a well known London restaurant, and marketing for a law firm and for a training and coaching organisation.

Susan Clegg has short stories published in *Matter* and *The Stinging Fly*. She was Highly Commended in the Writers & Artists Killer Fiction competition and was selected to pitch to a panel of agents and publishers at the Bloody Scotland crime writing festival. In 2020, her story, *Dogwood*, was shortlisted for the V. S. Pritchett Short Story prize, earning this review from Derek Owusu: *'A story that turns the mundane into magic, sleight of hand sentences that the eyes can't help but follow.'* *The Dolphin* is her debut novel and was longlisted for the Mslexia prize.

Chapter 1

Larry
February 1937

The last house was finished and the workmen stood about in the front garden. Larry watched them from the bedroom windows as he made his final inspection. They were smoking and larking about, pushing each other to see who would slip first on the icy ground. Around them the raw red brick of the new estate was half-hidden and silenced by mist, the men the only things alive in the frozen afternoon.

Larry moved on. He was pleased with this house. It was on a corner plot, near the top of the hill, and he'd done the brickwork on the front porch himself. It had been good to get his hands dirty again. He'd taken his time over it, adding herringbone details and extra steps to make a smarter entrance. Inside, the door furniture and skirting boards were good quality, though that had just been a lucky chance at the builder's yard. Sometimes a few small differences were all it took for a house to sell for £30 more.

He went downstairs and into the back garden to check the house from the rear. Like the front, the ground was a mixture of muddy clay and rubble with a tangle of brambles at one side. He walked slowly to the far end. Soon the ground would be levelled and a smooth square of turf laid, topsoil poured to make flowerbeds and paving placed in a strip around the edge. The people who bought it would see neatness and order. If, like most of the people who bought these houses, they came from the old part of town, they would also see progress. That pleased him too.

As he started back up the garden, his boot kicked something sharp and he bent to pick up a piece of thick brown pottery. It happened with all the houses they built – pottery, clay pipes, glass bottles, sometimes animal bones. The debris from twenty, fifty, a hundred years before worked its way to the surface as the new houses went up. There had been a farm on this land before and the farmhouse itself still stood at the top of the hill, all its fields now sold and built on. But the change was only superficial, Larry thought. Underneath, the land was always the land. What it really was, what had been put into it, you couldn't always tell, but it would rise up in the end. He fingered the fragment, wondering what it used to be, then threw it back down and walked on.

He went through the house to the front garden. The men were still joking with each other and Larry went over to them and lit a cigarette.

'It's all right, that house, eh?' one of them said.

'You've done a good job, lads,' Larry said. 'You can get off to the pub now.'

A cheer went up and they jostled each other out of the gate.

'You coming, boss?' someone asked.

'Not this time. Paperwork to do.'

'See you then.'

'See you.'

Larry finished his cigarette and watched them go down the hill. The light was dimming and cold had seeped into his boots and through his coat. Part of him wanted to go with them, to be one of the lads in a bright, warm pub, and a while ago he would have done it. But he was the boss and there was too much to lose to let his guard slip after a few drinks. He threw the stub of his cigarette into the mud and went back into the house.

It was gloomy inside and it seemed smaller, more cramped than before. His pleasure in it faded as he searched for the files he had left somewhere and he felt suddenly hemmed in. For the last nine months he had seen nothing but bricks and walls and the gradual enclosure of earth and air. He was doing a good thing, he knew that. Building homes for people, getting them out of their old, shabby houses and into somewhere clean and modern was worthwhile work. Profitable too. But everything he did was governed by the width of a brick, the length of a plank, the size of a plot of land. It all had to fit – he had to fit – and increasingly, it bothered him.

The files were on the kitchen window sill. He picked them up, ready to leave. But in the darkening cold he paused for a moment. There were a few days of paperwork left and then he would be done with these houses. People would move in and add their own ideas of beauty and convenience. A mother would stand where he stood, cooking. A father would sit in the room beyond. Children would play in the garden. They would make the bricks into a home, happy or otherwise. He wondered if they would feel constricted too.

He woke just after midnight. Rosemary lay turned away from him, her back hunched and swaddled in the blankets, muttering in her dreams. For a few minutes he lay still, hoping to reclaim some sleep, but as always these days, nothing came. He sighed and eased himself out of bed.

In the bathroom he ran a glass of water and drank it down, his bare feet freezing on the lino. The mirror above the sink showed a pale, creased-looking version of himself. 'What's up with you then, Larry Lambert?' he said aloud. 'What's got into you lately?' He might as well have been asking a stranger. His own face, his own self, told him nothing.

As he stood at the sink, a cry came from one of children's rooms and he tensed, waiting for it to stop. It went on. No words, just a plaintive wail, one of Roy's nightmares again. He tiptoed to the door. Rosemary's rule on night-time waking was strict – no comfort to be given. Nothing that might encourage further waking. But perhaps he could soothe the boy without her knowing. He crossed the landing and slipped into Roy's bedroom.

He was sitting up in bed, hugging the blanket to his chest, his face ugly with crying.

'There, son, shush now. Quieten down.' Larry patted his head.

Roy's body shuddered with sobs and he reached out to clutch at Larry's leg. 'I had a bad dream, Daddy. I'm scared.'

'It's all right, Roy. Back to sleep now. Don't wake your mother.' This was Rosemary's department, Larry thought. She knew what to do with Roy and Joanie, when to be firm and when to soften. He was at a loss when it came to the needs of the children.

'Stay with me, Daddy,' Roy whimpered.

'You're too big for that, son. Go to sleep.'

'Daddy, please stay!'

Larry hesitated, then laid Roy back on his pillow and sat awkwardly on the bed. 'Just for a minute, hear?'

Roy immediately curled up against him, still holding his leg.

Larry leaned back against the headrest and closed his eyes. The fox cub warmth of Roy's body warmed his as he drifted into a doze. And as he sank further into sleep, he began to dream of the sea.

June 1937

How best to put it to Rosemary, Larry wondered. He was standing on the back step, listening to her bathing the children upstairs. The garden was still bright with sunlight and swallows swooped for insects over the pond. He watched them skim fast across the surface and then, just as their wing-tips seemed about to dip under, lift effortlessly into the air.

There were good reasons for a seaside holiday. Fresh air for Roy and Joanie; no time off for three years; a gap between finishing one lot of houses and starting the next; and the money coming in was good now, they could afford to spend some of it. This was what he would say to Rosemary, he thought. She would understand those reasons. And though she wouldn't like the fact that he'd already booked the hotel, well, it was done now and how else could he be sure he'd get there?

What he couldn't explain, not even to himself, was his need to go to the sea. He had no connection with it. This land-locked part of England between the Midlands and the North had nothing to remind him of it. Yet he dreamt of it every night now, and even when he was awake it was there when he closed his eyes for a moment, spooling behind his eyelids like a film reel. It was always the same. He saw himself plunging below the waves into the vast rooms of the sea and swimming, with eels and plaice, with dogfish and herring, lolling in green, sunlit water and feeling it stretch away from him to circle the world. A peaceful happiness suffused him while the pictures played out.

There was a shout from upstairs, 'I hate you, Roy!' He heard a door slam and the sound of stormy crying. Purposeful footsteps crossed the landing and Rosemary's voice cut sharply into the evening, 'That's enough from you tonight, young lady.'

Larry sighed. Joanie and Roy's spats were regular and tiresome, blowing up out of a stray word or accidental nudge. He headed towards the bottom of the garden, away from the arguing. Tonight, he would discuss the holiday with Rosemary, tell her about his plans, make her as enthusiastic as he was.

'Why?' Rosemary asked. 'The children will only get out of their routine and then I'll have no end of trouble getting them back into it again.'

They were in the sitting room after dinner and she was darning a shirt. She bent her head to rethread the needle and Larry saw only the neat parting of her hair. He knew though that her lips would be pressed into the firm line that accompanied that tone of voice.

'It'll do them good, it'll do you good, to have a change,' Larry said, making his tone jolly to counteract hers. 'Norfolk, I thought.'

'The laundry will be shocking, before and after,' she continued. 'You don't realise how much work the laundry is.'

'But think how much fun we'll have – paddling, children playing in the sand, picnics. All free and easy.'

'And the cost, what about the cost?' she said, snipping

her thread and jabbing the needle back in the pincushion. 'It doesn't come cheap, that kind of thing, it doesn't come cheap at all.'

'There's plenty of money for that kind of thing now, you know there is. And July's the best time, before the next site's ready to start building. 19th of July. I've booked a hotel.'

She looked at him. 'So you've already booked it. I should have guessed. Well, then, I'd better start preparations, hadn't I?'

July 1937

The worst thing was that she'd been right, to some extent. He was standing on the quayside, smoking and looking for a fishing boat to take him out for a trip. It was a glorious morning, alive with sun and wind, and the idea of being out on the cold green water at last, surrounded by nothing and no one, was thrilling. But it was the first time on the holiday that he'd been at ease. Roy and Joanie, giddy beyond reason with crabs and salt water and beach clothes, bickered and fought constantly and Roy, completely exhausted at the end of each strange, exciting day, had wet the bed twice. Rosemary felt compelled to wash the sheet herself, to avoid the shame of the chambermaid doing it, so the laundry had even accompanied her on the holiday. And she refused to be free and easy. She brought darning or knitting to the beach each day as if even more shame would accrue if she was seen in public without work of some kind.

Larry ambled to and fro among the moorings. For two or three days now, he'd had his eye on the fishing boats, looking for a bit of form, so to speak. Not so much the catch they brought in but how the whole operation was run, and in particular the demeanour of the skipper. Spots of rust or flaking paint were sure signs to him that the engine must be neglected and the fishing tackle second rate. The skipper had to be equally trim and competent. A couple of boats had looked promising, The Dolphin and Patricia, and he scanned the quay now to see if they were in.

He felt marvellously loose here on the quayside, free and easy at last. There was perhaps a touch of guilt at leaving the children with Rosemary all day, but he reasoned that maybe things would be calmer without him.

There had been an unspoken war between him and Rosemary all week as he tried to indulge the children a little and she resisted. He would buy them ice creams as an afternoon treat and she would tut at the size, the price, the mess they made. All the joy of the ice cream was rubbed away until it was something to be eaten as quickly as possible, so it could be over.

She insisted on leaving the beach at what she called 'a respectable time' so the children could be in bed early.

'Let them stay up a bit,' Larry had protested. 'It's a holiday, they can sleep later in the morning.'

'I will not have those children embarrass me. They will not be running around the hotel garden at nine o'clock at night like those other hooligans. I am not having them show me up.'

Larry sighed. Rosemary's ideas of what was and wasn't respectable were unshakeable. He'd given in on the bedtime as he did on everything concerning the children.

Searching the harbour again, he saw that The Dolphin was in, neat in royal blue and white, her skipper busy sweeping the deck. He was a young man, early twenties

Larry guessed, sunburnt and muscular. Larry watched, half mesmerised by the swish of the broom. After a minute or two he realised that he was being watched too.

'You wanting a fishing trip, sir?' The man was grinning.

'Yes, yes, I do,' Larry stammered, embarrassed at being caught staring. 'How much?'

'It's three shillings, sir.'

'That's a bit steep, isn't it? The other boats don't charge that much.'

The skipper wasn't at all put out. 'Well, you could say that. But the other boats don't have my knowledge or my particular expertise. Coming along?'

He reached out a hand. Larry took it and climbed on board, aware that he hadn't actually agreed to pay the price.

'You go here, sir.'

Larry sat where he was told, in the stern.

'I'm William Pike, by the way. Everyone calls me Will.'

He started the engine and they pulled away from the quayside. Larry gripped the edge of his seat as they passed slowly through the harbour mouth and came out into open water. The sea at last.

The wind came at him like a brick wall and beneath him the boat shuddered and heaved. He leaned over the side and peered into the churning green water.

'Bit choppy today,' Will shouted from the wheelhouse. 'You feeling all right?'

Larry nodded and shouted back, 'Yes, I'm fine.' And it was, amazingly, true. No sickness, no fear, just exhilaration.

'We'll be able to start in about half an hour. Just need to get to a good spot.'

Larry turned to look at the land as it fell away behind them. From the boat the town looked cluttered, garish against the pure elements of water and wind. He wondered if his family were among the figures on the beach but he was too far away to identify anyone. Too far to see the flash of Rosemary's knitting needles as she turned the heel in a pair of socks, too far to hear Joanie's piercing shrieks as she ran in and out of the water, too far to see Roy's face crumple as yet another sand castle collapsed. He was far away from all of that and more thankful than he could say.

The boat went on and though the wind still blew straight through his shirt to his skin, the sun on his face was warm and he felt wrapped up and safe as if in a blanket. His eyes closed. Then there was an extra warmth on his arm and he woke to see Will above him, shaking his elbow.

'Shall we get down to business then?'

Larry looked about him, expecting to see rods and nets ready. There was nothing, just Will.

'Well, where is everything? Where's the fishing rod?' he asked.

Will laughed. 'No need for that is there?'

'What?' Larry stood up, beginning to feel anxious.

'I've seen you at the quayside, eyeing up the lads. Walking up and down, up and down. Seeing who you like the look of. Lucky you picked me, sir, or did someone tip you the wink about my fishing trips?'

'What?' Larry said again. Will was standing confidently before him, expecting something. 'You thought I was looking at the...the men? My God, that's disgusting.'

Will didn't move. He was close enough for Larry to smell the sweat on him, and see the dark hairs curling up from the neck of his shirt. They stood looking at each other, Larry with a high blush on his cheeks, the boat reeling beneath his feet, the sea churning beneath the boat.

14

'Are you sure about that, sir?'

'Of course I am. It's outrageous. I should report you.'

'The gentlemen don't often change their minds,' Will said. 'But no skin off my nose. As long as they pay.'

Larry said nothing.

'Well, we'd better be getting back then,' Will said equably. 'I'd like the three shillings now though, sir.'

Larry started to protest, then stopped. It would be too seedy to argue with him and being out at sea in a small boat with – well, a man who did the kind of thing that Will did would probably have no scruples at all about any kind of violence. He handed over the money and sat back down.

It took an age to get back to the harbour, a slow trudge against the wind. Larry was cold, his exhilaration long gone and replaced by a dread of seeing Rosemary again. What could he possibly say about the fishing trip? That he was empty-handed was bad enough, though she would assume that was his own incompetence and nothing more. About everything else he would just stay quiet. That was the best way.

He avoided looking at Will by leaning on the side and keeping his eyes on the water instead. But he was aware of him, all too close on the boat, and the tune he was whistling, *Pennies from Heaven*, stuck in his head. After a while his neck began to hurt and he was forced to sit up. They were close to the harbour mouth and he saw crowds of boats and gulls settling themselves on the water, ribbons of oil uncoiling on the surface around them.

'You could change your mind back again,' Will said suddenly, nearer than Larry had realised. 'For the same three shillings.'

He turned. Will was smiling, his face unashamed, beautiful.

Larry couldn't speak. He shook his head, letting the tears that had risen fall and blow away.

'All right,' Will said softly.

They passed into the harbour and slowly nudged up to the mooring. The boat bumped against the wall and Will leapt onto the quay, hauling the rope until she was securely tethered. Larry climbed off slowly, stumbling as his legs adjusted to solid ground. Will caught his arm and steadied him.

'Maybe you'd like a trip out another time, sir.' His hand was firm on Larry's elbow. 'Maybe we'd have more luck next time.'

Larry paused, noting the breadth of Will's palm on his skin, the roughness of his fingertips, the dirt under his nails. Noting them because there would never be another time. He began to walk away, towards the beach where his family would be waiting for him.

'Bye then, sir,' Will called.

Larry managed to wave.

Chapter 2

Joanie
September 1948

Joanie lay across two chairs in the Ladies Lounge. In twenty minutes, she would have to go downstairs to open up the main bar, but for now she lay on her back, out of sight behind the stacked tables, and stared at the ceiling. The upholstery, unused since they closed the lounge in 1941, gave off a faint smell of damp and smoke which she didn't mind at all and the velvet was comforting against her neck.

More than anything she wanted to sleep – she always did at this time of day, though the chance would be a fine thing, she thought. Sun had been pouring through the windows all afternoon and the dusty warmth pressing down on her eyelids was irresistible. She felt her limbs soften and go limp.

The sound of a door slamming jolted her awake. Through the table legs she saw her mother come down from the living quarters and pass the entrance to the Ladies Lounge as she went downstairs with the cash bags for the evening.

Rosemary paused and called out, 'Betty, here's the money. Joanie will be along soon.'

After a minute, Joanie heard coins being dropped into the till and then the drawer close with a ping. She sat up, sighing, just as Rosemary came up the stairs again.

'So that's where you got to,' Rosemary said. 'Time to open up. Betty's there already.'

'There's a few minutes yet,' Joanie said, stretching. 'Betty'll be all right on her own.'

'You need to be there keeping an eye on her.'

Joanie sighed again, but stood up.

'Make yourself presentable, for goodness sake,' Rosemary said. 'Your skirt's all crumpled at the back. And your stockings are crooked.' She pulled at Joanie's skirt and patted her hair.

Joanie shook her off. 'I'll do it.' She tucked her hair behind her ears and smoothed her stockings into place. 'There, that'll do. Good enough for a Tuesday night at The Dolphin anyway.'

When she got downstairs, Betty was sitting on one of the bar stools, smoking. She took a long draw on her cigarette as Joanie approached. 'Evening,' she said. 'Ready for the off then?'

No matter what she wore or how she did her hair, Joanie felt like a frumpy child when she was with Betty. Betty could make anything look stylish, even the Land Girl uniform she'd worn, briefly, during the war. Joanie could see that the black skirt she was wearing had once been Rosemary's, but it was unrecognisable now, transformed on Betty into something almost glamorous.

'I'll do the doors if you do the gate,' Joanie said.

'Right you are.'

Joanie unlocked the front doors and they both stepped out onto the terrace. A heavy, late afternoon sun lay across the flagstones, turning them into bronze, and house martins darted for flies above the roof.

'It's nice out here tonight, isn't it?' Betty said. 'Maybe it'll bring a few more customers in.' She went to open the gate and Joanie watched her go, envying her high heels and the ease with which she walked in them.

The outer doors were held open with lumps of stone. Joanie lugged them into place then gathered up some fallen leaves that had blown onto the terrace. She looked about for somewhere to put them, deciding in the end to drop them into the empty pool. For a few moments, she stood at the rim, remembering how at night the pool used to glow like a sapphire with its dark blue tiles and underwater light. Dad would never have let it lie empty, she thought, but then he never had to run the place virtually single-handed and in the face of years of shortages and rationing.

The warm evening did bring in a few more customers than usual. There was a pleasant hum of conversation as Joanie went about the place and even a few full tables on the terrace. The sound of Betty's laugh rang out regularly from behind the bar.

At the end of the night, Joanie emptied the till and began the cashing up. Betty started washing the glasses in the sink. One of her men friends had stayed behind 'to help'. He leaned across the bar to watch, leering and getting in Joanie's way.

'Come on, Frank, move over, will you?' she said.

'Sorry, sweetheart.' He shifted a couple of inches. 'You all right there, Betty? Shall I come and give you a hand?' He smirked. 'If you know what I mean.'

Betty giggled. 'Oh, stop it, you. Anyway, got a smoke?'

'You can't smoke while you're washing up. Here, I know...' He lit her a cigarette from his own and went to stand beside her, holding it to her mouth when she turned her head towards him.

Joanie continued to count the piles of shillings and pennies, ignoring the laughter and whispering behind her. When she was done, she noted the takings in the cash book and bagged up the float for the next day.

'Are you nearly finished there, Betty? I'll just take these upstairs to Mum, then I'll come back and lock up properly.'

'Nearly done,' Betty said. 'Frank'll help me dry them, won't you, Frank?'

Joanie didn't wait to hear his reply. She carried the cash bags upstairs and knocked on Rosemary's door.

'Is it just you?' Rosemary said from behind the door.

'Yes, Mum, just me.'

There was the sound of a key turning and the door opened.

'You're late tonight,' Rosemary said. 'How much?' She took the cash book and went to sit on the bed, running a finger down the In column. 'Five pounds, that's good.'

Joanie put the cash bags down on the bed. 'It was busy. People even came and sat outside.'

Rosemary nodded. 'Won't last of course. The weather's cooling off now. Winter won't be easy, though God forbid it's as bad as forty-seven. Even so, we might have to make some savings…'

'We aren't getting rid of Betty, Mum. Not unless you want to come and work behind the bar instead.'

Rosemary sniffed. 'Mmm, well, I should have sent that floozy back to London on VE day.'

'She's a good barmaid. She's popular with customers.'

'What's she doing anyway?'

Joanie thought it best not to mention Frank. 'Just washing the last of the glasses. I'll go down and lock up.' She went towards the door.

'Check she's done them properly.'

Joanie heard the key turn in the lock as she went down the hallway. She stopped outside Roy's room and knocked softly on his door.

'Roy, are you awake?'

A sleepy grunt came from inside and she opened the door. Roy was lying on top of his bed, fully clothed.

'What is it?' he said, without opening his eyes.

'Nothing. Just wondered if you were awake.' She picked up a book from the bedside table. *Spitfire Parade*. 'You're too old to be reading Biggles, aren't you?'

'None of your business.' He turned over to face the wall. 'Go away, I'm sleeping.'

There was a stale smell in the room and she wondered when he'd last had a bath.

'Anyway, Mum'll go mad if you sleep in your clothes again. Night.'

She closed the door behind her.

Downstairs, the lights were all off except over the bar. As she went towards the door, she jangled the bunch of keys she was carrying as loudly as she could. There were muffled sounds of belts and zips and Frank appeared suddenly from behind one of the pillars.

'Well, then,' he said, sweeping his hair back from his forehead. 'That's all the glasses washed and dried. Must be going.'

Betty sidled out from behind the pillar too. 'Thanks for helping, Frank. See you tomorrow?'

'It'll have to be Friday, love. There are some other things I have to do.'

'Right you are then,' Betty said. 'See you Friday.'

Joanie stood waiting by the open doors. A chilly breeze was blowing in from outside and she shivered a little in the draught. As he went out, Frank paused to light a cigarette and in the brief glow of his lighter she thought how good looking he was.

'Night, Joanie,' he said, and winked at her.

'Bye, Frank.'

She went outside to close the gate, waving Frank's car through and watching his rear lights fade and disappear. When she looked up, the sky was thick with stars and the moon was full and yellow.

Inside, doors locked, she went to switch off the lights in the bar. Betty was waiting for her with arms folded and a sulky expression.

'You could have given us a bit more time,' she said. 'It's no fun when you're in a bloody rush.'

Joanie didn't say anything, just flicked the light switch and headed for the stairs.

'All right, Joanie, I'm coming. Don't get all hoity toity.'

They went up together.

'You can go in the bathroom first, if you want,' Betty said. 'I'm going to have a cup of tea.'

'All right.'

Joanie washed slowly, all the tiredness she'd been putting off finally taking hold. She glanced briefly at her face in the mirror, just to make sure it was clean, then looked away. At this time of night, she was too worn, too colourless, for there to be any satisfaction in looking at herself.

Her room was cold and she changed quickly into pyjamas and jumped into bed. A hot water bottle would have been nice, but Betty was in the kitchen and she couldn't face her again. She wrapped her arms around herself and rubbed her feet against the sheets to warm them up. Wednesday tomorrow, which would be just the same as Tuesday, which was just the same as Monday. Sometimes she really wanted to scream.

When she went into the kitchen the next morning, Roy was at the table eating breakfast. He grunted a hello through a mouthful of toast and went back to reading the newspaper.

Joanie sat down and poured herself a cup of tea.

'Anything in the paper?' she asked.

'Not really.'

'Mum not up yet?'

'No.'

She cut a piece of bread and spread it with margarine. 'Any jam left?'

'Sorry, just finished it.'

'Oh.' She ate the bread without enjoyment. 'Well, anyway, what are you doing today?'

Roy folded the paper and took a drink of tea. 'Expect I'll have to drive Mum in to the bank again. Nothing, other than that.' He shrugged his shoulders.

'Don't you get bored? Don't you want a proper job?' Don't you feel bad that I'm working all the bloody time and you just do odd jobs here and there, she wanted to ask.

'I'll be called up for National Service soon. No one would take me on.'

'You can always help me out. Do a shift behind the bar. What I could do with a day off...' Joanie leaned back in her chair and closed her eyes. 'I'd have a lovely long sleep and then maybe a bath, a really deep one that uses up all the hot water. I'd do my hair properly for once and wear something nice, something silky and sophisticated ...'

Roy laughed. 'Then Clark Gable would pick you up and take you out for cocktails.' He patted her hand. 'Sorry, Sis, it's never going to happen. I'm not allowed in the bar when it's open, remember? Not old enough yet.'

'No one would find out. Just one day off, that's all I need, just one day.'

'Can you imagine what Mum would say? What she'd do?'

Roy laughed again and stood up. 'It'd be worse than the Blitz.' He made fighter pilot goggles with his hands. 'Heavy shelling from Mrs Lambert at two o'clock.'

Joanie stared at him. 'Roy, how can you joke about it?'

Roy put his hands in his pockets. Stared at the floor. 'Sorry, sorry. Didn't mean to bring it up.'

'Yes, well, just think before you speak next time,' Joanie said.

Roy was suddenly defiant. 'It happened to all of us, you know, not just you.'

Well, it doesn't look like it, Joanie wanted to say. 'All right, I know that,' she said eventually.

'Just because you go on about Dad it doesn't mean anything.'

Yes, it does, Joanie thought. Because you and Mum don't think about him at all.

'And it was seven bloody years ago. It's time you…' He stopped and looked at the floor again.

'I'm going downstairs,' she said. 'I've got work to do.'

The delivery from the brewery was due so she went out to open the gate. Despite the sunshine, the early morning air was cold, making her wish her legs weren't bare. Above her, the sky was a perfect sweep of blue. She leaned against the gate for a moment to gaze up at it. Then her eyes travelled down to take in the ragged fence of the field opposite and then the disused vegetable beds where The Dolphin's lawn had once been. Even when the command to Dig for Victory had been most shrill, they had never produced much and now they lay completely overgrown. I should clear them out and re-turf the lawn, she thought. That would tidy things up a bit. She stared at them a little longer, but didn't move.

What would Dad do? she wondered. If he came back now and saw the place so drab and unkempt, would he set to work building it up again or would the state of it defeat him? He would build, she was sure of it. Inch by inch, he would repair and re-gild it, even if it took a lifetime. A spasm of pity went through her. He didn't have a lifetime of course. His was over and done with. And she was just too tired to do anything about The Dolphin.

A horn sounded from down the hill and the delivery lorry appeared, making slow and noisy progress towards her.

She waved, watching it negotiate the gateway and drive into the yard. 'Morning,' she called, when it had stopped.

The cab door opened and the driver stepped out. 'Morning, Miss Lambert. Lovely day, eh?' He went to the back of the lorry to unhook the tailgate.

Joanie went to help. 'Isn't Patrick with you today?'

'He's gone and sprained his wrist, the silly lad. Off for a week they say.'

'Oh.' She was surprised at her disappointment. 'Oh well, shall I get my brother to help you?'

The driver rubbed his back with a pained expression. 'Would you, love? I'm suffering with the shrapnel today. It's playing up rotten.'

'I'll run up and get him.'

Roy came grudgingly, complaining that it wasn't his job to unload the lorry, just to organise the cellar.

'If you don't do it, I will,' Joanie said eventually, shaming him into action.

She had to help out anyway. Roy was so slow that the driver started checking his watch and grumbling about his other deliveries. Joanie took some of the smaller crates and at last they were done.

'See you next time,' she called as the lorry engine started up. 'Tell Patrick I hope he gets better soon.'

The driver waved and drove off.

Roy wiped the sweat from his face.

'I bloody hope he gets better too. I'm never doing that again.' He gave her a sly look. 'So, is he handsome then, this Patrick? The Prince Charming of the brewery?'

Joanie was annoyed to find herself blushing. 'Oh, give over.'

In the cellar, she checked that Roy had put everything in the right place. It wasn't too bad, but she tidied up some empty beer crates and bottles of wine. There was something calming about the cellar. Rosemary and Betty never came down here and Roy only when he had to. It felt like it was her place. Her bedroom was too close to everyone else so that she was conscious of every sound she made, every thought she had. And Rosemary's presence at the end of the corridor meant that she could never quite relax. The whitewashed cellar with its rows of beer barrels, though cold, was peaceful and private.

Once the cellar was tidy, she spent the morning the way she spent every morning; mopping, cleaning, restocking. It was part of Betty's terms of employment – arrived at through a series of sulks and threats to leave – that her shift started no more than half an hour before opening time. Joanie had to accept it, but the injustice rankled. It was Rosemary she resented rather than Betty as she mopped the beery floor and wiped cigarette ash from the tables. Betty, Joanie recognised, was simply doing whatever she could get away with.

When the floor and the tables were done, she went outside to sweep up the terrace. West-facing, it was still in shadow with a sharp jab of autumn in the air. Another winter coming. Oh God, another winter with the four of them stuck at The Dolphin. In the worst of '47 they'd been marooned up on the hill for two weeks, anxious at first, then bored and hungry, accusing one another of using too much tea or not taking their turn at breaking the ice for water. None of us came out of that well, she thought, and we don't have the reserves to cope again.

She swept up the cigarette ends and match heads that littered the terrace. Even a mild winter would be dismal. Custom dropped off once the evenings got colder, and the Circular Bar was closed from October until spring. It felt lonelier than ever up here on the hill, surrounded by darkness. What had made her father build The Dolphin here? Surely there would have been more custom if it had been closer to the houses he'd built, or on a main road at least. But then, everything was different before the war; maybe he'd planned to build more houses up here too. That would be nice, she thought, sitting down at one of the tables and resting her feet on the terrace wall. A little estate just across the road with people coming and going, maybe some girls her own age who popped into The Dolphin now and then, perhaps going on trips into town together.

'Oh, shut up, Joanie,' she said aloud. It was pointless to dream like this because it made the reality harder to bear. If Larry was alive, things would be different. She remembered the way he patted the wall reliefs as he walked around, or the wood of the bar, as if they were pets or children. The way The Dolphin gleamed like a constantly polished and buffed ocean liner. The way he seemed to be a different man when he was there. And he wouldn't let her work so hard, he would be fair. Self-pity brought tears to her eyes.

A squirrel hopped tentatively onto the bottom step, then, when she clapped her hands, raced towards the abandoned vegetable beds and hid itself in the tangle of weeds. She watched the foliage bend and shiver as the squirrel ran underneath. I should get back to work, she thought.

But thinking about her father triggered memories of the night of his death, as it often did. She saw the fires and explosions that erupted across the town, so clearly visible from The Dolphin. She heard again the planes overhead as she ran for the shelter. She'd gone on at Rosemary, asking her if they would be all right, if Larry would be safe fire watching, until Rosemary had shouted at her to be quiet.

'I don't know!' Rosemary had yelled. 'How can I when I don't know what's happening?'

She had started to cry then, and Joanie looked away and huddled up against Roy, her eyes and her fists squeezed tight.

The news about Larry came in the morning. None of them had gone to bed and when the bell rang, they were in the kitchen drinking watery cocoa. Joanie knew what the bell meant. They went together to open the door.

A man stood in the porch, grey haired and dishevelled, with streaks of dirt across his face and clothes. He carried a pair of binoculars which he held out to Rosemary.

'I'm Arthur Newsome,' he said. 'I do fire watching duty with your husband, Mrs Lambert. These are his.'

They sat on one of the window seats in the Circular Bar. Joanie remembered thinking it was the first time Rosemary had ever done more than stride through it. Rain battered the window behind them as Arthur told them what had happened.

'I'll take you to the hospital if you like, Mrs Lambert,' he said at the end. He cleared his throat. 'There's identification and so on.'

Rosemary nodded, looking grim but not really unhappy, Joanie thought. None of them had cried yet.

'Look after your brother,' Rosemary said, as she left. 'And both of you stay upstairs.'

They waited in the porch to watch Arthur's car leave. Roy fiddled with the door handle, staring at the floor. Joanie twisted a button on her dress. Everything inside her felt closed off, as if a shutter had come down.

The immediate problem of the pub only hit her when they went back inside.

'What about The Dolphin? Should it be open or closed?'

Roy shrugged. 'How should I know?' he said. 'Someone will come in, won't they?'

'But we need to decide. It's Dad's pub.'

They sat down again in the Circular Bar. Neither of them knew when the bar staff were due so they waited, Joanie watching the rain dribble down the window. Sitting there, in the place that Larry had cherished, it was impossible to believe that he wouldn't be coming back.

'I'm thirsty,' Roy said.

'What do you want?' Joanie asked.

'What is there?'

She looked over at him. He sat with his knees up on the window seat, a baffled expression on his face as he gazed out at the rain. It was her job to steer him through his first fatherless hours but she had no idea what she was meant to do. 'I don't know. Let's have a look.'

They walked across the room and slipped behind the bar.

'Are we allowed to do this?' Roy whispered.

'Yes, we are,' Joanie said loudly. 'Today we are allowed.'

They gazed at the rows of bottles. 'What do you want?' Joanie repeated.

'Something fizzy.'

She walked along the length of the shelves, calling out what was written on the bottle labels. 'Indian tonic water, soda water, ginger ale, sparkling orange.'

'I want fizzy orange,' Roy said.

Joanie picked up two of the bottles. There was a bottle opener attached to the bar which she had seen Malcolm use, so she twisted the bottles until the tops came off. Roy took out two glasses and she emptied the orange drink into them.

'Shall we add something else?' she said. 'To make it a special drink, a drink for Dad?' It felt like a very mature thing to say.

'Some cordial?' Roy said.

Joanie pointed to a bottle of brandy. 'What about that? That's what they have in films when someone's had a shock.'

Roy looked doubtful. 'I don't think we should.'

'Well, we've definitely had a shock.'

They stared at each other. Joanie wondered if she looked as pale and lost as Roy. He frowned for a moment, then nodded.

She opened the bottle. The fumes made her eyes water, but she poured a little into each glass. 'All right. What should we say?'

'We should say, To Dad. They do that in films too,' Roy said.

It felt so inadequate, Joanie thought. Surely they should say what he meant to them, what they would miss about him, something about his special qualities. All that she could think of was that he loved The Dolphin.

She lifted her glass. 'To Dad.'

'To Dad.'

They drank, then coughed and choked on the alcohol.

'Ugh,' Joanie said. 'That's disgusting.'

Roy grinned. 'It does something to you though, doesn't it?' He took another swig. 'Makes you all warm inside.'

Joanie almost offered him the rest of hers, but thought better of it and tipped it down the sink.

'Let's go and sit down. Someone must be due in soon.'

They went back to their seats. Roy leaned his head on the table and Joanie soon heard his breathing deepen and slow. She tried to stay awake, but the sleepless night and the brandy were too much. She settled a cushion under her head and was soon asleep too.

Now, remembering that bleak morning, she wondered what on earth she'd been thinking of, giving brandy to a ten-year-old boy. But there had been a need to do something out of the ordinary, to show that they weren't the same children anymore. To show that she wasn't even a child anymore.

She stood up and stretched, her legs stiff and cold. She ran on the spot to warm herself up. There had been trouble, of course. The bar maid had arrived and woken them. Then she had put up the Closed sign and sent them upstairs. Joanie remembered how Rosemary had reacted when she came back and smelled the brandy on them. She'd marched them to the kitchen and made them drink a glass of milk, watching as they forced it down.

'Today of all days you do this,' she'd muttered.

'It was for Dad,' Joanie protested.

'It doesn't make it right,' Rosemary said, her face drawn tight.

The enormity of her loss suddenly overwhelmed Joanie and she broke into great gulps of grief. Rosemary sighed, then put her arm round her until she quietened.

'All right, enough now. I won't say anymore. There's a funeral to arrange anyway.'

And she was gone, out of the room, leaving Joanie and Roy alone.

There were footsteps on the terrace behind her. Betty's voice brought her back to the present.

'Joining the League of Health and Beauty, are you?'

Flushed and embarrassed, Joanie stopped running. 'Just trying to get warm. Is it opening time?'

'Ten minutes. Your mum's just brought down the float.' Betty perched on the top step. 'I can give you a few tips, if you want.'

'What?'

'Beauty tips. You could make a lot more of yourself, you know. You've got a nice little face and your figure isn't bad. If you just showed off your assets a bit more.' She looked Joanie up and down and lit a cigarette. 'Have you ever had a boyfriend, Joanie?'

The question took her by surprise. Betty had a long line of Franks – and Johns and Harrys and Alberts – that she had courted and dropped when someone more promising appeared. Joanie had never seen her without a boyfriend for longer than Sunday to Friday. A face in the crowd at the bar would become familiar. He would buy them both a drink or two and flirt with Joanie a little. She'd know then that he was Betty's latest.

'When would I have time for a boyfriend?' Her laughter was unconvincing. 'Mum would scare him off anyway.'

Betty blew a perfect smoke ring.

'A little bird tells me that someone called Patrick tickles your fancy.'

Bloody Roy. Betty could winkle anything out of him.

'Well, the little bird hasn't got a clue about anything.'

Betty smiled, infuriating, knowing. 'Oh, really?' she said.

'I'm going to unlock the front door. And I think we might need some more ashtrays out here,' Joanie replied.

Inside, she was glad to be warm again. In the mirror on the wall by the door, she saw her reflection illuminated by a shaft of sunlight. She stopped. Dark hair hung like spaniels' ears around her face. She had always liked her hair. Her skin was pale and tired-looking and there were purplish circles round her eyes. A spot was forming just by the side of her nose. Her eyebrows were dense and untidy. Yet Betty had said she had a 'nice little face'. If Rosemary would only let her wear a bit of make-up, she could make something of herself.

She stepped back and surveyed her lumpy tweed skirt and sensible brogues. Everything about her said serviceable, workaday, and who could see beyond that? And when would she get the chance to be anything different?

She went to open up.

Chapter 3

Lottie
May 1968

Light was showing over the sea. At first, the smallest shift in the density of the dark, then a more definite paleness in the eastern sky. Eventually the sun shimmered up, turning the waves a silky purple and tinting Lottie's bare feet pink.

She pulled her blanket around herself and leaned back against the dune. The blanket smelled of smoke and so did her hair. She thought how delicious it would be to have a deep, hot bath when she got home, to wash away the sand and sticky sea salt. A bar of Bronnley's lemon soap waited in the cupboard to be unwrapped from its tissue paper – Lottie could almost smell its sharp, clean scent.

Somebody coughed and she turned to see who else was awake. The sleeping bags and blankets ranged around last night's fire formed a ragged circle, nobody moving. She wished she'd caught the last bus home but she had persuaded herself that sleeping on the beach would be a laugh. She flicked away a cigarette stub that lay next to her foot. It was all right for the others; they didn't have to go to work in the morning.

The coughing came again and with it a man wriggling out of a blue sleeping bag. He stood up and stretched, letting out a long, satisfied groan, then saw her and came over. She didn't recognise him from the party – there had been continuous arrivals and departures throughout the night – and there was nothing about him that made her want to talk to him. It was far too early to make unnecessary conversation. She nodded at him, huddled in her blanket, and stared at the sea.

'Hi,' he said, squatting next to her.

'Hi.'

'Amazing sunrise.'

'Yeah.'

He smelled stale and she guessed she was the same. She pulled the blanket up to cover her nose.

'It was a great party, wasn't it?' he said. 'A real laugh.'

'Mmm.' When did the buses start running? she wondered.

He leaned towards her suddenly and held out his hand.

'Hey, listen, I'm Dan. I didn't get a chance to speak to you last night.'

She reluctantly pushed the blanket aside and shook his hand. 'I'm Lottie.'

'So, are you hanging round the beach with this lot this morning? I think some of us are staying all day.'

'No, I have to get home.' She looked around for her shoes. 'In fact, I'd probably better get going now. Nice to meet you.' She stood up.

'You don't need to go yet, do you? It's really early.' His expression was annoyingly friendly. 'There's probably some booze left if we look for it.'

'I have to be at work so actually I do need to go.' She put on her shoes and folded the blanket then reached for her beach bag, stuffed the blanket inside and heaved it onto her shoulder. 'See you then.'

She headed for the road, sand leaking into her shoes and

getting between her toes. It was going to be an uncomfortable walk.

'Hey, hang on, can I give you a lift?' He ran to catch her up.

She stopped. 'Have you got a car?'

'Yeah, there look,' he grinned, and pointed to a grey Morris Minor in the car park. 'So, do you want a lift?'

She thought about the long walk up the hill with her heavy bag, weighing it against a short car journey with a complete stranger. 'OK, then.' He was annoying, but not threatening.

'Great, I'll just get my shoes.'

He hurried over to his sleeping bag where he retrieved a pair of grubby tennis shoes. She waited for him to put them on and hoped the journey wasn't going to be too excruciating.

'Where is it you live then, Lottie?' he asked.

'Up at the top of the hill.' After giving him directions, she felt duty bound to make conversation. 'What about you?'

'Got a bedsit just behind the High Street.'

It wasn't what she expected him to say. Everyone she knew still lived with their parents.

'Oh, are your mum and dad not local then?'

'They're out in Kenya.'

'Really? Is that where you're from?'

'Yeah. I left a while ago though.'

She looked at him properly for the first time. He was definitely older than her – maybe early twenties – and he didn't have the shaggy, unkempt hair of the other boys her age. He looked neat, kind, a bit square. She could imagine him wearing a safari suit.

'It's left here,' she said. 'Sorry to be taking you so far out of your way.'

'It's fine.'

She stared at the road ahead, then asked, 'What do you do then?'

'I work for an ironmonger, up round the back of the Esplanade.'

'Oh, I see. Good job, is it?'

He laughed. 'Not really. Though we've started selling plants and bulbs and that's more interesting. I like growing things. What about you? Or are you still at school?'

She hated it when people asked that. School was ages ago.

'I work at a cafe. Oh look, my house is just here. You can drop me at the corner.'

When the car stopped, she heaved her bag onto her lap and quickly opened the door.

'Thanks for the lift. That was really nice of you. See you some time.'

He looked up at her and smiled, about to speak, but she shut the door before he could say anything.

She knew he would turn up at the cafe. Someone would tell him where she worked and he would walk in and pretend surprise. And then she would have to make conversation while she was working (because none of the boys who came in ever thought about that) and – whether she liked him or not – eventually there would be the moment where he asked her out and she would have to answer in front of all the customers. At times, she wished she had a job that wasn't so public.

It was a couple of weeks before he came in. She was searching for a new notepad in the cupboard underneath the counter and when she straightened up, he was sitting at the table by the door. He waved. She sighed and went over.

'Hi, Dan.'

'Hi, Lottie. Didn't expect to see you here. How are you?'

'Fine, thanks. You?'

'Yeah, great, thanks.'

'So, what would you like?'

'Oh, let's see.' He peered at the board behind the till. 'What about a ham roll? And a coffee, please.'

'Milk?'

He nodded and smiled. 'This is a nice place. I haven't been before. Have you worked here long?'

She laughed. 'Only all my life. It's my mum and dad's cafe.' She pointed her pen towards her father behind the counter. 'I was practically brought up here. Anyway, I'll get your order. Won't be long.'

There was a sudden rush of customers and she managed to avoid serving him, sending over the new waitress instead. With a bit of luck, he'll take a shine to Maureen, she thought, watching her squeeze between the tables in her short, tight skirt.

She was kept busy at the till so it was easy not to look his way. When she did, he was smoking a cigarette and staring straight at her. She blushed and turned away.

There was a whisper in her ear. 'Got another admirer then?'

'Oh, shut up, Dad. He's not an admirer.'

Dan was still there when the lunchtime rush was over and there was no excuse not to go over when he beckoned.

'Everything OK?' she said.

'Fine, yeah, it was good.'

'Anything else?'

'Well, I wondered...' He was blushing now and she felt a pang of pity. Then he looked at her as if he knew what she was thinking and he shrugged his shoulders. 'Actually, nothing else, just the bill please, Lottie.'

'OK.' She felt both relieved and irritated as she rang up his order. If he'd done it, if he'd asked her out, she could have said no and that would have been that. They would both have known where they stood. Now, the question hung in the air and it would annoy her until it was dealt with.

She leaned on the back of a chair while he groped in his pocket for change, aware of her father watching from across the room.

'There you are,' Dan said, piling coins on top of the bill.

'Thanks.'

'Thanks, Dan. Well, see you around.'

'Bye then, Lottie.'

He shook her hand and left.

'I told you,' Bill called out when he'd gone. 'He's smitten, he is, smitten.'

Maureen lasted three weeks. She came in one morning and announced that she was leaving the next day to go to London where she wouldn't have to slave for the bourgeoisie. Lottie looked around at the customers – sensible raincoats, headscarves and flat caps, rarely spending more than a few shillings – and wondered who on earth she meant.

Bill dismissed her with a full day's pay and half the pot of tips.

'She's going to get a shock when the bourgeoisie aren't paying her wages anymore,' he said when she'd gone. 'Her big ideas won't last five minutes.'

'Oh, did she mean us?' Lottie said. 'I thought she was talking about the customers.'

'If she thinks London's going to be easy...' Bill said, and

then more softly, 'Well, she's got a bit more cash now anyway. Tide her over a bit.'

He dug around behind the till and, sighing, brought out the Staff Required notice they kept to hand. 'Better put this back in the window, I suppose.'

There were several applicants over the next few days, all unsuitable. Some of them stared too long at Bill's useless arm, some of them drank too many cups of tea, some of them assumed the job was theirs just by turning up. Lottie quickly tired of smiling at them and explaining what the work entailed.

'Can't you interview them, Dad?' she asked. 'I'm fed up with them all.'

'I'm no good at that kind of thing,' Bill said. 'Women are much better at picking up what people are like. Feminine intuition and all that.'

'Couldn't Mum do it then?'

'She'll do it if she's here, of course she will, but she's only in on your days off. So it's more likely to be you, love, I'm afraid.'

Lottie slept late on her day off, waking to a silent house. She yawned and pulled the covers up to her ears, picturing her parents hurtling about the cafe with plates of bacon and eggs. Half guiltily, half gladly, she rolled over and closed her eyes again.

She loved her job. When she stepped onto the pier in the morning and walked towards the cafe perched at the very end, she felt she was walking to a place that belonged more to the sea than the land. The water coiling and uncoiling round the pillars; the wind twisting in puffs and eddies as it caught in the cross bars and railings; the low, heavy sound of the waves like an engine beneath her feet. When she was a child, she imagined mermaids might drop in for tea one day, tucking their silvery tails under the Formica tables and asking for seaweed to go with their chips. On hot days when the windows were open on all four sides of the building, she'd waited for dolphins to leap through, finning over the till and the toaster before arcing back down again into the water. Even now, she felt something exotic might drift in from the sea, a shipwrecked sailor perhaps, or an albatross blown from the far south.

It was all she had ever wanted to do. There had been no question in her mind that she would leave school after her O levels and go straight to work at the cafe, but it had caused a huge row at home.

'You can do so much more with your life, Lottie,' her mother said. 'Don't get stuck here before you know what else there is out there.'

'You work at the cafe. Dad works at the cafe. Why is it OK for you and not for me?'

'Because you've got opportunities we never had. With your dad's war injury, it was hard to get a job afterwards. He was lucky that the cafe came up. And when I was your age, I had to do my duty and go to work. There was no choice.' Joanie paced up and down, an intense expression on her face. 'Your teachers say you could go to university. Nobody ever said that to me. Nobody ever thought I could do anything worthwhile. Don't throw your chances away.'

'But I don't want to do anything else.' She imagined being stuck in a lecture theatre or an office, wedged at a desk, breathing in stuffy air, looking through windows that showed only more buildings, more offices. Why would she choose that when she could spend her time doing things her way, out where the light and air and water were different every day? Why would she want to listen to someone else telling her what to do when she could do something she was good at?

'I just don't want you to end up trapped here with no other options,' Joanie said.

Lottie turned away. Her mother didn't understand anything.

They had gone on at each other for weeks until Bill intervened.

'Enough of this,' he said to her. 'I'm calling a truce. Lottie, me and your mum just want what's best for you.'

'But, Dad...'

He turned to Joanie. 'And we have to trust her to know her own mind. I think she'll be great in the cafe. She'll be a real asset to the business.'

'Bill, I just want her to have opportunities.'

'She's sixteen, Joanie. She's got a lifetime of opportunities ahead of her. There's always night classes and the like.'

Joanie frowned and left the room. It was one of the few times Lottie saw them disagree. She grinned and ran over to hug Bill, whispering in his ear, 'Thanks, Dad. We'll be a great team.'

And they were a great team. Within weeks it was obvious that she could run the cafe just as well as Bill or Joanie. She waited for her mother to start nagging again, but it never came. Maybe Bill had a word with her, maybe she'd given up. Either way, Lottie decided to say nothing more.

Now, two years on, she still loved being there. Even on days when the customers were rude and there wasn't a minute to breathe, let alone take a break, she found something richly satisfying about the place.

She slipped back into sleep now, dreaming of mermaids slinking over the railings, hair knotty with pearls, dripping bright seawater onto the floor.

When she got into work the next day, Bill was whistling happily at the coffee machine. He was always there by seven, putting the tea urn on to boil, bringing in the bread delivery a few loaves at a time with his one good arm. If her mother was driving him in, sometimes she went with him, but more often she liked to arrive by herself, walking down the hill and across the town centre so that the line of the sea came slowly into sight, until she was on the pier and above the waves.

'Good news, Lottie,' Bill called as she came in. 'Your mum saw someone for the job yesterday. Starts today at ten.'

'Thank God for that.'

At five to ten she laid a clean apron and notepad next to the till. There were only a couple of customers nursing cups of tea, so she gazed through the door at the people milling about on the pier, trying to guess which one might be the new girl. Only one figure was heading towards the cafe and that was Dan.

He grinned at her as he came in the door.

'Morning, Lottie. What do I do first?'

She stared at him. 'Hang on, you're not the new girl, are you?'

'Well, not the new girl, but I am the new waiter.' His grin widened and Lottie felt like screaming.

'Oh, I see. I didn't realise you were looking for a job.'

'The bloke I was working for retired, closed his business. First I knew about it was when I turned up for work and there was a notice on the door.' He shrugged. 'No more job.

And then I saw the sign in the window here the other day and spoke to Mrs Lennox. Oh, she must be your mum, yeah? Lovely lady.'

He was so annoyingly pleasant! Working with him was going to drive her absolutely nuts. How on earth could her mother have taken him on?

'OK, well, we'd better get started, I suppose,' she said reluctantly. 'I'll show you how it all works.'

Later, while Dan was trying to memorise the prices, she accosted her father. 'Why didn't you stop her, Dad? You knew it was him.'

'I was on the phone while she was talking to him. I only saw the back of his head. Didn't she say anything to you last night?'

'No, I was out, remember? Honestly, this is going to be a nightmare.'

'He seems quite good. He's picked it all up pretty fast.' Bill looked at her over the top of his glasses. 'So no scaring him off, eh? We could do with someone good for a change.'

Lottie turned away, frowning.

By the end of the day, she had to admit that he was a very good waiter, relaxed with the customers, swift around the tables, careful to get things right. And yet something about him got to her. He liked her, that was obvious, and he knew she didn't like him back, so why was he so damn confident?

As she turned the sign on the door to Closed, she wondered how she could say he'd got the job without being too enthusiastic or encouraging. She watched him chat to Bill about the Test match in an easy, blokey way, patting Bill on the back when he had a coughing fit.

She cleared her throat and they both looked up.

44

'Well, thanks for today, Dan,' she said. 'You've got the job as far as I'm concerned. Dad?'

Bill clapped Dan heavily on the shoulder. 'Welcome to The Pier-End Cafe, comrade! Glad to have you on board.'

He turned to pick up his coat and, giving Lottie a huge wink, went to leave. 'You lock up, love. I'll wait by the bandstand.' She could have kicked him.

Dan handed her the bunch of keys that was lying on the counter. 'You're really good at it, you know. Running this place.'

The bloody nerve of him! 'Thanks, but you're not really in a position to comment. Yet.'

It was the wrong answer because it made him laugh. 'You're right. Sorry. Listen, Lottie...'

Oh Christ, she thought, he's going to try again. Not now, not when she'd just become his boss. She strode to the door and opened it, calling over her shoulder, 'Look, Dan, we've employed you, you're a good waiter, we're comrades as Dad would say, but that's all. OK?'

He passed her in the doorway, his canvas jacket creaking and giving off the scent of campfires and wet grass. Outside, he waited as she locked the door and when she turned, he was smiling at her, utterly uncrushed. 'I like you, Lottie, that's all. Whatever you want is fine with me. Comrades it is!'

He gave her a mock salute and walked away, slowly disappearing into the crowds that still drifted around the pier.

Chapter 4

Larry
November 1937

Larry knew the place meant something before he knew what the meaning was.

He'd been driving around one Saturday morning as he often did, feeling a need to get out of the house and go somewhere. Joanie had asked to come too and they made their regular drive up to the new houses, slowing down to see who had moved in, what they'd changed, what they'd kept.

At the top of the hill they parked and he wound down the window. From there, they could see past the estate to the road leading back into town and the straggle of stone terraces that marked the old town boundary. When he'd built the new houses, they were isolated, red brick islands in the fields that surrounded them. Now, other buildings had sprung up along the road – more houses, small and cheaply constructed, he noted, a garage and even a cafe and shop selling cream teas and newspapers. They were dotted along the road at random, unplanned, ugly. Larry didn't like the way the town was creeping closer.

'Look,' Joanie said. 'The horses have gone.' She pointed down the hill to where a ramshackle livery stable used to stand. It was one of her delights on these drives to count the horses and make up names for them. But the field was empty and the stable doors gaped open.

'Where do you think they've gone, Dad?'

'I expect they've just moved them somewhere else, somewhere nicer,' Larry said. 'I wonder what they'll build there instead.' He started the engine.

'I don't want to go home yet,' Joanie said, pulling a sulky face. 'Can't we go somewhere else?'

'Well, where do you want to go? Mummy'll be cross with us if we're late back.'

Joanie folded her arms. 'I don't know. I just don't want to go home yet.'

Larry looked over towards the town, its dark roofs and chimneys crammed against a low grey sky. One of those roofs was theirs, though he couldn't tell which one. Beneath it, Rosemary would be cleaning the windows. Roy had told him this when they left adding, 'Mummy's going to let me help.' By now, Rosemary would be complaining about the rattling window frames and about Joanie gallivanting off. Roy would be bored and irritable. Larry didn't want to go home either.

He drove off slowly, uncertain what to do. A few hundred yards down the hill, a narrow lane crossed the main road, hardly more than a track. He braked as they approached it. 'What if we go down here?' he asked.

Joanie sat forward. 'Where does it go to?'

'I don't know. Shall we see?'

'Go on then, Dad! Let's go! Let's have an adventure.' She gave a little shriek of excitement as they made a sharp right turn.

High banks hemmed the lane on either side and the Austin brushed past faded bracken and great knots of old man's beard. Joanie reached out of the window and pulled at the tufts of silk as they passed. After a few minutes there

47

was a sudden dip downhill and leafless tree branches tangled above them. As they went lower, the trees grew black, sodden with damp and patched with vivid moss, until they reached a shallow ford at the bottom of the hill. Then the road went upwards again and soon the roadside banks levelled until they were gone completely and they came out into the open.

Larry stopped the van.

'Where are we?' Joanie asked. 'Can I go and look?' She was half out the door as she said it.

Larry got out too and walked over to a nearby gate. In front of him a field sloped away, with sheep crowded by the hedge and a bitter wind racing towards them through the grass.

Joanie climbed onto the gate and leaned forward, arms flung out. 'I can fly!' she shouted, her coat streaming behind her, dark hair pulling her face taut.

On the other side of the road was a strip of scrubland and then a fence. Larry crossed over to see what lay beyond it. The wind at his back pushed him forward through clumps of gorse and brambles and he tripped, almost falling into a ditch. Freeing his coat from a bramble sucker, he hauled himself up to the fence and gazed at the scene in front of him.

There was a steep drop below the fence, with a jumble of white rocks and a crow strutting, sounding its rough call. He turned to tell Joanie to come and look, and saw for the first time the whole shape of the hill and those surrounding it. The long fields reaching up to the crest, then the sudden fall. Like waves frozen just before they broke. Like a grassy sea.

In the afternoon, Larry got the stepladder and set it up outside the bay window. Rosemary could never reach to clean the top panes. He carried up a bucket of soapy water, balancing it with one hand.

Roy came out of the house with the sponge. 'I want to help.'

'It's a bit too high, son. Pass me up the sponge and I'll get started.'

'Mummy let me help her.'

'She wasn't on the stepladder. Pass me the sponge now.'

Roy sat on the bottom rung of the ladder, gripping the sponge between his knees.

'Roy,' Larry said, 'give it here.'

Roy didn't move. Through the glass, Larry saw Rosemary inside the sitting room, frowning at him and gesturing towards Roy. 'Come on now, let's have it,' he said.

'But I want to come up there.'

'It isn't safe. Look, Roy...' Larry shifted position to see if he could reach down and grab the sponge. As he moved, the galvanised bucket tottered and slipped from his hand. Warm water poured almost pleasantly down his leg before the bucket struck the back of Roy's head.

The boy fell screaming to the ground. Water trickled and pooled around him, foam covering him like a caul.

Larry jumped down and bent over him. Roy lay on his side, wailing and scrabbling at the ground, but there was no blood.

'Hush, hush, calm yourself now. Let me see.' He felt a lump just behind Roy's left ear and gently checked around it in case of further swelling.

'Get him up, get him off the wet ground!' Rosemary was suddenly next to him, pulling Roy into a sitting position, lifting him by the armpits. 'Take him and get him inside.' She thrust the sobbing child at Larry.

He lifted him and carried him into the house, hurrying through the hall, past Joanie halted at the foot of the stairs, and into the sitting room.

Rosemary was strewing the floor with newspaper. 'Here, put him down here where the rug won't get wet.' Larry laid him carefully down.

Joanie came to stand beside him. 'What's happened?' she whispered.

Rosemary began to undo and remove Roy's wet clothes. 'Oh, you silly boy. You're such a silly, naughty boy,' she said quietly, over and over again. 'Joanie, fetch me a towel. And bring his dressing gown and pyjamas.'

Larry stepped back and watched Rosemary strip and dry her son, then wrap him in his pyjamas and dressing gown.

'Right then, it's upstairs and into bed with you. Daddy'll take you.'

Larry bent to pick him up and saw that he was shivering and very pale. 'Do you think we need to get the doctor?' he asked, laying him down again on the sofa.

'I don't know,' Rosemary said. 'It's five shillings.' She looked down at Roy. 'I don't know,' she said again.

The doubt in her voice made Larry anxious. 'I'll go and get him,' he said. 'Joanie, help Mummy look after your brother.'

He flung on his coat and ran quickly to the van. The doctor's house was only a few streets away but in his agitation, it felt like driving through a maze. The doctor came immediately, offering reassuring words that Larry barely heard.

The examination was brief and Larry watched anxiously for signs of concern on the doctor's face. But as he put away his stethoscope, he said he was confident that there was no lasting harm.

'Let him rest for now. He'll be back to his usual self by the morning.'

Larry showed him out and watched him walk down the road, black coat blowing sideways in the strengthening wind. The upturned bucket was rolling on the path. He righted it, then folded the stepladder which was still poised by the bay window. He thought about leaving them there in the front garden but instead carried them through the house to the garden shed.

Dusk was crowding in and the wind-blown shrubbery bowed and shivered in the half light. In the house, all the upstairs windows were lit and from the shed Larry watched shadows pass from room to room behind the curtains. Rosemary would already have Roy tucked into bed with a hot water bottle and a cup of warm milk. He knew he should go and see him but he held back, full of self-blame. No doubt Rosemary would agree with him. If only he hadn't tried to get the sponge, if only he hadn't started cleaning the blasted windows in the first place.

Rain spilled suddenly out of the dark. He locked up the shed and slowly went back towards the house. As he reached the back step, something in the way the wind pushed at him reminded him of the morning, standing on top of the hill. He paused for a moment, remembering how the land was sea-green, the sweep and the swell of it. Then his old vision of the sea returned, flooding through him like a riptide, and mixed now with a memory of The Dolphin and the feel of Will's hand on his arm.

It was so sudden, so powerful, he had to grab hold of the door handle to stop himself collapsing onto the step. He'd thought all that was done with, but here it was back again, and he couldn't even tell if it gave him pleasure or pain. He blinked hard and opened the door, welcoming the light and warmth of the kitchen. If all this wasn't done with, if it didn't go away, what was he going to do? There was no way to live with it, no way to reconcile it with Rosemary, with Joanie, with Roy. The possibility of giving in to it, of leaving the life he had and choosing a new one appeared only for a moment before it evaporated again. So many barriers to cross, so much hurt and shame to endure, for him and others. He rubbed his temples and stared at the grain of the pine table, following with his finger the knots and whorls that wound round and round, leading nowhere.

He was still sitting there when Rosemary came in, startling him.

'Are you coming to see Roy?' she said. 'He's asking for you.'

'Yes, of course I am. I was just...I'm so sorry, Rosemary, I should never have let the bucket fall.' He stopped, waiting for her to heap blame on him.

It didn't come. Instead, she patted his shoulder briefly. 'Well, never mind that now. He's a strong-willed boy, a real little man.' She went to the door. 'Go and see him.'

Roy was sitting up in bed with Joanie sprawled across the foot, reading Peter Rabbit to him. Larry felt a stab of guilt as he saw the boy, his face small and vulnerable against the white pillow. To think what could have happened.

He ruffled Roy's hair, careful to avoid the bruise. 'How are you, Roy?'

'It still hurts a bit,' Roy said. 'But look, Mummy gave me milk and a biscuit. In bed.'

'Well, that's a treat, isn't it?' He glanced at Joanie who was lying on her back now, arms behind her head.

'Dad,' she said. 'I liked that place we went to today.'

'What place?' Roy asked. 'Where did you go?'

'It wasn't anywhere, son. We just stopped by the road somewhere.'

Joanie rolled over again. 'It was the top of a giant hill. You could see forever and it was so windy I could nearly fly.' She spread out her arms like wings.

'Can I go?' Roy asked eagerly. 'I want to see it too.'

'It's just a hill, Roy. Just a hill and a field and a road.'

'But it's not fair if Joanie goes and I don't.' He paused. 'And I got hurt, so I should have something nice. Can we go tomorrow?'

'Can we go again, Dad?' Joanie added.

They looked at him, waiting for him to agree. He looked back at them, wondering if he could do it.

Larry half hoped Rosemary would find a reason to stop them from going. But something about Roy's accident had softened her, temporarily at least. 'It'll be a nice drive out if we wrap up warm,' she said. So, on Sunday afternoon they put on coats and gloves and hats and piled into the van.

The narrow lane was less mysterious than it had been the previous day. Larry drove cautiously, worried that this time the hilltop would have no meaning for him. What if it was just any old hill? What if it wasn't?

His heart was beating fast as they splashed through the ford and began the uphill climb. When they reached the top, he parked and pretended to adjust one of the dashboard controls while the others got out.

It's just a place, he told himself. Just a place that reminds you of the sea, and the boat, and... that's all. He stepped out onto the grass. Joanie and Roy were running round the gorse bushes, pretending to fly, and Rosemary was at the fence, staring into the distance. All around him the hills came in green waves and he knew then that this place would always remind him of The Dolphin. He knew too that this was as close to the sea as he could ever get. He shivered.

Rosemary called his name.

'Just a minute,' he called back, taking a deep breath. Then he straightened and went over to her, attempting his ordinary walk, putting on his ordinary face.

'It's a fine view, isn't it?' he said.

'Very nice. Very impressive.' She turned to him. 'So, is this your next project then?'

'Project?'

'You've got that look about you. That look you get when you're thinking about something, when you're planning something.'

Larry smiled uncertainly, wondering what he'd given away.

'And you were so keen to come out here. Is it going to be more houses then? That view will sell them for you, no trouble at all.' She was looking about as if assessing the site. 'Not just semis though, not here. You want something a bit special up here.'

'Well,' Larry said. 'I don't really know just yet.'

'Detached, that's what you want. Something with a bit of class. In fact...' She moved closer to him, a light in her eyes. 'What you want to do is build a house up here for us. It's about time we had some benefits, saw some of that modern living.'

'You want to live up here?'

'Not on our own. There'd need to be other houses too, a nice little estate of detached houses. You could call it the Hilltop Estate or Hillcrest or something like that.'

She kept talking while Larry stared at her, hating every

word she said. The thought of this place being cluttered up with houses and cars, with cookers and candlewick bedspreads, with dahlias and butter knives and all the dreary accessories of living, made him queasy. But Rosemary had fixed on this now, he could see that. She was walking about, plotting the number of houses, where they would fit, the size of the gardens.

'It's early days, Rosemary,' he called. 'Don't get too excited. I haven't even bought the site yet.'

'Well,' she said. 'You'd better get onto it, hadn't you?'

January 1938

The film was nearly over. Larry had barely noticed the plot and couldn't have named one of the actors, but he was grateful for the dark and not having to talk to anyone. Beside him Rosemary sat slightly forward in her seat. Her face, lit silver by the screen, was rapt.

The change in her surprised him every week, although they had been coming to the Gaumont on Saturdays since before they were married. In the warm dusk of the cinema, the hard contours of her face dissolved and each time he glanced over, he saw hope, fear, anxiety and joy bloom in sequence across her features. Only here did she show emotion.

He sank lower in his seat, turning over the question about the hilltop site. He had sought out the owner and bought the land. Partly because he couldn't bear the thought of anyone else building there, partly to placate Rosemary. But now she kept up a monologue about how she wanted the house to look, what kind of windows it should have, which direction the bedrooms should face. He had said as little as he could, made her no promises, and hoped desperately that planning permission would be refused. Though even that might not stop her, he thought.

He looked up at the screen. *The End* appeared in flowing script as the lights came up and the national anthem began to play. He and Rosemary stood and he watched her everyday face return as the music finished.

A heavy sleet was falling when they stepped outside, with a north wind driving it straight at them. They hurried towards the bus stop, collars up and heads down against the weather.

Rosemary stumbled into a puddle of slush, splashing both of them with muddy ice. 'Oh, really!' she exclaimed.

Larry took her arm to guide her, but a particularly spiteful blast sent them both staggering across the pavement.

'We can't wait out here in this,' he said. 'Why don't we go to the pub over there?'

'Don't be ridiculous. I'm not going in there.'

'Rosemary, look at the weather. We'll freeze out here.'

'You mean you want a drink.'

'No, I mean that we'll freeze out here. Look at you, your teeth are chattering and your coat's soaking wet. Come on.'

She frowned but looked towards the glowing windows. 'The Star. Is it a respectable kind of place?'

'It's just a normal pub,' he said. 'Not Sodom and Gomorrah. Look, we can catch our deaths out here or we can go in. I know what I'm going to do.' He stepped towards the doorway.

'All right then. Just until it eases, mind.'

Larry pushed at the door to the lounge bar and held it open for her. A wave of smoke and beery warmth rolled towards them, mixed with the smell of damp wool. He nudged Rosemary forward and closed the door behind them.

It was an ordinary pub, near identical to dozens of others, built with now faded Victorian splendour. But to be there tonight when all he'd expected was a cold bus ride home gave Larry renewed hope. Things would work out, he was sure they would. Perhaps he could talk to Rosemary now, persuade her that the hill is the wrong place for a house.

'You sit down and get warm,' he said, pointing to an empty table. 'I'll get us something to drink.'

From the bar, he watched her sit primly at the table, handbag held in her lap. She surveyed the room and he did too, to see what she saw. The pub was busy. Men were gathered in clumps and pairs, with the odd loner leaning against the bar. Among them, the few women stood out brightly, like spring bulbs in bare earth. But they weren't Rosemary's sort and he could imagine all too clearly what she thought of them.

He took their drinks back to the table. 'I got you a brandy,' he said. 'I think you need it. Medicinal purposes.'

'What's that you've got?'

Larry held up his glass and turned it to the light. The liquid in it shone an oily gold.

'Whisky,' he said, relishing the word. 'That'll warm me through.'

He leaned back in his chair. Lit a cigarette. 'It's a nice little place, this,' he said. 'Not a bad little spot at all.'

At the next table, three young men and a girl were talking and laughing, the girl as loud as any of them. Her lips were a deep crimson, her blouse a fleshy pink. Larry watched one of the men move his hand to touch her arm, then slide his fingers under the sleeve of her blouse. Saturday night, Larry thought, everything happens on Saturday night.

'Warming up a bit?' he asked Rosemary.

She nodded and he noticed that her brandy was half gone already. 'Want another one?'

'I don't think so.'

'Go on, Rosemary, it'll do you good. And we need to dry off in here for a while longer. It's still foul outside.'

'A very small one then.'

He finished his own drink and went up to the bar. The whisky was unfurling inside him, his cheeks reddening in its warmth. He looked over at Rosemary, sitting closed and narrow in her chair, her gaze fixed on the table. She didn't know how to be happy, that was the trouble. She set so many conditions on it that it would never happen. Larry sighed. And there was so much pleasure to be had from a pub, he thought, not just the drink but the conversation, the company, the belonging. He listened now to the noise around him – the talk of football and work, the jokes and banter, the laughter of men at ease with each other. There wasn't a better place to be.

He made his way back to the table, setting Rosemary's drink in front of her.

She took a sip of brandy and suddenly leaned towards him. 'I never came out on a Saturday night when I was that age,' she said, gesturing to the girl on the next table. 'Mother would never have allowed it.'

Larry watched as the girl took a long drink of beer, then smiled across at him. He looked away quickly. 'Times do change, don't they?'

'I didn't complain though. Not once. I did my duty.'

He nodded, half listening.

'Poor Mother.' Rosemary's voice cracked as tears gathered in her eyes. 'She didn't get an easy time of it.'

He watched her dab at her eyes, feeling both pity and resentment. Her mother had dominated her, filled her with ideas of what her life should be – the husband, the home, the children, all struck from a preordained mould. Rosemary had not once questioned whether this was the right thing to do, even when it was clear as glass that reality would never live up to her expectations. No wonder she was unhappy.

But nobody had it easy, he thought. It's a hard life and then you die, his mother had told him countless times. He could see her now, work-roughened hands, worry lines drawn deep on her face, no time to be soft or loving. I don't want that life, he said to himself.

'Listen, Rosemary, I need to talk to you about the site on the hill, about the house.'

'And I didn't either,' Rosemary continued. 'First nursing father, then her.' She sighed, then lifted her head a little and wiped her cheeks. 'What did you say?'

'Building the house. The site on the hill.' He turned his glass round and round on the table. 'Maybe we can find a better location, somewhere closer to town. Up there on top of the hill, well, think of the inconvenience.'

She said nothing, but looked at him steadily.

He drank a little whisky. "It's not the right place for a house, not for our house.'

'Why not?' Some of the steel was back in her voice.

'Because...' he said, then stopped. An idea hit him with an almost physical force. It arrived complete in every detail, as if he'd already done it. 'Because I'm going to build a pub there.'

Rosemary's expression changed to puzzlement but he ignored it and carried on, as much for himself as for her.

'Nothing ordinary. This will be exceptional, really exceptional. It'll bring in people from miles away, coach trips even. I can see it now, every inch of it. It will be a beautiful place.' The image of it shimmered in front of him.

'You'd rather build a pub than a house for your family?' Her voice was icy cold.

He ignored her, tuned in only to the image he had in his head. 'We could live there too! It'll have all mod cons, masses of room.'

Rosemary stared at him. 'You honestly think I would live in a pub? That I'd let my children live in a pub?' She gave a hollow laugh. 'Have you gone mad or is it just the whisky talking?'

'All right then, we won't live there, but this is what I'm going to build, Rosemary, this is what that site's for. I'm certain of it.'

She stood up, began to put her coat on and was already on her way to the door. 'I think you've had enough for one night. This is just a stupid, drunk idea. I'm going home.'

Larry downed his whisky, grabbed his coat and hat, and hurried after her. Outside, the sleet had stopped but the wind still blew, whipping their faces with cold, wrapping their wet coats round their legs. They made their way to the bus stop without a word and stood in silence waiting for a bus to arrive.

For once, he was glad to walk the babysitter home, to have an excuse to be alone again, even in the bitter cold. He dropped her off, then took a detour around the edge of the park. It was quiet, the light from the street lamps caught and held by the perimeter trees. Beyond that was a still pool of darkness. He could think here.

Plans. Elevations. Materials. Costs. He seemed to know

everything already, as if his mind had been working without telling him. I knew it was the right place, he said to himself, I knew it was right for something. He longed to get started straight away, would have gone out there now and started digging if he could. There was so much to be done. Rosemary would need to be appeased, somehow. Perhaps she would come round to the idea by herself, perhaps he would have to convince her. He didn't want to think about that.

He paused for a moment and closed his eyes, picturing the pub sailing on the hill, permanently cresting a wave. The Dolphin.

Chapter 5

Joanie
February 1949

Joanie knew something had happened as soon as she went into the kitchen. When she opened the door, Roy was standing by the window and Rosemary was reading a letter at the table. The kettle was whistling on the stove. It had been a busy lunchtime and she was looking forward to sitting down with a peaceful cup of tea, but that seemed unlikely now. She went over and took the kettle off the heat.

'What is it?' she said.

Rosemary pushed the letter towards her. It was short and official looking. Joanie only had to glance at the contents to know what it was.

'When do you have to go, Roy?'

'Two weeks on Thursday.'

'He has to go to Oswestry,' Rosemary said. 'Oswestry, for goodness' sake. He'll hardly ever be able to get home. And what's he going to get up to if I can't keep an eye on him?'

'I'm not going to get up to anything, am I? I'll be too busy marching and being bawled at and cleaning out latrines.' Roy trailed off, a look of disgust on his face.

Joanie couldn't think of anything to say. She didn't know what the army would be like for Roy, but she could imagine all too clearly how life at The Dolphin would change without him.

Since the night of the Blitz, Rosemary had changed. Joanie had watched her mother focus on Roy, giving him all her attention, though not noticeably her affection. She started calling him the 'man of the house', telling him how big and strong he was and how all the girls would fall for him. She gave him the best of their rations and anything extra that came their way. More clothing coupons than was fair were spent on Roy so, unlike the rest of them, he never had to tolerate underwear that was falling to pieces or shirts that had been worn to transparency.

She made a pot of tea and sat down. Rosemary would be unbearable without Roy to distract her. She would turn her attention to Joanie, but not in the same way, not in a motherly way. After Larry's death, Rosemary had changed towards her too, treating her almost as an adult. 'A woman's role is to do her duty,' she had told Joanie. 'I did mine. It's your turn to do yours.'

Surprised and pleased at first, Joanie took on the responsibility of counting the takings that the bar staff brought up at the end of each shift. Sometimes it was a rush to get home from school in time to get them done. Then Rosemary started bringing her the stock sheets and sending her down to the cellar to check them. It was more and more difficult to fit in her schoolwork and harder still to maintain friendships.

She sipped at her tea, pushing back the mounting sense of injustice. One morning she woke up and realised that, without any clear decisions on her part, she had left school and was more or less running The Dolphin.

'Pour me one then,' Roy said. 'You won't get many more chances.'

Joanie took a cup of tea over to him. She glanced at the letter again. 'It says you've got an advance on your pay.'

'Four shillings,' he said. 'Not much, is it? Not for what they expect from me.'

'You never know, Roy, you might enjoy it. You'll be going somewhere new, doing something different.'

'Huh.' The look of disgust returned. 'It's bloody slave labour, that's what it is.'

'Language, Roy!' Rosemary said. She stood up, ready to leave. 'Anyway, I've got a lot of organising to do before you go.'

Joanie heard the door of her room close and lock.

'At least you'll be getting out of here,' she said. 'God, I'd do anything for a change of scenery.'

'You wouldn't be saying that if you had to do fucking National Service.'

Joanie watched him as he sat at the table and lit a cigarette. He was tall but childish, barely needing to shave, utterly wrapped up in himself. She suppressed a feeling of triumph and wondered how he'd survive.

The morning of Roy's departure was bitterly cold. Feathers of ice patterned Joanie's window and her breath fogged the air above her face. She lay in bed, willing herself to get out. 'Three, two, one,' she said out loud, throwing back the bedcovers. The slap of cold on her skin made her gasp. She dressed quickly, putting on her thickest jumper and Betty's old land girl breeches that had somehow become hers.

Roy and Rosemary were already eating breakfast. The kitchen was rich with the smell of fried eggs and bacon and her mouth began to water. How long was it since she'd had a proper cooked breakfast?

'Is there bacon?' she asked hopefully.

'There wasn't enough for two,' Rosemary said. 'And Roy's

got a long journey ahead of him. There's an egg though.'

Better than nothing, Joanie thought, lighting the flame under the still greasy frying pan. She cracked in the egg and watched it spread and whiten, then frill at the edges. After a minute she added a slice of bread, turning it until it was golden and glossy with fat. She slid everything onto a plate and sat down.

There wasn't enough of it, but it was delicious, with an elusive scent of the bacon that had been cooked in the pan. She closed her eyes and chewed each mouthful slowly, making it last.

'Come on, Roy, hurry up,' she heard Rosemary say. 'The taxi's booked for seven. Joanie, are you coming to the station or not?'

Joanie opened her eyes. She hadn't thought about that. 'Do I need to? Do you want me to come, Roy?'

He shrugged. 'If you want to. It's no skin off my nose.' He nodded towards her breeches. 'Not sure if you're suitably dressed though.'

'For goodness' sake, Joanie, you can't go into town looking like that,' Rosemary said. 'Well, you'll just have to stay here and I'll take him. Fetch your case, Roy, and we'll wait downstairs.'

Roy stood up slowly, almost languidly, with an arrogance that Joanie was certain hadn't been there the day before. He must be feeling like he's a man, she thought. I expect that'll get knocked out of him soon enough.

She went downstairs with them to watch for the taxi coming up the hill. Although it was barely daylight in the yard, a clear sky rose up in the distance. On the hills beyond The Dolphin where the early sun had reached, she could see a pale pink glitter of snow.

A thought struck her. 'Have you said goodbye to Betty? She wouldn't want to miss you.'

Roy's face flushed crimson and he put his hands in his pockets. 'I said it last night.'

'Oh, I see. Well, I'll tell her you got away all right. Here's the taxi, look.'

They went out to the gate and Joanie unlocked it. Rosemary climbed into the front seat while Roy put his bag in the back. He turned to Joanie. 'Bye then. See you in a couple of years.'

She laughed. 'You'll get leave, silly.' He looked like himself again, stubborn and self-centred, and when she said, 'I hope it's all right, I hope you like it,' she meant it.

The taxi went slowly down the icy hill while she watched, stamping her feet and shivering, until it had disappeared.

There was time for another cup of tea before she had to start work so she sprinted back to the kitchen. Huddled by the stove, warming her hands on her cup and jiggling her cold feet, she wondered what Roy's blush had signified. He'd had a schoolboy crush on Betty ever since she arrived. Maybe he'd finally declared himself. The thought of it made her smile.

An old cardigan of Rosemary's hung on the back of the chair and she folded it up and rested her head. There was a lot to think about, but the early start, the warmth after the cold, the wireless playing in the background, all made her drowsy.

When she woke up, Betty was sitting opposite her. She was wearing her dressing gown and her hair was in curling papers. 'Roy's gone then?' she said, lighting a cigarette.

'Yes.' Joanie checked the clock. 'Mum should be back quite soon, I think.'

'All right, was he?'

'He wasn't quite himself, but that's only to be expected.'

Betty smiled. 'Well, he's a man now. Off to do a man's job.'

'He did say goodbye, didn't he? I asked him ...'

Betty smiled again, then started to laugh. 'Oh yes, he said goodbye.' She leaned forward.

Joanie could see orangey patches of make-up still stuck to her cheek.

'Did he tell you anything about last night?'

Joanie shook her head.

Betty sat back in her chair and blew out a cloud of smoke. 'Oh, well, if he didn't tell you...Mum's the word.'

Joanie sipped her tea, fuming. She refused to play Betty's games. For a while they sat in silence.

The urge to ask the question was almost irresistible. She was about to say something when a horn sounded outside. 'Oh blast! I'd forgotten about the delivery.' She jumped up and went towards the door.

Betty called after her. 'Hope he likes your outfit.'

Joanie ran down the stairs, cursing herself for falling asleep, for forgetting to change her clothes. It was too late now. She paused at the door to the yard. Patrick was already unloading, rolling the beer barrels down from the lorry. He seemed able to control them with a flick of his wrist, effortlessly guiding them down from the driver at the top of the ramp, then lining them up ready for her to open the door to the cellar.

She walked over slowly, fidgeting with her jumper and breeches as if they could somehow be made more alluring. 'Morning,' she said as brightly as she could. He was whistling *In the Mood*, handling the barrels in time to the tune, but he stopped when she spoke.

His hair was bright as a fox pelt in the sunshine and his eyes seemed shot through with light. 'Morning, Joanie. It's a cold one today, eh?'

She smiled uncertainly, hurrying to unlock the cellar door and heave it open. It occurred to her that there was no one to put the barrels in place once they were in the cellar. That had been Roy's once-a-week job. She folded her arms and restrained herself from kicking at the wall. No doubt Rosemary had assumed she would just take over.

'Something wrong?' Patrick said as he brought over the first barrel.

She lifted her hands helplessly. 'Roy's gone off today for National Service. There's no one to sort out the cellar. Oh, I'll just have to do it.' She switched on the light.

'Hang on, Joanie.' Patrick's hand was on her arm. 'Can't someone else do it? One of the bar men?'

'There's only me and Betty. And I'd like to see Betty's face if you suggested she do it.' The idea of it made her smile and the more she thought about it, the funnier it seemed. She began to laugh out loud and once she'd started, she couldn't stop.

'It's just about the last thing she'd ever do ...' She was off again, conscious of him watching her. Finally, it was all out of her. She took a deep breath and wiped her streaming eyes. 'Oh dear, sorry. I don't know where that all came from.'

He smiled at her. 'That's better. You always look so worried. You need a good laugh now and then.' He strode into the cellar. 'Come on then, where do you want them? I'll sort them out for you.'

The driver called out from the lorry, pointing at his watch.

'Won't be long,' Patrick called back. 'Just a few minutes.'

The cellar was quickly organised, faster than if Roy had

done it. Joanie brought in the lighter crates of drinks and then they were done. They leaned against the wall, both slightly out of breath. She felt horribly red-faced and hot in her thick woollen jumper. 'Thank you so much for helping,' she said. 'I'll have organised someone to do it by next week.'

'I thought you said there wasn't anyone else.'

'No, well, I'll have to find somebody.'

'I can do it if you need me to, Joanie,' he said.

'He wouldn't be very happy,' she said, indicating the driver.

Patrick laughed. 'Oh, I'll sort it with him. A pint'll do it. Honest, I'd like to help.'

He was very close, their shoulders almost touching. She didn't dare look at him. 'Well, thanks, Patrick. That's a weight off my mind. Look, I'd better get on.'

'That's that then. See you next week.'

She watched him jump up into the cab of the lorry. The engine started and as it moved off, his hand waved from the window.

She'd forgotten about Betty's little mystery and only remembered halfway through lunchtime. It was a quiet day and the few customers who were there seemed disinclined to chat. Betty was idly washing some glasses, humming to herself. Joanie went over and began to dry, hoping she was in a good mood.

'Was Roy all right when you saw him last night?' she asked. 'Do you think he was worried about going?'

'I think he was bleeding terrified,' Betty said. 'He was nearly in tears.'

'Oh dear, poor Roy. Were you able to make him feel better?'

Betty dried her hands on the tea towel and turned to her.

'Nosey Parker. You're just itching to know what happened, aren't you?'

But Joanie could see that she was almost as keen to tell.

Betty moved closer. 'Thing is, your mum had a word with me a few days ago. Wanted to know what I thought of Roy. Well, you know your mum isn't one for cosy chats so I asked her right out what she was getting at.' She lowered her voice until Joanie could barely hear her. 'Turns out she wanted me to...well, in her words *make sure he's a real man*. She was worried he was...' She stopped, looking faintly embarrassed.

'Worried he was what?' Joanie whispered.

'One of those perverts, a poof.'

Joanie stared at her. 'What?' She didn't know which piece of information was more startling, that Rosemary thought this about Roy or what she'd asked Betty to do. She was lost for words.

Betty was fiddling with her nails. 'I was a bit aggrieved at first, but then I thought, poor old Roy, going off to God knows where, no fun on the horizon for months. So I, well, you know. Anyway, your mum's happy.'

When lunch was over Joanie went down to the cellar. She dragged a beer crate into a corner and sat on it, pulling up her knees and wrapping her arms around them. There had been too much change for one day. She closed her eyes and wished that Malcolm was there.

She hadn't thought about him for a long time, but sometimes he was the only person in the world she wanted to see, the only one she trusted to do the right thing. When Larry died, she'd searched through his desk for Malcolm's address and written to tell him what happened, begging him to come to the funeral. He replied weeks later, apologising for missing it. *Larry was a fine and decent man*, he wrote, *and the best of friends to me. You must always be proud of him.*

He wrote often after that, wanting to know everything that was happening at The Dolphin, even offering her advice on what to do. *Remember to move the window seat cushions away from the glass in cold weather so they don't get damp from the condensation. If you can get any, lemon juice cleans the copper reliefs a treat.*

And always there was a solicitous comment for her: *Take care of yourself, Joanie, and don't take on too much responsibility.* He seemed to know how hard things were, even though he was miles away.

When did he come back for that last visit? Was it before the war ended or after? She hugged her knees tighter in the chill of the cellar and tried to remember.

It was after, of course. Newly eighteen, she was finally allowed to work behind the bar and Rosemary had summarily sacked the latest barmaid and installed Joanie as a cheaper, more pliant alternative. Betty was already there, her land girl days long over, and Joanie could see her touching up her hair and putting on a smile as she always did when a good-looking man came in. When Joanie turned to take a look at Betty's latest target, she saw Malcolm.

He was older, naturally, and thinner, but still smart in his demob suit and still smiling. Oh, the joy when he walked straight past simpering Betty and gave Joanie a long hug. She started to cry and he too had tears in his eyes.

'Well, look at you,' he said. 'The very grown-up Miss Lambert.'

It was early evening and still quiet, so she took him up to the Ladies Lounge.

'Don't you use it anymore?' he asked sadly, brushing a finger through the dust on the bar.

'We just can't,' Joanie said. 'It's hard enough to find staff to keep downstairs open. Betty's the only one who's stayed longer than a few months.'

He wandered around the room, taking in the spotted mirrors, the cracked paint, the empty shelves behind the bar. For the first time in years, she saw them too and she was embarrassed at The Dolphin's shabbiness. But if Malcolm came back, she thought, maybe things could be made right again.

'It's hard to see the place without Larry in it,' he said. 'It doesn't really feel like The Dolphin.'

'We did our best,' Joanie said. 'I tried to keep it the same.'

He nodded and sat down. 'I know. It's been hard times for everyone.'

'Are you...well, what I mean is, what are you planning to do now it's all over?' She stared down at her hands, almost afraid to hear the answer.

'I'm wondering that myself, Joanie. It's not quite how I thought it would be, coming back to civvy street.'

She cleared her throat and lifted her head a little. 'You could always come back here.' It came out as a whisper.

For a moment he said nothing, then he sighed. 'I've thought about The Dolphin so often. On a busy night with a good crowd in, it's as good as anywhere. Better than most. But The Dolphin without your dad...I don't know, Joanie.'

Please, please, please, she wanted to say.

He patted her hand and smiled. 'But it's the best offer I've had yet. Let me think about it.' He stopped speaking, and stood up, adjusting his tie. 'Good evening, Mrs Lambert.'

Joanie turned round.

Rosemary was standing at the entrance to the Ladies Lounge, severe in her black coat and hat. 'Mr Gardiner,' she said.

'Malcolm might want to come back here, Mum. Wouldn't that be perfect?' Joanie couldn't help but blurt it out, even though nothing was decided. She squeezed Malcolm's hand.

Rosemary was suddenly next to her, pulling her roughly away by the elbow. 'You're needed in the bar, Joanie. Go on.' She pushed her towards the stairs.

'Mum, for goodness' sake.'

'Downstairs, thank you.'

Joanie went down a few stairs then stopped and crouched down, out of sight of the Ladies Lounge. She could hear their voices clearly.

'Mr Gardiner, there is no question of you coming back to work at The Dolphin. Do you understand?' Rosemary's voice was harsh.

'It was just an idea, Mrs Lambert. Joanie asked me and I said I'd think about it. The poor girl's worked off her feet.'

'I'd like you to leave now.'

'I should say something to Joanie.'

'Go please. And if I find out that you have contacted either of my children, I will call the police.'

'There's really no need, Mrs Lambert.'

'And you know what the police mean for people like you.'

Joanie craned her neck to hear Malcolm's reply, but there was only silence. A few seconds later he appeared at the top of the stairs, Rosemary behind him.

'So sorry, Joanie,' he whispered as he passed her. 'So sorry.'

It was much too cold in the cellar to sit for long, and Joanie shivered. There was nothing to be gained from remembering these things. The past was the past, it was done with, gone, and it was no help to her at all.

The cold, clear weather held for almost a week. Then, overnight, a fierce gale blew in, funnelling so much rain onto The Dolphin that Joanie felt they were being specially targeted. Just opening the gate in the morning required mackintosh and wellingtons and even then, the rain seeped inside. By Saturday, all her clothes were damp. She set up the bar for the evening feeling dowdier than usual, and even more so when Betty came downstairs in a new dress.

'Like it?' Betty twirled round the Circular Bar, the skirt of her dress floating up and spreading like ink in water.

'Oh, you've got a New Look dress! Where's it from?' Joanie had never seen so much fabric in one garment. She reached out to touch it. It was silkily cool and rich, like dipping a finger into a cold pot of cream.

Betty stopped spinning and smoothed her hands down the bodice and over her hips. 'Frank had it sent up from London. It's just gorgeous, isn't it? I might have to marry him!'

'You can't wear it for work though, Betty. What if something got spilled on it?'

'Well, I wanted to ask about that, Joanie.' Betty gave a little giggle and looked coy. 'Frank really wants me to come to this dinner tonight, that's what the dress is for really. Big business deal and all that. What if I had the night off tonight and covered your shift tomorrow lunchtime?'

I should say no, Joanie thought. Too short notice and a five-hour shift on my own on Saturday night isn't the same as a quiet two hours on Sunday lunch.

'You'd get a whole day off then,' Betty pointed out. 'Since we aren't open Sunday nights.'

Joanie nodded slowly. It would be too dispiriting to work with Betty anyway, not with the way she looked in that dress. 'All right then, but you have to do all the setting up tomorrow too. I'm not even going to get out of bed.'

'Course I will. Thanks, Joanie, you're a pal. Listen, you can be my bridesmaid!'

A horn tooted outside and Betty rushed to get her coat and handbag. 'I reckon he might even pop the question tonight. Wish me luck!' She blew a kiss and was gone.

Joanie went slowly into the main bar. She tried a twirl, but there was no swish of satin. Utility rayon, she thought, rubbing the fabric between her fingers. The opposite of glamour.

By nine o'clock only a handful of customers had come in. She could hear the wind battering the windows and now and then rain hit the glass like gravel. What if I closed early, she wondered. Then I could curl up in bed with a book and a hot water bottle. She pictured Betty at the dinner, all sparkling conversation and fancy food. Perhaps there would even be champagne. She sighed.

The door opened with a crash and a noisy gust of wind blew in, rattling the glasses on the shelves behind the bar. Joanie looked up, preparing her face for the next customer, and saw Patrick walking towards her. He was wearing a suit and a loud patterned tie and he looked both older and younger than he usually did. Her cheeks blazed.

'Hello, Joanie,' he said, leaning on the bar. She thought she saw his cheeks redden too.

The glass she was drying slipped and she almost dropped it. 'Hello, Patrick.' For a moment she twisted the glass to and fro, not knowing what to do.

'Can I get a drink?'

'Oh, yes. Of course you can. Sorry. What would you like?'

'A whisky please. It's a rotten old night out there. Think I deserve one.'

She poured out a measure for him. 'That's what my dad used to say: a whisky warms you through. Water?'

'Just a splash. Here, I'll do it.' He added a little water from the jug, then took a sip. 'That'll do fine.'

Joanie smiled, but could think of nothing to say and was relieved when another customer came up to the bar. When she was done with the order she turned back to Patrick. He was gazing around with an amused look on his face.

'I didn't realise what this place was like inside,' he said. 'I've only ever seen the cellar. It's a bit much, isn't it?' He began to laugh. 'Like a bleeding opera house or something.'

Joanie blushed again, at once embarrassed and defensive. 'It's how Dad designed it. So it wouldn't be like anywhere else.'

'You can say that again. In fact, I remember now.' He leaned across the bar and tapped her arm. 'When I first started working for the brewery they told me about The Dolphin, what a queer kind of a pub it was. The fairy castle on the hill they called it. I'd forgotten about that.' He laughed again, then cleared his throat. 'How are things then, Joanie? Not running it all on your own again, are you?'

Her skin murmured where he'd touched her. She picked up a cloth and began to wipe down the bar. 'Well, Betty's got the night off. Anyway, it's quiet.'

'Found someone else to help you out yet?'

'I haven't really enquired. I mean, you've been so good with the cellar and everything so it hasn't been too bad. And to be honest, the way business is just now, I don't think we can take on anyone else.' She wondered if this was indiscreet, but she didn't care. 'The only thing is, with Roy gone, none of us can drive. So we're a bit stuck up here at the moment.'

'How do you get away on your days off then?'

She laughed. 'Oh, there haven't been many of those lately.'

There was an awkward pause. Was he meeting someone? Or had he actually come in to see her? He stood up and she thought he was about to leave. She reached for his empty glass. 'Would you like another one?'

'Well...' He sat down again.

'On the house. To say thanks for your help.' Rosemary would be furious if she knew, Joanie thought. Free drinks were strictly against the rules. She poured him a double.

'Cheers, Joanie.'

More customers came in and she was busy for a while, but always aware of Patrick. She circled him as she went about collecting glasses and emptying ashtrays, feeling his gaze on her, like a ship in the beams of a lighthouse. He was still there as closing time approached and the bar began to empty.

She brought over a tray of dirty glasses. 'I'm going to have to close up, I'm afraid.'

'Already?'

She nodded. 'Sorry.'

He stood up. 'Well, thanks for the drink. I'll see you on the next delivery then.'

She remembered again how drab she looked that evening and how her hair had been blown to ruins by the wind. 'Yes, see you then.' How stupid she had been to have any hopes. Hoping was always stupid.

At the door, he turned. 'Listen, Joanie, I've had an idea. Why don't I teach you to drive?'

'What?'

'If you can drive you won't be stuck here anymore. You can go anywhere you like.'

'But...'

'Come on, it's a great idea. I can borrow one of the brewery vans. When's your next day off?'

She looked at him, trying not to be hopeful again. But he looked hopeful too. 'Actually, I'm off tomorrow.'

'Then we'll start tomorrow. Two o'clock?'

She smiled. 'Two o'clock.'

She woke early on Sunday. The sound of the kettle whistling reached her from the kitchen and she heard Betty's door open, then footsteps cross the landing. She yawned, stretching luxuriantly in the warmth of the bed. There was no need to get up for hours.

Rosemary wasn't happy, of course. Joanie had told her about the arrangement for Sunday when she brought the evening's takings upstairs. 'Betty will do it all,' she said. 'From start to finish.'

'What on earth made you agree to such a stupid idea? I've told you a thousand times, she can't be trusted.'

'Oh, don't start that again. I trust her.'

'Well, you'll have to check up on her.'

'Mum, I haven't had a proper day off in months. I am not checking up on Betty.'

'Well, pop down at the end of lunchtime, make sure the till's right, and there isn't any stock missing. It won't take long.'

Joanie took a deep breath. 'I won't be able to do that because I won't be here. I'm going out.'

Rosemary looked at her sharply. 'Oh? Where are you *going out* to?'

It was too much to tell her about Patrick. 'Just out somewhere, into town probably. I deserve to get away from The Dolphin for an afternoon.' Just thinking about it made her heart beat faster.

Rosemary had said no more, though Joanie knew there would be more questions later. But that was later. She pulled the blankets up to her ears and closed her eyes. For now, there was just the delicious sense of anticipation.

She had arranged to meet Patrick further down the hill, out of sight of The Dolphin. He hadn't asked her why. At ten to two she put on her coat and went downstairs. The bar was quiet as she passed through and Betty was deep in conversation with one of the customers. She noticed that dirty glasses had accumulated on several tables and there was a puddle of beer under one of the chairs, but she forced herself to turn away. Hurrying to the door, she slipped out before anyone saw her. At the gate, she began to run. The rain had stopped, but it was still windy and her coat flew behind her like wings as she raced down the road.

After a few hundred yards she slowed, gulping in air and smoothing down her hair. He should be just round this bend, she thought, and closed her eyes for a moment. She heard the wind humming in her ears. The snap of twigs under her shoes. The in and out of her breath. She opened her eyes. He was just round this bend.

He kissed her just after he'd explained about the gears and the clutch. She kept her eyes open. His were closed and she could see little movements in his eyelids and a pale blue ribbon of vein running up his temple. She was surprised at the fleshiness of his mouth and faintly embarrassed by the

79

moist sucking noises their kiss made. But when he whispered, 'Oh, Joanie,' and pulled her closer, her insides did a little flip. She closed her eyes too.

It seemed a long time before the kiss ended and they drew their heads apart. He leaned back and sighed. 'You know, I only made up the driving lessons so I could see you. But I bet you guessed that anyway.'

'Really?' He had wanted to see her that much! 'Honestly, I didn't have any idea.'

He turned towards her and touched her hair. 'We can still do them if you like. Someone needs to know how to drive. And it's a good excuse, if you need one.'

Joanie wondered what would upset Rosemary the most. She smiled. 'You haven't met my mum yet. I don't think she'd be very keen on me learning to drive. Too much freedom. Or on me having a boyfriend.' She stopped, blushing. What a stupid thing to say! He'd think she was one of those ghastly clingy girls she'd read about, girls who started planning a wedding as soon as they shook hands with a man. 'Well, anyway, I'd rather she didn't know anything for now.'

He stroked her cheek. 'Have your other boyfriends been hidden away too?'

'Oh, there haven't really been any boyfriends before.' She gave a half laugh. Was lack of experience something to be ashamed of or not? She didn't know. But he had used the word boyfriend too. She smiled.

'What, none of your customers ever asked you out?'

She shook her head and he laughed, surprised. 'You're unique, the only bar maid in town who hasn't...' He trailed off.

'There's always been Betty, you see. She gets all the attention.'

'Well, I'm glad. That means I get you to myself.' His arms were round her waist again and his lips were close against her neck. 'All to myself.'

Later she had a go at driving. The van, smaller than the one he used for deliveries, but bigger than it looked, veered horribly towards the middle of the road and then stalled. Patrick restarted the engine for her and she edged jerkily back to the verge.

'Oh dear, it's not very easy, is it?'

'You just need practice. Nobody's born knowing how to drive. It takes time.'

She sighed. 'Talking of time, I suppose I'd better be going home soon.'

The rain had started up again, misting up the windscreen so she felt cocooned there behind the wheel. They sat silently for a while, hands touching on the leather seat, the damp bringing out the scent of old beer from the back of the van.

'Will you be able to get away next Sunday?' he asked.

'I'll try. I'll have to come up with a good excuse though. Mum's bound to suspect something. And Betty.'

'They can't stop you coming out, Joanie. You're an adult; you're allowed to do what you want.'

It sounded so easy, so clear cut.

'I know.'

She looked down at her lap, stopping herself from crying. It wasn't as simple as Patrick said. She couldn't remember ever doing what she wanted. There were the things that had to be done, the things that other people wanted her to do, the things she ought to do, before she could decide what she herself wanted. Most of the time she didn't even let herself think about it.

He took her face in his hands and turned her towards

him. 'Do you want to do this again?' His eyes were almost colourless in the grey rainy light as he looked straight at her.

She took a deep breath. 'Yes,' she said, 'I do.'

She got back to The Dolphin as daylight was starting to ebb. The windows were dark, all except for Rosemary's, where a dull pink glow came through the curtains. Joanie shivered as she went inside and up the stairs.

In her room, she switched on the electric fire and huddled in front of it. The elements slowly turned red then orange and she watched them brighten, smiling to herself. When her shins got too hot, she lay down on the bed. Any minute now, Rosemary would come in and ask her where she'd been, but for a few precious minutes she curled up on the bedspread, cradling the secrets of the afternoon inside her.

Rosemary knocked and came in, all in one go. Joanie was sitting up by then, flicking through a magazine.

'You're back from gallivanting about then.'

'Everything all right at lunch?'

'You'll have to check the takings. Betty didn't do them properly, just went off to her room before I could ask her about them.'

Joanie remembered Betty's dinner the previous night. 'Was she wearing a ring? She thought Frank might propose on Saturday.'

Rosemary snorted. 'I pity the man who puts a ring on her finger.' She dropped the takings bag on Joanie's bed. 'Anyway, where did you get to this afternoon?'

Joanie felt herself blush and bent down to put her magazine on the floor. 'Oh, just for a walk. Round and about.'

Rosemary stood looking at her for a moment longer, then

went to the door. 'We're eating at six,' she said. 'You need to come and do the vegetables in fifteen minutes.'

'All right,' Joanie said, avoiding her eyes.

As soon as she heard the wireless go on in the kitchen, Joanie tiptoed out of her room and knocked on Betty's door. 'Are you there, Betty?'

There were noises inside and the door opened a little.

'Hello.' Betty sounded tired.

Joanie went in. A scarf had been thrown over the bedside lamp so the light in the room was a dim amber. Betty was sitting on the bed in her dressing gown, smoking. The air was heavy with the scent of stale cigarettes. The dress, the beautiful floating dress, lay crumpled on a chair.

'Well, did he?' Joanie started to say, then stopped. Betty didn't look like a newly engaged woman. It was hard to tell in the gloom, but Joanie thought she'd been crying. 'What happened last night?'

Betty lit another cigarette. 'Nothing worth mentioning.'

'Frank didn't propose?'

For a few seconds, Betty said nothing, then she mashed the cigarette into the ashtray. 'Turns out he's already married. So no, no proposal.' Her voice was shaky.

'Oh, Betty.'

'Not unless you count the proposals I had from the men at the dinner. But then, they weren't anything to do with marriage.'

'Oh, Betty,' Joanie said again. 'I'm so sorry.'

Tears were running down Betty's face. Joanie sat down beside her.

'That's why he wanted me there, that's why I was at the dinner.' She was sobbing now, Joanie's arm round her heaving shoulders. 'He thought I'd sleep with them and then he'd make a big sale.'

Joanie offered her a hanky and stroked her hand. 'He seemed so keen on you. I can't believe it.'

Betty blew her nose and pushed her hair behind her ears. 'You've got the right idea, Joanie. Don't have anything to do with men. You can't trust them, not even the nice ones.'

Joanie looked at Betty's blotched, puffy face and hoped she wasn't right.

Chapter 6

Lottie
September 1968

Lottie hurried to unlock the cafe door, rain and sea spray hammering at her back. The sea was churning round the pier supports, brought high by a spring tide and a fierce wind. The water seemed just a few inches below her feet.

Inside, she took off her coat and hung it up to dry. The walls of the wooden building were shivering in the wind, draughts blowing in through gaps she'd forgotten existed. It felt as if the whole place could take off at any minute. She loved days like this.

She put the tea urn on to boil and brought in the bread. Rain had seeped underneath the plastic sheet that covered the crate and some of the rolls were ruined. She was sorting through them, deciding what to keep and what to throw away, when Dan arrived.

'Morning, Lottie.'

The weather had un-neatened him, his hair sticking up over his forehead, his cheeks ruddy as a child's. Lottie suppressed a smile.

'Are we really opening up on a day like this?' he asked. 'There's nobody out there.'

'We are,' Lottie said. 'It could all die down by lunchtime and if any of the regulars come along, we have to be open.' She peered out of one of the windows. 'Anyway, it's exciting.'

Dan came to stand next to her and they watched the lead-thick sea roiling below. 'Is Bill not in?'

'He'll be in later. He's got a doctor's appointment this morning.'

Slowly they made the cafe ready, stopping often to see what the weather was doing. Rain found its way under the door so Dan wedged in a wad of tea towels to stop it spreading. One of the windows rattled so much it seemed about to crash from its frame so Lottie jammed paper napkins into the gaps. It felt as if they were patching up the Ark.

When Bill hadn't arrived by eleven o'clock, Lottie rang home. There was no reply. She stared at the rain dribbling down the window and wondered if she should be worried.

At half past twelve the first customers came in. An elderly couple, they laughed as they shook out their sodden raincoats, patting their faces dry with paper napkins. 'It's like Armageddon out there!'

When they'd gone, she rang home again. Still no answer.

Dan made her a cup of tea. 'Maybe he's just gone off for a jaunt with your mum.'

'On a day like this?'

'Or maybe the car's broken down, the engine could have been flooded or some such thing. They could be waiting on the roadside somewhere.'

She gave him an alarmed look and he trailed off. 'Anyway, they'll be fine. They're a great pair, your mum and dad.'

'Mmm.'

'Have they had this place long? Seems like they've got it all down to a T.'

She knew he was being kind, trying to stop her worrying, but there was a sort of comfort in talking about it. 'Years and years. Dad bought it just after the war, I think, then

Mum came to work for him and they've been here ever since.'

'Ah, so they met here?'

'Yes, romantic, isn't it?'

Dan laughed. 'Passion brewed in the tea urn! Love sizzled with the sausages!'

'Don't get any ideas!' she said quickly, but she smiled at him.

He went to wash up their cups. She stayed where she was, watching him at the sink and wondering how long it had taken for her parents to fall in love. She'd heard the story of how they met a hundred times, making them tell it over and over again throughout her childhood.

'I came on the milk train after the van I was driving broke down,' her mother had told her. 'It was October 1949 and I was looking for work and a fresh start after my mother died. I walked round the town but nothing was open, so I went out along the pier, further and further until I was almost in the sea. When I saw the cafe and went inside, it was all pale green, as if it really was under water. And your dad was there, bringing in a crate of lemonade from the door, one bottle at a time.' Here, she would lean towards Lottie and whisper, 'He was swearing because he wasn't very good at it, what with his bad arm.'

'So there I was,' her father would continue. 'Bringing in those damn bottles when this skinny little thing appears and says can she help. Well, I laughed at her, of course. And blow me down if she didn't pick up the whole crate and bring it inside. I offered her a job on the spot.'

At that point they always smiled at each other and her father would say, 'Your mum's the strongest person I know.'

'And your dad's the most intelligent.'

She'd honed the story in her mind over the years, smoothing and polishing each scene until it played like a film. All the details were there in her head – the early morning sun, the chilly air, the salty seaweed smell of low tide drifting up from the beach. She used to like acting out Bill's part as much as Joanie's and she knew by heart what Bill had said when Joanie picked up the lemonade crate: 'Well, I never! I could use a strong girl like you. Want to come and work for me?'

'Want another cup of tea, Lottie?' Dan called, looking at her with concern.

'No, I'm fine. Listen, thanks for being so nice, Dan.'

He shrugged his shoulders. 'Anytime, Lottie.'

At twenty past one, another customer appeared and stayed for fifteen minutes, but no one else came in. She and Dan played cards at the table by the door.

At a quarter to three, Lottie looked out and saw her mother struggling towards the cafe, the slight figure wavy and lopsided through the rainy glass. It must be bad news, she thought, watching her approach, not wanting to know.

Dan opened the door and bustled Joanie inside, getting her a towel for her hair and making her take off her shoes. He fetched newspaper to stuff inside then put them to dry near the oven. 'Coffee, Mrs L, or a tea?' he asked.

'Coffee please, Dan,' Joanie said.

Lottie sat down opposite her mother and waited for her to speak.

Joanie sat with her hands folded in front of her. 'Your dad went to the doctor's this morning.'

'I know.'

Lottie fiddled with the cruet set, rolling the salt cellar across the table until a few grains spilled out. She brushed them to the floor and waited for the worst.

'In fact, it wasn't the GP, it was a specialist.'

Dan quietly put two cups of coffee down on the table and went back behind the counter.

'Was it? What kind of specialist?' Here was the worst, she knew it.

Joanie took a sip of her coffee. 'He was a lung specialist. And he had some news.' She took another sip then continued in the same level voice. 'Lottie, your dad's got TB.'

'TB? But that's a horrible thing.' Wasn't it something old people had, or poor people? The disease that people in books died of?

'They think he's had it for some time so it's quite established.'

Lottie began to cry, tears springing faster than she could wipe them away. From the corner of her eye, she saw Dan put a pile of paper napkins on the table. She picked one up and blew her nose.

'Come on now, Lottie.'

There were no tears in Joanie's voice, no grief. Why aren't you crying, Lottie thought, why aren't you upset?

'Is he...will he...?'

'They're starting treatment straight away. And these days there's a lot they can do with antibiotics and so on. Chances are he'll be fine.'

The tears didn't stop.

'Lottie, listen, you can't do this when you see him. You mustn't upset him.'

But he's my dad, Lottie thought, my lovely dad.

She had always been a daddy's girl. She went to her mother for the practical things – the plaster for a grazed knee, the tying of shoe laces – but her father supplied the comfort. Even now, she often curled up against him on the sofa in the evenings to watch TV. Nothing made her feel safer than resting her head on his shirt front and feeling the bulk of his chest through the starchy cotton. His smell of Palmolive soap and fried bacon was the most comforting thing she knew.

One of her earliest memories was of him pushing her on the garden swing. She was about four, she supposed, and wearing her favourite yellow and white striped dress and a blue cardigan. She could still remember the stiff hem of the dress catching against her knees as the swing went forwards and the scratchiness of the cardigan where it touched her bare skin. She was talking away to Bill as she swung and he was making her laugh, tickling her legs. Then there was an awful lurch as she leaned back and the chains slipped out of her hands, the ground smacking her hard a second later. She remembered a high blue and white sky and warm air on her face as she lay on the grass, pain shooting through her body. And then she was cradled, stroked, the deep rumble of her father's voice making it all right again.

She looked at her mother across the table, drinking coffee and dabbing at her lips with a napkin. Her face gave nothing away; it never did. Her father whistled when he was happy, threw stones in the sea when he was angry, and smoked pipe after pipe when he was miserable, which was hardly ever. Her mother was always the same. Careful, practical, sensible. Never angry, but never joyful either. There was a guardedness about her that never let up, as if she couldn't quite relax, even with Lottie. Yet Lottie had memories – she was sure they were real, not just imagined – of Joanie holding her, playing with her, of the two of them whispering and laughing together. When had that stopped? It must have been around the same time she fell off the swing, when she was four and full of questions that Joanie never answered.

She blew her nose. 'Where is he?'

'He's at home, resting. He'll have to take things easy from now on.'

'What's going to happen then? How are we going to manage?'

'Don't worry about it now, Lottie. Come on, let's close up and go home. He'll be wanting to see you.'

Lottie had forgotten about the storm outside, about Dan discreetly hovering behind the counter. She looked through the window at the rain, still hurling itself across the pier. She'd had no idea he was ill, hadn't noticed anything unusual about his cough. And all along there had been this dark secret inside him. The afternoon was getting dim, long before the usual time, and the storm no longer felt exciting. It seemed hard now and cruel, wanting to harm. Succeeding.

The atmosphere in the cafe changed. When customers asked where Bill was, Lottie told them the truth. She couldn't lie about a thing like that. On the days when Bill felt well enough to come in and help set up, it was painful to watch him move so slowly around the place, to hear him struggling to get his breath. He always left before customers arrived.

After one particularly bad morning, when all he could do was sit at a table and fold napkins, he beckoned Lottie over.

'I think it's time we called a spade a spade,' he said, fiddling with his shirt cuffs. 'I'm not up to it anymore.'

Lottie stared at the table top, wishing she could disagree with him.

'It's down to you now, love. Your mum'll help out when she can, but I think I'll be needing her too.' He paused to cough. 'Anyway, you and Dan are a good team. You'll work it all out, I know.'

He smiled like he used to smile, as if he could put anything right, and she wondered how much effort it cost him.

They took on a new waitress, but she didn't stay; neither did the next one nor the one after that. Lottie took out the old sign from under the counter and hung it on the door without much hope.

'I can't see that we'll get anyone. Not anyone good anyway,' she said.

'Could your mum do any more shifts?' Dan asked.

Lottie shook her head. 'Dad really needs her at home.'

'Look, maybe there's another way,' Dan said. It was nearly closing time and the cafe was empty. He was putting the chairs on the tables and Lottie had started to sweep up. 'I had an idea the other night.'

'Oh yes?'

'Why don't we go for a drink and we can talk about it?'

Surprised to find herself blushing, she kept her head down and carried on sweeping. 'OK then.'

They went to a pub on the Esplanade, huge and bright and noisy. It was the kind of place she hated.

'What do you want?' Dan shouted when they reached the bar.

'Lager and black, please.'

She looked around while he ordered the drinks. It was busy, with a faint haze of perfume and hair lacquer in the air, mixed with all the potential of early evening. Three girls were trading banter with a group of men standing at the bar and she watched them laugh and preen, wondering who would end up with who at the end of the night.

'Here you are,' Dan said. 'Anywhere to sit?'

'Can't see anything.'

'What about that corner over there? We can lean against the wall anyway.'

They made their way between the crowded tables to a corner near the window, squeezing in behind a rowdy group of men in suits and ties. It was getting dark outside and the interior of the pub was reflected in the glass. Lottie stared at the animated scene, golden against the blue of the dusk. The reflection looked a lot more glamorous than the real thing.

'We can go somewhere else if you want,' Dan said. 'You don't look like you're enjoying it here.'

'Sorry, it's fine. Just a bit loud. So, tell me the idea then.'

Dan leaned towards her and she strained to hear him.

'Well, we either need to get someone else in to work or we need to change what we do so we don't need as many staff. And we can't seem to get anyone to stay so...'

'Change what?'

'The food. You see, if we don't make everything to order, it wouldn't take as much time. Then we only need two people to run the place, not three.'

'But how would we make cooked breakfasts if not to order?'

'We wouldn't. We'd have to take them off the menu. And chips. And all the other things like that.'

One of the men on the table in front of them was leaning back in his chair, smoking, looking her up and down with a leering smile. She edged closer to Dan and tried to focus on what he was saying.

'We could make up sandwiches during the morning, when it's quieter, and wrap them up ready. We can still do cakes and toast and the like, no problem.'

'No more hot food?' That would change everything. It wouldn't be Bill's cafe anymore. But what other choice was there? She sighed.

'It's just an idea,' he said.

She saw the group of men glance up at her and nudge each other, then they suddenly broke out into loud laughter. She thought she heard the word 'jailbait'.

Dan turned and stared at them. 'Let's go somewhere a bit more civilised,' he said.

They went towards the door, more raucous laughter following them. Dan took her hand and kept hold of it even once they were outside. It had started to rain and they hurried to stand under the canopy of the shop next door.

'Bad choice of pub,' he said. 'Sorry.'

'It's OK.' She looked at him. 'Thanks for getting us out. And thanks for the idea. Let's give it a try, shall we?'

She was conscious of the warmth in his fingers as they wrapped more tightly round hers.

'Well, thanks for listening, comrade,' he said.

The street was busy, people hurrying past them as the rain grew heavier. The canopy began to drip and make puddles by her feet. She turned to look in the shop window and saw their reflections again. They were amber in the streetlights, surrounded by the black and glitter of rainy pavements. Dan was smiling and she realised that he always smiled. She turned back again and reached up to kiss him. She wanted someone who always smiled.

Chapter 7

Larry
June 1938

Mud didn't bother Larry, nor rain. A drizzle had started about seven o'clock but in the long midsummer evening he hardly noticed it. He tramped across the ditch where the foundations for the tower had been started, checking the angles with a theodolite. His instructions had been precise and he was glad to see that they had been properly followed. The main part of the building was already taking shape, with the position of the internal walls marked out in string. He paced through them, measuring, making sure enough space had been left for the double doors he wanted to order.

By half past nine the light was beginning to dim. He wiped the mud from his boots as best he could and went to sit in the van. The rain had grown heavier, draping itself across the hills, mixing greyly with the last of the light. He drank the last drop of tea in the thermos, feeling chilly now in the damp air.

If he could, he would have stayed on the site all the time and forgotten about his other jobs. Getting the right workmen wasn't easy and keeping them was harder still. He really needed to be there to monitor what went on. There were constant complaints that he expected too much from them and that he was harder here than on the other sites. Larry ignored the overheard comments about him being obsessed. He would make no compromises. It had to be right.

He threw the dregs of the tea onto the grass and started up the van. For a moment, the wheels spun in the mud and he had a brief flash of hope that he might have to stay overnight and could wake up on the hill in a June dawn. Then the wheels caught, the van moved and he was on his way home.

Rosemary had left him a plate of ham salad on the kitchen table together with the post from the morning. He opened a bottle of beer and sat down, riffling perfunctorily through the letters until he saw one from the bank. He tapped it against the table top a few times, eating a mouthful of salad before he opened it.

'... *Must advise you that your account is overdrawn to the sum of £53 7s 5d. Please make arrangements forthwith or I will have to terminate ...*'

He'd been hoping it was less, small enough not to mention to Rosemary. He could have juggled a few things to cover up £10, even £15, but not this. It must have been the French oak for the window frames. That or the copper for the roof of the tower. He rubbed his eyes and took a swig of beer. For all he knew, it could have been one of the lads swindling him. He'd let so much slip lately.

He heard Rosemary's footsteps cross the upstairs landing, padding from the bathroom to the bedroom, and wondered if this was a good time to talk to her about the bank account. He finished the salad and rinsed the plate in the sink. Of course, there could never be a good time to talk to her about the bank account, or anything else. Since the evening at The Star, she had virtually stopped talking to him. And then he was hardly in the house anyway, always up at The Dolphin site or busy with one of his other projects.

He sat down at the table again, thinking through the different ways he could approach the subject. He really had no idea how she felt. He knew what she thought about manners, hygiene and what constituted respectability, but how she felt about the children, about himself, about the rest of her life was a mystery. How did she feel about their marriage?

He remembered their first meeting. During what would be her final illness, Rosemary's mother had demanded a sun porch be built on the back of the house. Larry was appointed as the builder and on his first visit, the old woman ordered him to push her wheelchair so she could show him how she wanted things done. Rosemary hovered behind them, carrying a blanket and a sun hat to cover every eventuality.

Once he started work and spent more time at the house, he began to feel sorry for Rosemary, so put upon by her bully of a mother. There was a porcelain bell which her mother rang whenever she wanted to summon her daughter and its chime sounded all day long.

One day, Rosemary had just brought him a cup of tea when they heard it ring.

'Doesn't she ever give you time off?' he'd asked.

'She wants to make sure things get done properly,' Rosemary said. 'She can't bear being ill, you know, she always used to be so energetic.'

'You should have some time to yourself, go out and have a bit of fun,' Larry said, starting on the brickwork again. 'What do you like? Dancing? Going to the pictures? Enjoy yourself for a change.'

When he looked up, Rosemary was staring at him, her eyes bright. With an awful jolt, he realised that she thought he was asking her out.

'Meet up with some friends,' he added lamely. Her expression was suddenly stricken and a deep blush spread from her neck to her forehead as she turned away. He might as well have slapped her.

The following day he hardly saw her. When she brought him tea, she left the cup in the doorway of the porch without speaking. At the end of the day, he called out, 'Goodbye then. See you tomorrow,' but she was upstairs and didn't answer.

The day after that he waited for her. When she put the cup of tea down, he called out, 'Rosemary, hang on a minute. I wanted to ask you something.'

She was halfway back through the doorway. She stopped and looked at the ground.

'Look,' he said, climbing around the piles of bricks and bags of cement, 'I wonder if you'd like to go to the pictures with me one night next week.' Her face was in profile so he couldn't clearly see her expression.

She dropped her head and was silent for a moment. 'What a very kind invitation,' she finally said. 'But I'm not sure Mother would think it's a good idea.'

'Oh, surely she won't mind,' Larry said, determined to right his wrong. 'I'll ask her this afternoon when I take up my invoices.'

Permission from her mother was granted, though in a frosty and suspicious manner, and the date for the outing fixed.

Now, sitting in the kitchen, Larry wondered what kind of marriage was possible from such a botched start. His intentions and Rosemary's had always been at odds. He lit a cigarette and finished the last of the beer, remembering things he hadn't thought about for years.

After the trip to the cinema, he considered that he had done his duty. He had been pleasant and conversational in what he hoped was a friendly way, more like a brother than anything else. He came to the house the next day in a good mood and was fitting a window frame when Rosemary appeared.

'Hello, Larry,' she said with a new little laugh.

'Morning, Rosemary.'

She didn't move away or ask if he wanted a drink so after a moment he said, 'Wasn't too late for you last night, was it?'

'No, not at all.' She came over to where he was working and looked up at him. 'I had a lovely time.'

'It was a good film, wasn't it?' he said, reaching up to take a measurement and avoiding her eyes.

'Mother would like you to have tea with us later. About four o'clock.'

He was so startled he dropped his tape measure. 'Oh, no, I don't think that's a very good idea.' He gestured at his work clothes. 'I'm far too mucky for that. And I don't want to delay getting this finished. Your mother wouldn't like that, would she?'

'She doesn't expect it to delay you much. We'll be in the kitchen at four.' Rosemary went off, humming.

Larry leaned back against the wall, aware that something inescapable had been set in motion.

For the rest of the day he worked hard, doing the heavy jobs that he normally put off. Perhaps if he was grimy and sweaty enough, they would change their minds. Or maybe he could injure himself with one of his tools and have to go home. At lunchtime, as he sat on the floor with his sandwiches, he ran his thumb over the saw blade. He pressed and the calloused skin tore a little, but didn't bleed. He pressed harder, pulling his thumb back over the metal until the quick flesh stung. A red line drew itself across the ball of his thumb, then thickened and smudged. He blotted it with his handkerchief and went back to his lunch.

At four o'clock he heard the kitchen door open.

'Larry,' Rosemary called. 'Come and have some tea.'

He took off his boots, dusted down his clothes then stepped carefully through the hall into the kitchen. Rosemary was standing by the range waiting for the kettle to boil. Her mother was seated at the table, directly facing the door.

'Good afternoon, Mr Lambert.' She spoke as soon as he entered the room.

'Afternoon, Mrs Parker. It's very kind of you to invite me for tea. I'm not really dressed for it though.'

'Here, sit on this,' Mrs Parker said. She glided away to pick up a cloth from the dresser and Larry realised that she was in her wheelchair. 'Just spread it over the chair. It'll keep the worst off. We'll sponge down afterwards.'

'Tea, Larry?' Rosemary said, bringing the teapot to the table.

He nodded and sat down. In front of him were trays of small triangular sandwiches, a seed cake on a glass cake stand and a platter of jam tarts. Placed around them were plates, cups, saucers, teaspoons, knives, so many that the tablecloth was almost invisible. He felt huge and awkwardly male.

'Fish paste or tomato?' Mrs Parker asked.

'Oh, fish paste, thanks,' Larry said, taking two and putting them on the plate he hoped was his.

'And how is the sun porch coming along? I want to make use of it before winter sets in.' When she reached for the sugar bowl, he noticed that her hands, chalk white and garlanded with veins, were trembling.

'It'll be ready well before that. Just the windows and doors to fit then it's over to the decorators for the inside. I expect my bit to be finished in about a week.'

There was silence for a moment as they all sipped tea and Larry saw a thin dribble leaking from Mrs Parker's mouth. He wondered what illness she had.

She wiped her chin with a napkin and said, 'So is the building trade in good health? My husband always said a good builder is never short of work.'

'It's not bad, Mrs Parker, not too bad. Plenty of work for a one-man band like me.'

'Is it your own business?'

'Well, if you can call it that. It's what my dad did. I just carried on where he left off.' What did they want to hear? Larry had no idea if he was saying the right things.

Mrs Parker bit into a jam tart and spoke through a mouthful of pastry, 'Has he passed on then?'

'Yes, and mum too. The flu.'

'Mmm. A terrible time. Any other family?'

'Just a sister. She's in Northumberland now, married a soldier.'

Rosemary pointed at the seed cake, 'Would you like a piece, Larry?'

'Well, I really should get back to work.' He stood and as he did so his leg caught the table top, making everything rattle. 'Sorry. Clumsy of me.'

Mrs Parker wheeled herself round towards him and said, 'Before you go, Mr Lambert, I believe Rosemary is very keen to see the concert at the Music Hall next week.'

'Oh, that's nice.' He was about to wish Rosemary a

pleasant evening when she turned to him, her face at once hopeful and embarrassed. Then he understood what her mother meant.

He cleared his throat and it was a moment before he could say, 'Well, would you like me to take you to the concert, Rosemary?'

She nodded and said, 'That would be very nice.'

He knew then how it would be.

The kitchen was cold now and his cigarette just ash in the saucer. He read the letter from the bank again then put it in his coat pocket. He would talk to Rosemary about it tomorrow.

He was busy the next day, driving between different sites. At the workshop they were building for the parks department, the foreman came up to him.

'We've got a problem here, boss.'

'What is it?'

'We're short of a load of piping. Got the trenches in for water but can't go any further till we get the pipes. And that's holding everything right up.'

Larry looked around. The workmen looked slack and slow and there was none of the usual noise and banter. He did a rapid calculation of how much time – and money – would be lost if they couldn't keep working.

'I'll get it sorted, soon as I can.'

He got back in the Austin. So there was piping to buy now. And the wages to be paid on Friday too, he couldn't get out of that. He reached for cigarettes in his pocket and felt the letter there. He sighed, then started the engine and set off for home.

Rosemary appeared from the kitchen as he came in, a saucepan of potatoes in one hand. 'What are you doing home?' she asked.

He made a fuss of taking his boots off by the door, and she'd gone when he looked up.

He took the letter from his pocket and with reluctance went towards the kitchen. Without the children there, the house was quiet, only the sound of Rosemary mashing potatoes. To be home at this time of day felt furtive. Someone else might have taken the opportunity for a bit of hanky-panky, he thought. The idea almost made him laugh.

When he went into the kitchen, she was pricking sausages and dropping them into the frying pan.

'What is it then?' she said. 'The children will be home for their lunch in a minute.'

Larry passed her the letter and watched her face as she read it. He was impatient to get it over and done with, to get on with his work, and he tried to make light of it. 'It's just bad timing really. In a couple of weeks, it'll be fine, when the house by the bridge gets sold.'

But she leaned back against the table and folded her arms. The letter drifted to the floor. 'So you're asking me for money? Again.'

'I wish I didn't have to, Rosemary, I honestly wish there was another way. But I have to pay the wages on Friday and there's some piping to buy.'

'For the pub?' He saw her eyes flash as she leapt at that possibility. 'Because if you think I'm funding that idiotic scheme, you'd better think again, Larry. That's what's brought this on, isn't it? You're spending all the money up there and you're not looking after the rest of the business, the work that keeps a roof over our heads.'

'It's for the parks workshop, Rosemary, not the pub. That's all done separately.' It was a lie, but it felt true. The pub was far removed from the rest of his life. 'Listen, I know the savings account is meant to be for the children but this really is for them. To keep the business going.' He stopped, tired of pleading.

She turned back to the frying pan. 'If my mother knew where her money was going...' She poked at the sausages with the fork and fat spurted out, hissing in the hot pan.

The back door was open to let out the smoke and he went and stood on the step, looking over the garden. Yesterday's rain had left a misty damp that made the bushes especially full and green, enclosing the garden like a secret place. A wet summer scent rose up from the ground. He thought of the bracken he'd cleared up on the hill and how leaf fragments had got into his clothes and skin so he stank of it for days. He thought of the coconut smell that blew over the building site when the gorse flowered. Just sort this out, he told himself. Sort this out and you can go back there.

When he turned back inside, Rosemary was watching him, her face sharp and unhappy, and for a moment he saw himself through her eyes. A disappointment as a husband. A mediocre father. An ungifted businessman. Whatever she'd hoped for from their marriage, he was certain he hadn't provided it.

He heard the front door open then and the sound of Joanie and Roy clattering through the hall into the kitchen.

'What are you doing here, Dad?' Joanie asked, sliding into her seat at the table.

'Wash your hands first, young lady,' Rosemary said, tapping her on the shoulder. 'And you.' She steered Roy towards the stairs before he could sit down.

While the children were in the bathroom, she took out the cheque book from the drawer.

'Well then, how much?' she said, writing the date.

The light in the kitchen had faded and he saw that a quiet drizzle had started up outside. Rosemary looked tired, old. He supposed he did too. There was something more in her face though, a sadness that was usually blotted out by her bitterness and anger. A sadness that this was all their marriage was, and that neither of them had the power to change it.

'I'm sorry,' he said. 'I'm sorry I'm not...' Someone else, he wanted to say, someone who could make this different.

She had written the pound sign and was waiting, her pen poised to write the figure. 'Sixty,' he said.

At midnight he stopped trying to sleep. He got up, dressed, and went out to the van.

The darkness on the way up the hill was cloudy and thick, the headlights petering out in a spongy mist. It was colder than he'd thought. He parked by The Dolphin and pulled his coat tightly around him, folding his arms across his chest. Below him was mostly blackness, seeded here and there with faint lights. He watched the headlights of a car move slowly across, vanishing and reappearing like code.

Memories crowded in on him, as if sitting in the kitchen last night, he'd opened up a stopcock and couldn't shut it off again. He closed his eyes and listened to the sounds of the night. Birds settling in the bushes, a fox's high shriek. The past insisting he remember.

Their wedding had been in April, on a cold bright day. Waking far too early, he had dressed, shivering, not long after dawn. He combed his hair and made the bed carefully, conscious that Rosemary too would be sleeping in it that night.

Downstairs he brewed a pot of tea but couldn't face anything to eat. He roamed from room to room, noticing how much the house was changed. Rosemary had been coming in to make things ready, scouring the place of the old, soft dustiness that he'd lived with since his parents died. The worn armchairs in the sitting room wore new antimacassars like bandages, Goss china knick-knacks crowded the mantelpiece. A smell of furniture polish and bleach filled the house.

At nine o'clock he put on his coat, then took it off again. He couldn't turn up at the church in his old tweed. There were still hours to go but he left the house anyway, striding out onto the pavement as if he was in a hurry and turning away from the direction of the church. A brisk wind blew at him as he walked.

He felt constricted in his suit, and too formal to be wandering the streets. People might notice. He set his mind to calculating costs for the storage sheds he was building for the council. Nothing fancy, but a difficult site with odd nooks and crannies that made it hard to plan. For a while he was engrossed in the minutiae of bricks and roofing slates until he remembered why he had the job in the first place. One of the councillors had been at Mrs Parker's funeral and approached him to do the work. 'A favour to Rosemary,' he had said, shaking Larry's hand and patting Rosemary's shoulder. 'Think of it as an engagement present.'

He tried to picture her now, getting ready to be married. Was she joyful? Nervous? Afraid? None of those emotions seemed right. He crossed a road and increased his pace. Determined, that's how he imagined her. She would be putting on her dress and veil, buckling the straps of her shoes, and she would be determined to marry him, Larry Lambert.

The road ran past a printing works where the clatter of machinery reached him from inside. Three men in brown coats stood around the doorway, smoking, and Larry longed to be there too, having a normal day with a tea break and a few laughs and work to do. One of the men caught his eye. He had blonde hair and a broad face and he nodded at Larry, as if he'd sized up his situation and understood. If I could be him, Larry thought, just for today.

He checked his watch; still an hour and a half before he was due at the church. The walking had warmed him and he slowed now and lit a cigarette. He had walked almost to the edge of the town where small factories and workshops began to dwindle into mean little fields and shabby farm buildings. The road narrowed. Up ahead the pavement came to an end and he stopped. A thin horse watched him from the far corner of one of the fields and he wondered what kind of a life it had there, and whether it had ever had a better one. He hoped so.

When the cigarette was finished, he threw the stub to the ground. The wind worried at it for a few seconds, fuelling a brief glow, before it rolled into the mud and faded. He put his hands in his pockets and turned back towards the town.

Then a cramp in his foot brought him back to the present, sitting in the van with the smell of damp wool rising up from his coat. For a moment he imagined there might have been a different ending to the story, an ending where he didn't turn up at the church, didn't put the ring on Rosemary's finger, didn't kiss her stiffly on the lips. But what might have been evaporated in the chilly air.

He got out of the van and took the path over to The Dolphin. In the dark it was a black shape, but he knew his way around it as well as he did his own house. He wondered what would happen to the place if he had to abandon it. The whole enterprise felt precarious, as if the building had shifted closer to the cliff and could slide away from him at any time. He stepped into the space that would be the lounge bar, touching the half-built walls with his fingertips. The chilly smell of mortar and the physical fact of bricks and timber reassured him. They were real. The past was gone, its story fixed. But however unwanted, however wrong the story was, it had led him to this and about this he was more certain than anything. Whatever the obstacles, he would overcome, he was sure of that.

Chapter 8

Joanie
February 1949

As the week went by, Joanie tried to come up with an excuse for going out again on Sunday. Another walk, a trip into town, a bicycle ride; none of them were convincing enough. She wondered about confiding in Betty, but after Frank's betrayal she was so listless and morose that Joanie could barely get her to pull a pint of beer. Conversation was beyond her, let alone inventive excuses.

On Wednesday night, she took the takings upstairs as usual. Rosemary unlocked the door and Joanie saw that she was already in her nightdress with her hair plaited. She passed her the cash book and noticed that her finger was shaking as she checked the figures.

'Are you all right, Mum?'

Rosemary lay back on the bed. 'I've been rather off this evening.' Her face was pale and she was shivering.

'You get into bed then,' Joanie said. 'Get some sleep.'

Rosemary pulled up the covers and closed her eyes. 'Put the takings in the safe before you go.'

'Where's the key?'

'Dressing table drawer. Under the petticoats.' Her voice was weak.

Joanie found the key and unlocked the safe. There was a heavy mechanical clunk as she turned the handle and opened the door. She put the takings inside and locked it again.

'Good night then. I'll come and see how you are in the morning.'

Rosemary was no better the next day and struggled to lift her head when Joanie came in. 'I have to go to the bank today,' she said, then collapsed back onto the pillow. 'Oh, for goodness' sake, help me up, Joanie.'

'Mum, you can't go, you can't even sit up.'

Rosemary tried again and collapsed again. She gave a long sigh. 'You'll have to go instead then. The taxi's booked for ten.'

'What do I need to do?'

'Just pay in the money and get some change for the till.' Her eyes closed. Joanie stood by the bed for a moment, looking at her pallid skin and the lank plaits of hair on the pillow. It was unsettling to see her mother anything less than formidable.

She made Rosemary a cup of tea. If she did this unasked, it would hopefully be enough. Waiting for the kettle to boil, she gazed out of the window, wondering how she could get away on Sunday if Rosemary hadn't recovered. It would be harder to justify. She sighed. But still, a taxi ride into town was a bit of a treat. Perhaps she could have a quick look at the shops while she was there. It was ages since she'd done that. The kettle whistled and she made tea, slowly stirring it as she thought about the possibility of buying a New Look dress for herself. Then she could wear it the next time she saw Patrick. With a jolt she remembered he would be arriving with the delivery soon. She took the tea to Rosemary's room, carefully placing the cup on the bedside table.

'Cup of tea for you, Mum.'

Rosemary grunted, but didn't open her eyes. Joanie closed the door and ran downstairs to wait for Patrick.

They kissed quickly in the cellar once the driver was back in the lorry.

'Are you set for Sunday?' he whispered, running his hands up her back and over her hair.

She put her cheek against his. 'I don't know. Mum's ill. I don't know what to tell her.'

'Look, I'll go to the same place as before. You're working Sunday lunchtime, aren't you? I'll get there at three and I'll wait for you. If you aren't there by four, I'll know you can't get away.'

'Will you wait for me all that time?'

'Course I will.'

He kissed her again. 'Try and come, won't you?' Then he waved and was gone.

At ten o'clock she was sitting on the window seat in the Circular Bar, waiting for the sound of the taxi coming up the hill. She had on her best hat – how long was it since she'd worn it? – and the one pair of shoes that she never wore for work, old but un-scuffed. She'd checked that Rosemary was still sleeping and warned Betty that she might have to open up by herself.

Betty nodded her agreement and said blandly, 'Have a nice time.'

The attaché case with the takings lay on the seat and for a moment Joanie wondered what she could do if she ran off with the money. She stood, pulling her gloves on and off, imagining herself on the French Riviera, drinking champagne from a shallow glass, watching yachts skim the surface of a sun-dazzled sea. She lifted her head, imagining the sea-soaked breeze and the southern sun on her face.

There had only ever been that one trip to the seaside, when she was ten, but the smells and textures remained with her, here in the chilly February morning. Warm sand, salt water, bleached wood. A necklace of cold green sea as she swam. The mysterious places that lay beneath her kicking legs. The rhythm of waves wearing stones into pebbles, pebbles into sand.

A car horn hooted and she shook her head to clear the memory. The cash would get her nowhere more exotic than Skegness. She gathered up her things and went outside.

The taxi ride was over far too quickly and the bank took only a few minutes. By half past ten she was finished. She calculated that she needed to be back at The Dolphin in an hour which left her forty-five minutes. She heaved the attaché case full of change under her arm and wandered down the High Street, gazing into the window of the drapers, choosing which outfit she'd buy if she had the money.

Next door was the milliners, its window full of frothy spring hats. There was one in particular, a neat straw made daring by an undulating brim and a spray of large roses on one side. It would suit her hair and her face shape, she could tell, and if she wore it with a dress like Betty's she would look, for once, 'Like a million dollars,' she whispered aloud. There were no prices on the display and she imagined her mother's voice, 'If you have to ask the price, you can't afford it.' She opened the door and went inside.

The shop was light and feminine. There were glass cabinets and dainty tables with artful arrangements of hats and gloves. Joanie felt her spirits soar.

A young woman sat on a velvet stool in front of a large triple mirror, trying on a hat that was almost not there, a cloud of tulle and flowers around her hair. She jumped up as Joanie came in. 'Oh dear, you caught me trying it on. I couldn't resist.'

She laughed awkwardly and took off the hat. There was a luxuriously loud rustle as she put it in a box, folded tissue paper over it and put on the lid. 'It's just so beautiful. Can I help you, madam?'

Joanie took a deep breath. There was no fustiness here, no damp, no mildew. The shop smelled new and fresh. It had nothing to do with duty or being grateful for small mercies. It didn't make do and mend or eke out a meagre ration. It was about pleasure and prettiness and glamour.

'I'd like to try on a hat in the window, please.' She smiled at her own audaciousness.

The shop assistant smiled back. 'Of course. Can you show me which one?'

Joanie pointed it out.

'Ooh, that's a lovely one, madam. Very chic. Now, sit down here and see how it looks.'

Joanie's reflection jumped into the triple mirror. She took off her old hat, so shabby now in the smart surroundings, and gingerly put on the new one. She was right. It suited her perfectly. All three of her strained forwards to peer at this new version of herself.

'The hat looks gorgeous on you though, madam. Brings your eyes out lovely.'

Joanie adjusted the brim and tried to stop gazing at herself. 'How much is it?' she asked, the words coming out in a whisper.

'I'll just check for you.' The assistant trotted over to the counter. 'That one's a guinea, madam.'

A guinea! She couldn't possibly pay that much for a hat. Rosemary would think she'd gone mad. She suppressed a giggle. Well, she felt a little bit mad today. And it wasn't as

113

if she had anything else to spend her earnings on, small as they were. A couple of pairs of stockings and a jar of cold cream were all she'd bought in the last few months. Her ration book still had plenty of coupons left. That was one thing about working all the hours she did; she never had to worry about overspending.

She stood up and held out the hat to the assistant, 'I'll take it please.'

'Oh, I am glad,' the assistant said. 'I always like it when the customer buys exactly the right thing.' She chattered on while she packed the hat into a box, finishing it off with a thick blue satin ribbon. 'Golly, that'll perk you up for the rest of the day, won't it? A brand new hat.'

'It certainly will,' Joanie said. She took out her purse and laid the money on the counter, her heart beating faster as she picked up the hat box. She had never bought anything so expensive in her life.

On the way home in the taxi she tried to think of what she would say to Rosemary. With luck, there would be no need to say anything for a day or two, if her mother kept to her bed. But she simply had to show the hat to Betty. This was an opportunity she couldn't possibly miss. And Betty would know, from the label on the hatbox alone, that it wasn't a cheap purchase.

She sank back in her seat, watching houses and gardens stream past the window. Why couldn't she just tell the truth? 'I bought an expensive hat because I liked it and I'm going to wear it when I meet my boyfriend on Sunday. Oh, and he's teaching me to drive.' There was nothing awful about any of it, nothing dirty or wrong. She sighed. But it wasn't what Joanie Lambert did. Duty, duty, duty – that was her role. Always and, as far as she could see, forever.

The taxi turned up the hill towards the estate Larry had built so many years before. The houses still looked modern, but the rawness was smoothed and they were settled in the landscape now. They belonged. A woman in a green coat walked along the pavement. A postman leaned his bicycle against a wall. An elderly man with a white dog let himself into one of the houses. Joanie had a glimpse of a bright hallway. They had no idea that the man who built their homes had died in a fire, that his daughter was in a taxi driving past, that she wished she had a life like theirs instead of her own.

At The Dolphin, she carried in the hatbox and attaché case and dropped them onto one of the tables in the bar. A cold draught blew from the French windows where Betty was out on the terrace, slowly wiping a cloth across the glass. She picked up the hatbox and went outside.

'I'm back, Betty.'

'Hello, Joanie.' Betty barely glanced at her but her eyes brightened as she took in the hatbox. 'Oh, what's that you've got there then?'

Joanie opened the box and parted the tissue paper. 'I just had to get it. Couldn't resist.' With care, she put it on.

Betty looked at her, then she began to smile. 'You've gone and got yourself a boyfriend too, haven't you?'

Joanie felt her cheeks flush.

'Come on, Joanie,' Betty said. 'House of Juliette hats don't come cheap. And I've never seen you show much of an interest before.' She touched the roses and stroked the curve of the brim. 'It's lovely. Suits you.'

'Don't say anything to Mum, will you, Betty? I haven't worked out what to tell her yet.'

'Course not. It's not as if we're having cosy chats by the fire anyway, me and her.'

'Is she up?'

'No, still in bed I think.' Betty gave the glass a final polish and they went back inside.

'I'll just take this upstairs,' Joanie said, picking up the attaché case. 'Back in a minute.'

In her room, she looked for somewhere to hide the hatbox, but quickly gave up. It was too large to fit in the wardrobe and its aura of expense made it horribly conspicuous in the plain surroundings. Anyway, she wanted to look at it, to make sure she really had bought it. She put it on the table at the end of her bed and took the attaché case to Rosemary's room.

Rosemary was sleeping, breathing heavily, the pink eiderdown bunched up around her head. Joanie went over to the dressing table and removed the safe key as quietly as possible but it clunked loudly in the lock. Rosemary stirred but didn't wake. Joanie put the bags of change inside and locked it again.

Betty had opened up by the time she came downstairs and a couple of customers had already arrived. Betty leaned on the bar and beckoned her.

'Come on then, Joanie, spill the beans. It's that brewery boy, isn't it? What's his name?'

'It's Patrick,' Joanie said. 'He's terribly nice.'

Betty gave her a long look, as if she knew everything. 'Be careful, Joanie. Don't get carried away, will you? First love is dangerous.'

'Dangerous?' Joanie laughed, but Betty had turned away, an odd, lonely look on her face.

By evening, Rosemary had recovered a little. Joanie took up some tea, ran her a bath, and changed the sheets while she was in the bathroom. She opened the window and tidied up the bedside table, pleased to have things clean and fresh again. That would put Rosemary in a good mood too, she hoped. If she was going to tell her about Patrick, and it would have to be soon, before Rosemary became suspicious, it was best if all potential irritants were removed.

Despite the prospect of this conversation, she was happy as she busied herself around the room. Sunday wasn't so far away and she was certain that she would find a way to meet Patrick, with or without Rosemary's knowledge. And when she saw him, she would be looking her absolute best.

Rosemary climbed back into bed and wrapped a shawl around her shoulders. 'Make me a cup of Bovril, Joanie. I need to build up my strength again.'

'Anything to eat, Mum?'

'Not just now. I might manage an egg later.'

Joanie brought the Bovril and told her that everything had gone well at the bank. 'All the change is in the safe and I put the bank book in with it.'

'I'll check it when I'm feeling better,' Rosemary said. 'It's such a nuisance taking ill like this.'

'I could go to the bank again for you, if you like,' Joanie said. 'I don't mind.'

Rosemary didn't seem to have heard. 'And what a nuisance that Roy's away too and there's no one to drive.' She sighed loudly. 'Taxis are so expensive.'

Joanie could hardly believe her luck. 'What if I learned to drive then?' she said. 'The van's sitting there doing nothing at the moment. I could learn to drive and I could take you to the bank like Roy did. And there are other errands I could do.'

'Oh, driving's no job for a girl, Joanie. Far too technical.'

'Some girls drive, Mum. Loads did it in the war. Someone's

offered to teach me, in fact. It would be a shame to miss the chance.' She went over to the window, fussing with the curtains so she wouldn't have to look at her mother.

'I really don't think so, Joanie.'

Joanie spun round. 'Oh, please, Mum. It would make such a difference.'

She had been too enthusiastic. Betrayed herself. Rosemary straightened up a little in bed and stared at her. 'Who's offered to teach you then?'

How much should she give away? 'It's Patrick, one of the drivers from the brewery. He saw we were in a bit of a fix without Roy. I'm sure he'd be very good.'

'How much?'

'Oh, he wouldn't charge. It would be a...a friendly gesture.'

Rosemary took a sip of Bovril. 'What does he want instead?'

Joanie blushed a deep crimson as Rosemary continued, 'Don't be so naive, Joanie. There's no such thing as something for nothing. So does he want free beer? Something else?'

'Honestly, Mum, it's just because he's a friend. In fact...'

Rosemary cut in. 'I know! He's after Betty, isn't he? Trying to get into our good books to get a chance with her.' She looked pleased with herself. 'Well, you take him up on the offer, Joanie, but don't let him anywhere near that trollop. It could be very useful.'

Spring arrived on Sunday. The sun had some warmth at last and when Joanie walked down the road to meet Patrick, she noticed fat leaf buds on the beech trees and a faint glimmer of green in the woods. The dank smell of winter had all but disappeared. She was wearing the new hat but somehow it didn't make her as happy as when she'd bought it.

Rosemary, fully recovered now, hadn't even commented when she was getting ready to leave. 'Just pick up what you need to know as quickly as you can, Joanie,' she'd said. 'We don't want you wasting time on these lessons.'

And now that her mother knew where she was and who she was with, the afternoon was tainted, as if Rosemary's narrow mindedness and distrust were following her. Maybe Patrick really was interested in Betty and he was using Joanie to get to her. Or perhaps he had some other motive. By the time his van came into sight, she was doubting whether she should be there at all.

He was leaning against the door, hands behind his head, face turned up to the sun. Tears welled up. She stopped and searched her pockets for a handkerchief.

'Joanie?'

His blurred figure came towards her and she felt the wool of his coat against her cheek, inhaled the peaty smell of the tweed.

'What's wrong? Has something happened?'

She found her handkerchief at last and blew her nose, turning away from him in embarrassment.

'What's wrong?' he asked again.

'It's nothing.' She sniffed and wiped her eyes. 'Nothing at all.'

'There must be something. Here, look at me.'

She shook her head, aware that the beauty of the hat would be cancelled out by red eyes and a blotchy face. In the hundreds of times she'd imagined this meeting over the last week, she had been laughing or alluring. She had never thought she would cry. More tears gathered. It should have been so wonderful.

He cleared his throat. 'Look, if it's that you don't want

119

to be here, if you'd rather not meet again, well...that's fine.'

That was it then, it was over. All that Rosemary said was true. He wasn't interested in her, was bored already. She should have known it. He hadn't meant a word he'd said.

She turned to face him. 'Oh, I see,' she said and attempted a laugh. 'Just when Mum's agreed to driving lessons too.'

'Has she?'

'Yes, but...well, never mind if you don't want to.'

He grabbed her arms and looked straight at her. 'I want to. I thought you didn't.'

'Oh, but I thought you didn't.'

He pulled her close until she could hardly catch her breath. 'Don't scare me like that, Joanie,' he said, kissing her.

'You'd tell me, wouldn't you, Patrick?' she asked. 'If you didn't want to see me. You wouldn't leave me wondering. Please say you wouldn't.' It was somehow terribly important.

'I always want to see you; I've spent the last week longing to see you.' He stroked her hair.

'Will you promise me, though? I couldn't bear it if you just went off somewhere and I didn't know.'

'Promise.'

After the driving, they sat close together on the front seat of the van. The sun was getting low and the sky, huge and empty, had turned a pale, cold yellow. Joanie watched the trees darken to silhouettes.

'Penny for them,' Patrick said.

For some reason she'd been thinking about the long-ago trip to Norfolk. 'What's the furthest away you've ever been?'

He thought for a few moments. 'Not far really. I went to Lincoln once. And Mablethorpe another time. Don't know which is furthest.'

'Do you ever want to get right away from here? To

somewhere completely new?' An awful thought suddenly struck her. 'Oh, but you'll be called up! National Service, like Roy.'

He looked despondent. 'I know. I'm just waiting for the letter. It could come any day.' He tried to laugh it off. 'That'll be somewhere new all right. A year and a half of somewhere new.'

Joanie couldn't speak. It was such a cruel trick. Everyone who mattered had been taken away – Larry, Malcolm, even Roy, if he counted. And now Patrick, just when she'd found him.

He squeezed her hand. 'Let's not think about it. It could be months before it happens. And they're so bloody incompetent they might miss me out altogether!'

She smiled, agreed it might never happen, and leaned in closer to him, knowing that there wasn't the slightest chance that he would be missed.

Chapter 9

Lottie
January 1970

The sound of coughing woke Lottie. She lay with her eyes closed, waiting for it to stop, but it didn't. She heard the click of a light switch and footsteps going to the bathroom. The toilet flushed and the footsteps went back again. Then the coughing lessened and the light clicked off.

Sometimes in the morning there were pale threads of blood in the toilet bowl. She guessed that it had been a bad night and her mother had flushed away too many bloody tissues to clean off every trace. Every time she saw those thin red lines on the white porcelain, they startled her. Now, she turned over and tried to go back to sleep. In the end she turned on the radio, twisting the dial until a Joni Mitchell song came on and she fell asleep.

The next day both her parents were in the kitchen when she came downstairs. It was rare for Bill to be out of bed and she went over and kissed him, hugging his bony shoulders.

'Morning, Dad.'

'Morning, love.' His voice was weak, barely more than a breath.

Her mother put a cup of tea on the table in front of him and he took a sip, wincing at the heat.

'I fancy a fry-up for breakfast,' Lottie said. 'Sunday treat. Shall I do one for you too, Dad?'

Bill smiled and shook his head.

Joanie made a tutting noise. 'You know he can't eat heavy food, Lottie.'

'Just asking, just being nice.'

She took the frying pan from the cupboard and threw in a nub of dripping. When it was hot, she laid in two strips of bacon and broke in a couple of eggs, leaning on the counter while they cooked. The window was clouded with condensation. When she rubbed away a patch of it, she saw that the garden was coated in a heavy frost.

'Looks freezing out there,' she said.

'Better wrap up warm when you go out,' her mother said. 'Are you seeing Dan today?'

'We're going to the beach.' Lottie didn't want to think about leaving the warmth of the kitchen. 'Not till lunchtime though.'

With the sputter of the frying pan and the kettle beginning to boil she could almost ignore the sound of her father's laboured breath and intermittent coughing. She rattled the pan loudly on the burner then slid everything onto a plate.

Joanie tipped cornflakes into a bowl, poured on milk and began to eat. Bill sipped tea. Lottie sliced into the eggs, watching the yolk flood out and circle the bacon. None of them spoke.

It was getting hard to remember what Sunday mornings used to be like, the kitchen full of noise and steam and the Sunday papers spread over the table. She would smell the cooking before she'd even got out of bed. The radio would be on full blast, her father singing along when a Sinatra song played. It used to be happy, she thought, as she chewed her bacon. Sunday morning always used to be happy.

'Mind if I put the radio on?' she said.

Bill nodded. 'That'd be nice.'

But it only made the silence more obvious. There was nothing to say these days. Even simple conversations petered out in the huge wasteland of things they couldn't talk about. The future, the past; they were equally painful. Lottie was as guarded as her mother, censoring herself before she spoke in case she used the wrong words.

Strangers in the Night came on. She watched her father tap his fingers on the table top, silently mouthing the words, and it was suddenly all too much.

'Actually, I've just remembered I arranged to meet Dan a bit earlier. I'd better go.' She ran out of the room, flung on her coat and scarf and hurried to the front door.

Outside, the air was so cold it hurt to inhale. She wrapped her scarf round her face and walked quickly, then ran down the hill. The pavement was icy in places and several times she almost fell, but she carried on recklessly until she reached the bottom. Out of breath, she leaned against a lamppost and closed her eyes. Her throat was raspy with cold and her fingers were almost numb. The corns on her little toes throbbed painfully. But she was glad of the discomfort, glad to be distracted, and unzipped her coat to let in more freezing air. Then she ran towards the beach.

By the time she saw Dan walking towards her through the sand dunes, she could barely speak. She was shivering so violently he had trouble putting his arms round her.

'Christ, Lottie, what's going on? Your lips are blue. How long have you been out here?'

'Don't know.'

'Look, you have to get warm. Come and get in the car. Can you walk?'

She stood with difficulty and he hooked one of her arms

round his neck. They stumbled to the car and he helped her into the back seat, then fetched a rug from the boot. It was so like Dan to have a rug in his car, she thought. He always had the right thing.

He tucked the rug round her and took her hands in his, rubbing them until she felt the blood work its way back to her fingertips.

'I can't feel my feet,' she said.

He took off one of her shoes and with her foot on his lap, he flexed her toes and rotated her ankle, his fingers warm through her sock. She leaned back and stared at the roof of the car.

'Dad's dying,' she said.

Dan paused, then continued flexing and rubbing.

'I don't know what to do.' She began to cry.

'You can't do anything,' Dan said. 'I wish you could. I wish I could. But we can't.'

She pulled her foot away and pushed off the rug. Opening the car door, she climbed out, strode across the car park. The wind was flecked with sea spit, sharp against her face as she walked towards the sea.

'Lottie!'

Dan came up behind her and she walked faster. She could hear the creak of his jacket as he followed her.

When she reached the damp sand at the tide line she stopped. The beach was empty, the two of them the only solid things against the water. The only warm things in the bitter cold.

When she got home from work, the house was hushed, like always. Most days, Lottie parked the car and sat for a few moments, readying herself to go inside. Then she would get out and open the front door quietly, tiptoe to the kitchen and begin to make dinner, waiting for her mother to leave Bill's bedside and come downstairs. Only then did she feel it was all right to turn on the radio and let noise back in.

But today the atmosphere was particularly still. She stood at the foot of the stairs and listened. No coughing, no laboured breathing. When she went into the kitchen there was a note on the table: *Lottie, we've gone to the hospital. Not an emergency. Don't worry. Come when you can. Mum.*

She ran back out to the car, fumbling with the key as she tried to unlock it, stalling the engine twice. Then she drove, breaking the speed limit for the first time since she passed her test.

He'd been in hospital often and every time she was afraid he wouldn't come out again. He was so frail. With every cough another piece of him seemed to evaporate. She raced through a set of green lights and careered into the hospital car park, then ran towards A&E, leaving the car parked at an angle.

She didn't believe her mother. Going to hospital in an ambulance was the definition of an emergency. When Joanie said, 'He's had a peaceful night,' or 'He's a bit perkier today,' it meant nothing. He wasn't any better; he just hadn't died.

At the reception desk, she gave his name. The nurse checked a clipboard. 'He's been admitted,' she said. 'Manley Ward, second floor.'

Lottie pressed the button for the lift, then changed her mind and took the stairs. At the first landing she paused and leaned against the wall to catch her breath. A door slammed somewhere above her, then footsteps squeaked on the steps and another door slammed. How many others were like her, waiting on landings or loitering in corridors, delaying their visit to the bedside? Desperate to see someone, but unable to face their weakness, their illness, their death?

She started up the stairs again, her feet heavy. On the second floor, she took a deep breath and set off down the corridor towards Manley Ward.

He'd been here so frequently he called it his home from home. Lottie saw him straight away, in his usual bed, lit up by the low evening sun streaming through the window. The heavy light gleamed gold on every surface except his skin, grey against the white pillow.

Her mother was sitting on a plastic chair by the bed, her hand in Bill's. She looked up as Lottie approached.

'Hello, love.'

'How is he? What happened?'

'He had a bit of a wobble at home so we came in. Just to be on the safe side.' Her voice broke, and when Lottie looked at her, she saw she'd been crying. Through the long months of Bill's illness, Lottie had never seen her cry. Her heart began to race.

'What kind of a wobble?'

'He was coughing a lot and something came out. So we thought it best to come in.'

Lottie bent over to kiss Bill and saw the dried blood at the corners of his mouth. His eyes were closed and his breathing was faint.

'Mum, is he OK? Honestly?'

Joanie paused, then shook her head. 'I don't think he is, Lottie.' She gave a huge juddering sob.

Lottie pulled up another chair. They sat, side by side, watching the slight rise and fall of Bill's chest as the sun moved past the window and the lights of the ward were turned on.

It was nearly midnight by the time they left the hospital. Joanie drove, carefully, sensibly, still crying. Lottie sat in the passenger seat, hugging her knees and staring at the road ahead.

At home they sat in the kitchen. After a while, Lottie said, 'Do you want something to drink, Mum? Tea? Brandy?'

Joanie smiled a lost little smile. 'We had brandy when my dad died. I made my brother have some even though he was only ten.'

'Your brother?'

'My brother Roy.'

Lottie stared at her. 'But, Mum, you never told me you had a brother.'

Joanie put her hand on Lottie's. 'I know, love, and I will tell you about him. But not tonight, OK? We've had enough tonight.'

Lottie nodded. 'OK.'

Early in the morning, she drove to the cafe to put up a Closed notice. It was a grey, windy day, the sea full of brisk little waves and she shivered as she unlocked the door. With the black marker pen they used for the daily specials she wrote a sign. *Closed due to family bereavement.* She stuck it to the door then phoned Dan.

'It was about eleven o'clock last night. When I looked at him, he just wasn't him anymore.'

Dan was silent.

'Dan?'

'I'm here.' He cleared his throat. 'Are you OK?'

She paused, not sure how to describe what she felt. 'I'm just sad, really sad.'

'How's your mum?'

'I can't tell.'

'Can I come over, would that be all right?'

It surprised her how much she wanted to see him. 'Will you? That would be really nice. I'm at the cafe.'

'I'll be there in ten minutes.'

When he opened the door, she ran and flung herself at him, clutching his coat and squashing her face against his chest. He put his arms around her and there they stood, so close Lottie could scarcely breathe.

'Poor Bill,' Dan said eventually. 'I'm so sorry, Lottie.'

'I know,' she said. 'It's just not fair.'

'He was one of the kindest people I ever met.'

'I know,' she said again.

Dan broke away and reached for a paper napkin to wipe his eyes. 'It won't be the same here, will it? I mean, I know he hasn't worked in the cafe for a long time, but now he won't ever be back and that feels so wrong.'

Lottie gazed round at the tables and chairs, the green blinds pulled down over the windows, the Victoria sponge under a cloche on the counter. All so familiar that she barely noticed them but now they were infused with loss and the knowledge that Bill would never see them again. There was grief that he was gone, relief that she didn't have to wait for him to die anymore, loneliness too. And something else she couldn't define.

Dan sat next to her, wiping his eyes. She leaned against

him, glad to have someone there, glad it was Dan. Then she reached up and turned his face towards hers, kissing him hard. With her other hand she felt for his belt buckle and undid it, pulling down his zip and sliding her hand inside.

'Lottie?'

She manoeuvred herself onto the floor, bringing him down with her, the chairs skidding noisily out of the way. Her jeans pushed down, the coldness of the floor was a shock against her back and buttocks. But then he was there, his skin warm against hers, life racing through him, through her.

'Let's get married,' she said

He lifted his head. 'What?'

She wanted the future, the whole huge living future, not the past. 'Marry me, Dan.'

June 1970

The wedding was much too soon. Everyone said so when Lottie told them about it, if not to her face, then later to her mother. Let things settle down, don't rush into anything, give yourself time to grieve. She heard the same advice from everyone.

But she didn't want to wait. Even in the first horrible weeks after Bill died, when waking up meant realising all over again that he was dead, she was sure she wanted to get married. She had an image of herself and Dan striding into the future, hand in hand like the pioneers on Bill's old socialist pamphlets. Young. Strong. Purposeful. Ready for anything.

The only thing she wasn't sure about was her mother. She

had come undone in such an unexpected way since Bill's death. She was absent, abstracted, almost dreamy. Lottie couldn't tell what was going on.

She noticed it first on the day of the funeral, when they were getting ready to go to the church. The car was due in twenty minutes and Lottie was waiting in the kitchen, already in her coat.

'Do you want a cup of tea before we go, Mum?' she called out.

When there was no answer, she went upstairs. Joanie was sitting at the dressing table, wearing her black dress and an old straw hat with a ragged spray of roses pinned to one side. She didn't seem to notice Lottie enter the room.

'Mum, do you want a cup of tea?' Lottie asked again.

'I found this when I was going through some of your dad's things,' Joanie said, putting her hand up to touch the hat. 'It cost me a guinea in 1949, more than anything I'd ever bought in my life, and it was the most glamorous thing I owned.' She smiled. 'Hard to believe now.'

'The car will be here soon, Mum.'

'I thought I looked the bee's knees in it. I used to wear it on Sundays.' She took off the hat and put it on the dressing table. 'When I wanted to impress someone.'

Lottie sat down on the bed, half wanting to know more, half wanting to get her mother back to the present.

'Roy used to tease me. I said I'd tell you about Roy, didn't I?'

Lottie nodded. 'But you don't have to, not today.'

'He was four years younger than me,' her mother said, ignoring her. 'Still is, I suppose. I don't think you would've liked him, Lottie. He was ghastly, to be perfectly honest; never had any sympathy for anyone but himself.' She sighed.

'It's so long since I've seen him though and he was only seventeen when I left. Perhaps he's mellowed.'

'Why didn't you keep in touch? After your mum died, I mean?'

Her mother paused. She looked at Lottie as if about to speak, then looked away again.

'Oh, well, he was in the army, you see. National Service. All the men had to do it then. And I came here. So we lost contact.'

'Didn't you try to find him?'

'I've thought about it, but what would be the point?'

Lottie stared at her, wondering why she knew so little about her mother's history.

The car had arrived then and they'd gone off to the church, busy with other things, other emotions.

In the weeks leading up to the wedding Lottie went to bed exhausted, her head forever spinning with lists of things to do. She would lie staring at the gap between the curtains, wishing that it was all over, that Dan was lying next to her in their own bed in their own house and that she never had to make another decision again.

The house was the most unexpected outcome. Lottie had assumed that they would share Dan's cramped bedsit. The only other alternative was for them both to live with Joanie and she didn't want to do that. Not long after the funeral though, Joanie had passed her an envelope at breakfast one morning.

'This is from your dad. Something he left for you.'

Lottie prepared herself for the rush of emotion that came with anything connected to Bill. There was a cheque for £500 inside. 'What's this?'

'So you and Dan can put a deposit on a place of your own. Your dad would hate you to be paying rent to some Rachman in a seedy flat.'

'But where's it from?'

'A policy he set up to look after us. Once he knew, he thought everything through.'

They were silent for a while. Lottie imagined Dan and herself in their own house, free to do whatever they wanted. She smiled, then felt guilty at her pleasure.

'If we have our own place, will you be all right?' she said.

'I'll be fine. I'll be absolutely fine.'

'But are you sure, Mum? By yourself?'

'I'm a grown-up, Lottie. I've done harder things than live on my own.'

The day before the wedding, Lottie had a last fitting for her dress. Joanie had sewn yards and yards of polyester silk into a puff sleeved, high necked affair that even had a small train. It took up most of the space in the spare room, where it hung from the door, and when Lottie took it down, she was immersed in slippery whiteness for ages before she came out into the light again.

She stood on a chair while Joanie checked the hem. 'Looks OK from here.'

'It's good enough. What about the cuffs? How do they feel?'

Lottie stretched out her arms. 'They're fine. I can move anyway.' She looked at herself in the mirror, smoothing down the long skirt panels. 'It looks lovely. Thanks, Mum.'

'First wedding dress I've ever made. I'm glad it turned out well.'

'Didn't you make yours?'

Joanie shook her head and bent to put the sewing box away. 'There was still rationing then, no material for anything glamorous.'

'What did you wear? I don't think I've ever seen any photos.'

'Oh, just a smart suit. We didn't really bother with photos.'

Lottie watched her mother straighten up, the lost, dreamy expression crossing her face again. Then she blinked and was back to normal.

Something made Lottie ask again, 'What, nobody took even one photo? Not Granny or Grandad Bill?' She had only a hazy memory of her grandparents, now long dead.

'There might be one somewhere. I don't know.'

Lottie climbed down and stood in front of her mother. 'I'd really like to see, now that I'm getting married myself.'

Joanie gave her a look that was almost desperate and went out of the room. In less than a minute she was back, holding a black and white photograph on a cardboard mount. She handed it to Lottie.

The photograph was taken in front of the registry office in town. Bill and Joanie stood arm in arm, smiling, sunlight making them squint. Bill wore a light-coloured suit and a wide tie, his buttonhole of white flowers matching Joanie's small bouquet. Joanie's suit was full skirted, the jacket open over a white blouse. And she looked fat, fatter than Lottie had ever known her. She peered more closely. No, not fat, pregnant, heavily so. It was so unexpected she felt herself flush with embarrassment, for herself or her mother she wasn't quite sure.

Joanie was jiggling her foot and tapping the back of the chair with her fingernails. 'As you can see, it wasn't the kind of wedding you took photos at,' she said quietly. 'There

134

weren't any guests except the witnesses. We asked a passer-by to take that one. It's the only one.'

'So it was a shotgun wedding?' Lottie winced as she said it.

Joanie leaned towards her. 'No, it wasn't, Lottie. Whatever it looks like, your dad and I chose to get married. We loved each other and it was what we wanted. Nobody forced us into it.'

Lottie noticed the date written across the mount in blue ink. 14th March 1950. Only a month before she was born. How mortifying it must have been, humiliating even, to get married in that state. She stared at the photograph again. They didn't look embarrassed or humiliated though. They looked really happy.

Joanie took the photograph from her. 'It's all in the past now anyway. You need to be thinking about your wedding, not mine. Come on, let's get that dress off before you spill something on it.'

A week later, when the excitement of the wedding had died down, Lottie lay in bed, woken by the dawn chorus swelling outside. There was something wrong about her mother's words. *Your dad and I chose to get married,* she'd said. But the date on the photograph didn't make sense. Joanie arrived in town in October 1949. Five months later she and Bill got married when she was seven or eight months pregnant. How could that be?

The sound of rain drifted through the open window together with its cool, damp scent. She turned over and hugged Dan's sleeping back, sifting through the possibilities. Did they meet somewhere else before, have one night of passion, and then Joanie found Bill again when she knew she was pregnant? But if that was true, was the story of how they met a lie? Or was Joanie already pregnant when she arrived and walked out along the pier? Lottie dismissed that straight away. Bill's name was on her birth certificate, William Lennox, written in thick blue-black ink. And anyway, not for one minute could she imagine her mother in that situation. Sleep began to pull her down again. She'd tell Dan in the morning and they'd work it out together.

When it came to it though, she didn't say anything. She and Dan set up the cafe as usual, talked about normal things, and it felt wrong to bring the subject up, as if by doing so she was betraying her mother. As she wiped down the tables and filled the sugar bowls, she wondered if she could ask Joanie outright what happened. But even thinking about the conversation made her cringe. She would have to ask such awkward, intimate questions and be ready for awkward, intimate answers. It was the kind of conversation people had in films, not in real life. And how much did it matter anyway?

She turned the sign on the door to 'Open' and stepped onto the pier. Sunshine was drying the wooden planking, the night's rain evaporating in wisps of steam. Beneath her feet the sea lay placid, the sound of the waves as gentle as breathing. She could live with it, surely. What difference would it make to be told where and when she was conceived? Her parents were her parents, that was the important thing. She didn't need to know anything else.

August 1971

Lottie missed the old money. When she counted the takings at the end of the day, the new coins seemed insubstantial and light. As if they weren't worth much. She kept a jar by the till for the pre-decimal coins that came in and she liked to weigh them in her hand now and then, rubbing her fingers over the big heavy pennies with their long-gone monarchs and rolling the lumpy threepenny bits across the counter.

She and Dan had converted prices and costs accurately, and she was sure they didn't make mistakes with change, but their takings were down. Even on the hottest days, the money that came in was less than in previous years. Despite the three of them working hard to make it pay, the cafe had lost its momentum, its energy, since Bill died. She no longer regarded it as wonderfully other-worldly. Nor did the blurring of land and sea make it somewhere special. It was just an ordinary cafe now.

But it wasn't just the cafe. On the beach, there were wide stretches of empty sand between holidaymakers, and even in August, the boarding houses along the Esplanade had Vacancies signs in the windows. People were spending their new money in new locations.

She and Dan talked about it in the garden one evening. It was unusually warm and humid and they lay side by side on their tiny patch of lawn, hoping for a breath of wind to cool them.

'You know Margaret, next door to Mum?' Lottie said.

'Yeah.'

'I met her on the High Street today. She's back from two weeks in Spain. Lucky thing. You should see how tanned she is.' She stared up at the starless sky and sighed. 'That's the trouble though, isn't it?'

'What, that Margaret's got a tan?'

She kicked his leg. 'That people are going on holiday to Spain and places like that.' She sighed again. 'I mean, I'd love to go too, but that's what's hurting the takings.'

Dan touched her arm. 'We could always go and visit Mum and Dad if you want to go somewhere hot.'

'That's not what I meant.'

He carried on, 'I could take you to the Rift Valley. It's like nowhere else on earth.'

Lottie said nothing for a few moments. Dan's parents had not been able to come to the wedding. It had been arranged too quickly, they said, and they couldn't leave their farm at such short notice. Instead, they had come over at Christmas for a strained week together in Lottie and Dan's small house. Lottie had cringed at their out-of-place clothes, their loud exclamations over the cost of everything, the number of times they commented on how 'unhygienic' it was to live so close to other people. She had realised, despite Dan's nostalgic talk of sunrise over the plains and the journey from the farm to Lake Turkana, that his parents were almost as much strangers to him as they were to her.

'It'd be expensive to get there though. And we couldn't really leave the cafe,' she said.

'That's true,' Dan said, a note of regret in his voice.

A plane crossed the sky, the engines faint above them.

'Anyway, I've had an idea,' Dan said.

Lottie smiled. Dan always had an idea. 'What is it then?'

Dan rolled over onto his stomach and leaned his head on her shoulder. 'Bulbs,' he said. 'A mail-order bulb business. Low start-up costs because we've already got a greenhouse and I can spend as much or as little time on it as I want. Then if the cafe keeps getting quieter, there'll be another income to keep us afloat.'

'But do you know anything about bulbs? Or mail-order?'

'When I worked at the ironmongers, remember? I grew

them then. And it's not like they're difficult. I'll start off with something easy like snowdrops or daffs.'

Lottie watched the plane disappear into clouds.

'What do you think?' Dan asked.

'Will it bring in enough to make a difference?'

He shrugged. 'It'll be something. And everything helps.'

As the school holidays came to an end, Dan began work on the bulb business. Lottie helped him heave sacks of compost and crates of flower pots into the greenhouse. She covered for him in the cafe when he went off to the wholesale nurseries to buy his initial stock of bulbs. She spent long evenings writing Latin names on labels and sticking them on the pots. And all the while she wondered if they should be making the cafe more viable instead.

She said nothing. Dan was so pleased with his idea and so certain it was going to work. In quiet periods at the cafe, he drew up plans for building a bigger, better greenhouse. While she wiped down the tables and folded napkins, she ran through other possibilities but came up with nothing that was workable. She watched Dan calculating measurements and costs, frowning in concentration. So much effort was going into the bulbs. If he would put as much into the cafe perhaps they could make something of it.

Joanie was surprised when Lottie told her what he was doing. 'There's no need for that is there? Seems like a waste of time.'

'You know we haven't been very busy lately, Mum. This might help a bit.'

They were sitting on the beach. It had been one of Joanie's days to work at the cafe and they had stopped for an ice cream before going home.

139

'Is that what he's been doing today then?' Joanie asked.

'He's building a new greenhouse.'

'Is he? Does he know what to do?'

'I think so. He used to have to do things like that on his parents' farm.'

The beach was emptying. Lottie watched a straggle of families trudge towards the steps with their bags and deckchairs, sunburn reddening white shoulders and necks, tired children complaining. She wondered if Dan did know what he was doing or if it would end up a bodged job, leaky and leaning.

'My dad was a builder,' Joanie said suddenly.

'Was he? I didn't know that.'

'He built houses, a pub, all kinds of things. He was quite successful at one time.'

This was more information than Joanie had ever volunteered before. All Lottie knew about her grandfather was that he had died in the war. There were no photographs of him and she wondered what he looked like, if there was anything of him in her. She didn't even know her mother's maiden name.

'What was he called?'

Joanie didn't answer and when Lottie looked over at her, she had the absent look that meant she wasn't listening. Perhaps she was thinking about her father the way Lottie thought about Bill. It occurred to her for the first time that both she and her mother had lost a father at a young age. How miserable that must have been. Lottie hugged her knees and felt immensely grateful that Dan had been there when Bill died.

And now Joanie was widowed young too, or at least long before she might have expected. How small her family was, she thought, how disconnected from previous generations. She nudged her mother's arm and tried again, 'Mum? What was your dad called?'

Joanie pushed the end of her ice cream cone into the sand and stood up. 'Well, time we were getting home,' she said.

Chapter 10

Larry
July 1939

At the end of each night, Larry poured himself his first and last drink of the day. With all but the wall lights turned off, he settled at a table in the main bar, slowly sipping his whisky. Around him, he felt The Dolphin calm itself after the noise and bustle of the evening, as it returned to being his alone.

Tonight though, Malcolm was there too. He had spent so long washing the glasses and wiping down the bar that Larry felt obliged to ask him if he'd like a drink. He accepted a whisky and they took their drinks outside. The terrace was one of The Dolphin's grand gestures, one that Larry was particularly proud of, with its broad steps leading down to the lawn and the pool set like a jewel into the paving. Sitting there by the water, Larry didn't mind Malcolm's presence. From the moment he walked through the door, Malcolm had understood The Dolphin almost as well as Larry.

'What a beauty,' he'd said in his soft Scottish accent. 'What an absolute stunner.'

Larry had hired him as manager on the spot.

For a while, they sat in silence. Then Malcolm said, 'That was some night, wasn't it? I've never seen the place so full.'

Larry nodded. 'They're coming round to us. I knew they would, in the end.'

'There was a party came all the way from Buxton. Did you see them? The arty-looking lot in the corner.'

'Buxton? Really?' Larry smiled broadly. 'Well, would you believe it?'

'It'll be a goldmine, this place. You know it will.'

Larry leaned back in his seat and stretched his legs. He'd got something right at last, something good. The Dolphin was getting busier every week. All it needed was a warm summer to bring out the crowds, a steady autumn, and by Christmas it would all be plain sailing.

'You're doing a fine job, Malcolm,' he said. 'I mean it. You've got a gift for this kind of thing, I can tell.'

'Oh, it's just about paying attention,' Malcolm said. 'Keeping an eye on everything and everyone, all at the same time.' He stood up. 'Well, I'd better get back home before the landlady locks me out again. I'm on a warning already.'

'Oh, she's that kind, is she?' Larry said. 'A bit of a battle axe?'

'You certainly wouldn't call her timid,' Malcolm laughed, then gave a sigh. 'I think it's time to start looking for new digs. Somewhere a bit more liberal.'

'Why not move in here?' Larry said it without thinking. 'The Dolphin?'

'Plenty of room upstairs. I built it with living quarters. Want to see?'

'Well, yes,' Malcolm said. 'But are you sure?'

'Come and have a look,' Larry said. 'It's through the door in the tower.'

They went through the Circular Bar and climbed the stairs up past the Ladies Lounge on the mezzanine. Larry unlocked the door at the top. The public rooms below had acquired the patina of six months use, but up here it still felt new. As they walked from room to room, the bare floorboards bounced echoes down the corridor.

'No furnishings, of course. But I'm sure we can find some bits and pieces for you. A bed, at least.'

He'd forgotten how much space there was. Each white room seemed huge, his reflection in the black windows more than life-size. 'And the kitchen and bathroom are top-notch, look.' He showed Malcolm the emerald green tiled bathroom. 'I thought about moving up here myself.'

'Why didn't you?'

'My wife wasn't so keen on the idea.' He ran a hand across the tiles. They were smooth and cool as seawater. 'Anyway, if you move in, you'd be doing me a favour. The place'll be more secure and having you on hand will be a big help. Not that I'd be coming after you to work all hours, of course. So, what do you think?'

'Well, if you're offering it, I'll say yes.' Malcolm held out his hand and Larry shook it. 'Thanks, Mr Lambert.'

'We can work out the rent later,' Larry said. 'When do you want to move in? I expect you'll need to give notice to your landlady.'

'Oh, I'll sort her out, don't worry,' Malcolm said.

They went back downstairs. Larry went to collect their glasses from the terrace and he stood for a moment by the pool, feeling the warm night air on his skin. He could hear Malcolm wheeling his motorbike out from the shed but there was no other sound.

'Will you be all right up here by yourself?' he asked him as they locked up. 'There's no one else roundabout for a mile or two.'

'Being up here on my own sounds like heaven! No one

to bother me and no one for me to bother. Thanks again, Mr Lambert. I'll see you tomorrow.'

Malcolm started up the bike, pausing for a moment to adjust his helmet. Larry watched insects cross the beam of the headlight and a moth flutter towards its centre. Then Malcolm turned the bike towards the road, gave a wave and accelerated away.

Driving between building sites the next day, Larry found he was smiling. Having Malcolm live in would be a weight off his mind. The Dolphin was vulnerable at night, now that people knew it was there and although nothing had happened yet, its remoteness made Larry uneasy. He took the cash from the till home each night but that wouldn't stop thieves wrecking the place to look for it. The copper roof on the tower and the brass fittings on the doors and windows could be stripped and sold for scrap without a thought for their intricately beautiful design of seaweed and dolphins. He couldn't bear that to happen. Yes, Malcolm living in was a very good idea.

He arrived home at six to find Rosemary listening intently to the wireless. Her sewing lay untouched in her lap and she sat hunched forward, one ear up close to the set. Before he could say anything, she held up a finger to hush him, so he gave her a wave and went into the kitchen. Joanie was at the table eating bread and butter and reading a magazine.

'Hello, love,' Larry said, patting her hair. He looked around the kitchen. There was no evidence of cooking. 'Dinner not ready?'

'Not yet. Mum's been listening to the news.'

'Oh.' He checked the teapot on the table. It was cold. 'Make me a cup of tea, will you, Joanie love?'

She rolled her eyes, but put down her magazine and went to fill the kettle.

Larry sat down. 'What's that you're reading?' He picked up the magazine. The Picturegoer. 'Does your mother know you're reading this?'

'Of course she does, she buys it.'

'Does she?' He flicked through a few pages of smiling film stars. When did she start buying that kind of thing, he wondered.

They waited for the kettle to boil. Larry watched Joanie spoon tea leaves into the pot and put milk in his cup. Then she picked up her magazine again and leaned against the sink to read. She seemed to have shed all her childishness recently. At twelve she wasn't tall, but she was strong. Strong mentally too, Larry thought, and self-controlled. He had seen her sometimes when Rosemary laid down the law. Joanie's face showed neither anger nor upset, showed nothing at all in fact. If she did as she was told, it was only because she chose to.

He heard the wireless click off and Rosemary hurried into the kitchen. She took out onions and a slab of liver from the larder, calling out, 'Joanie, peel the potatoes, there's a good girl.'

The kettle began to whistle and Joanie made the tea for Larry, then started on the potatoes. Rosemary chopped the onions and flung them into a pan.

'Anything on the news, Rosemary?' Larry asked.

'There isn't a war yet, if that's what you mean,' Rosemary said.

'Good, that's good to hear.'

She flashed him a contemptuous look. 'As if it bothered you. As if anything bothered you except that bloody pub.'

He couldn't remember her ever swearing before and certainly not in front of the children. Joanie stood still, the peeler in her hand, staring at her mother.

'Now, Rosemary...' Larry began, then stopped.

She was stirring the onions so hard that pieces sprang out of the pan. He took a sip of tea and tapped his fingers on the table, saying nothing. She was silent too, as she sliced up the liver and dabbed each glistening strip with flour, dropping them into the pan with the onions.

Joanie had gone back to the potatoes and threw him a look as if he ought to do something. But what was there to do? Or say? She was right. The Dolphin had taken over, pulled him in, drowned out the rest of his life. He longed to be there in the evenings, longed to go there now. He was neglecting his other work, cutting corners and advantage was being taken, but he couldn't make himself care. He didn't even care that Rosemary had sworn in front of Joanie.

'Well,' he said. 'I think I'll get off up there a bit earlier tonight. Got a feeling it'll be a busy one.'

'There'll be no dinner left,' Rosemary said without looking round.

'That's all right. I'll sort myself out.'

He went upstairs to wash and change. It was always a suit for The Dolphin, a suit, a clean shirt and a splash of cologne.

As he combed his hair in the hall mirror, Joanie came and sat on the bottom step.

'Can I come with you, Dad?'

'Don't be silly, love.' He wondered about a folded handkerchief in his breast pocket but decided against it.

'Please.'

He rubbed at a stain on one sleeve of his jacket, annoyed

he hadn't noticed it sooner. 'Fetch me a damp cloth, Joanie. This spot's a stubborn one.'

'I don't want to stay here,' she said when she brought it. She looked towards the kitchen as she spoke.

The clatter of cutlery and saucepans grew louder. Larry could almost hear the sizzle of Rosemary's anger.

He sighed. 'Look, love, I can't take you. It's Friday night, it'll be busy and it's not a place for children anyway. Maybe you can go tomorrow, in the morning.'

'Oh, you don't care!' Joanie shouted and stamped up the stairs.

Larry took her and Roy up on Saturday, telling Rosemary that he was taking them out for a drive. Joanie sat beside him in the van, trailing her hand out of the window just as she had the first time. He felt only partially forgiven. A heavy heat lay over everything, only relenting when they reached the top of the hill.

Malcolm was opening up and the children went to help him. Larry walked through the public rooms, checking that everything had been properly set up. He felt a thrill of anticipation as he breathed in the smell of a freshly opened pub.

Saturday lunchtimes were generally quiet and he liked to sit and read the newspaper on one of the window seats. He fetched a glass of soda water and went to the circular bar. The view was best here, with the land falling steeply away beyond the window. From the right spot, it looked as if the whole building was airborne.

He watched Malcolm arranging glasses behind the bar. Joanie and Roy were trying to do the same, giggling as Malcolm teased them about their wobbly attempts at a pyramid. Malcolm suited the place so well, Larry thought, with his suits and his glossy silk ties. And he knew how to talk to people, never getting it wrong, even with Roy.

There was a commotion at the main door and through the archway, a crowd of seven or eight bustled in. Malcolm steered the children back towards Larry and went to greet them.

'Having fun?' Larry asked.

Joanie nodded and then all three turned to watch the group. With much banter and playfulness, the young men and women settled themselves in the lounge bar, the women smoothing down their skirts as they sat, the men patting their pockets for cigarettes. Sleek and well-groomed, they looked as if they would be at ease anywhere.

While he was building The Dolphin, Larry gave little thought to who would come, only that he wanted it done. But now his customers were unfailingly interesting to him. He watched the group order their drinks, heard their sharp, educated voices and their easy laughter. So these were the kind who came to The Dolphin – people who arrived in large cars, wore expensive clothes and were utterly confident of who they were and their place in the world. It amazed him that they wanted to come to a place that he had created for himself.

He glanced at the children.

Joanie was leaning forward in her seat, her eyes fixed on the group. 'Those shoes are beautiful,' she whispered, pointing to a woman wearing bright green, high-heeled, lizard-skin sandals.

Roy was watching the group too, but with an expression that reminded Larry rather too much of Rosemary. She would think the group vulgar and the women fast. Even though Roy was far too young to have formed the same opinion, like her, he distrusted anything different or unusual.

Then Roy laughed. One of the men was making silly faces at him. Joanie laughed too, both of them suddenly returned to childishness. Larry's eyes filled with sudden tears and he turned to wipe them away.

The hot weather continued. Each day Larry thought it would break, but no relief came and he felt heavy and slow, the heat a physical weight he couldn't shrug off. His workmen were listless, carrying half the usual number of bricks in their hods, stopping often for cigarettes. More time lost, more money lost, more grist for the bank manager's letters. But Larry left them alone and said nothing. Tempers were short enough already.

When he came home, Rosemary was absorbed in the Daily Telegraph or the news on the wireless. She barely answered his questions about Europe but gave him a withering look that implied he should be following events himself. He noticed dust had started to settle on some of the furniture and his shirts were carelessly ironed. Roy and Joanie were left to occupy themselves for hours at a time, Rosemary only rousing them to help with cooking or to run an errand. Larry felt he had no role in the house anymore.

Only at The Dolphin did the tension lift, slipping away as he drove up the hill to the fresh breeze at the top. He started to go there at lunchtime as well as in the evening, dreading the moment when he would have to return home.

He was there when the weather finally broke. It was a Thursday afternoon and so hot that the heat had risen right up the hill, bringing a dusty inertia to The Dolphin. The last customers had gone and only Larry, Malcolm and one of the barmen were left. They cleared up slowly, taking their time to wipe each table, polish each glass. When the barman cycled away at half past three, Larry went outside to tidy up the terrace. After a minute, Malcolm joined him.

'I'll just check down the end of the lawn there,' he said. 'I think some of our charming customers have been chucking their glasses in the border.'

The air was grey and thundery and as Larry rearranged the chairs and tables, he felt spots of rain on his arm. It came silently at first, evaporating on the warm stone of the terrace, but then falling faster and heavier until it was like standing in a waterfall. The sky was almost black and he could only just see Malcolm at the far end of the lawn, making an attempt to run for shelter. Lightning flared above them, catching Malcolm in an attitude of surprise. Thunder like a slammed door came instantly afterwards. Through the noise of the storm, Larry heard another sound and peered into the murk to see what it was.

Malcolm was laughing. When the lightning came again, Larry saw that he had taken off his shirt and was standing with arms outstretched, laughing wildly. He was pale as an owl in the gloom, his hoots and giggles rising like a song above the rain.

Larry stood watching him, water dripping from his chin, his nose, his eyebrows. He felt it stream from his fingertips as if his whole body was turning to liquid. He couldn't move, could only watch the dim figure capering at the end of the lawn. Then Malcolm came towards him, becoming solid again, his features sharpening as he approached. Larry could see the thinness of his torso, the dark hair on his chest, the pointed nipples. The beauty of him.

'That was...' Malcolm began to laugh again. 'God, there's

so much bloody rain!' He looked Larry up and down. 'And you stayed out in it too! Look at the state of us!'

Larry felt the weight of Malcolm's hand on his shoulder, the smell of rain and sweat and skin that came off him. Malcolm's face was close to his and he noticed a spray of freckles across his cheekbone and that his jaw was turning bluish as his beard grew through. The urge to touch his cheek was overwhelming.

'I think we should get inside, Malcolm,' he said.

They retreated into the porch. The rain on the roof was deafening and they stopped to watch as it poured from the gutters and drainpipes and raced across the terrace. Larry looked down at his sodden clothes and felt suddenly foolish. What on earth was he going to say to Rosemary?

'I'm freezing,' Malcolm said, his teeth knocking together. 'We need to get changed.' He started towards the stairs in the tower. 'Some of my things are upstairs already. I thought I'd bring them over a few bits at a time. Hope that's all right with you. There's probably a shirt you can borrow at least.'

Larry followed him up to the living quarters.

There was still no furniture but Malcolm took him into one of the bedrooms where a tea chest of books and a suitcase sat in a corner. He opened the suitcase and rummaged through the clothes. 'Let's see. Clean shirt. Socks. That's all I've got.' He straightened and handed them to Larry. 'Will they do, Mr Lambert?'

'Thanks, Malcolm,' Larry said. 'Look, please call me Larry. Mr Lambert sounds so formal.'

'Right ho then. Larry,' Malcolm smiled.

'I'll go and get dried off.'

He took the clothes and went into the bathroom. With

152

the rain running down the window and a greenish light reflected from the tiles, it felt more than ever like being under the sea. A faint echo of his old dream came back to him. He sat on the side of the bath with his eyes closed, trying to deny what he'd felt when he saw Malcolm in the rain. Trying, and failing.

After a while, he began to shiver. He opened his eyes and stood up. What was the point in thinking about it anyway? He took off his wet shirt, drying himself as best he could. The storm had been so violent that he'd felt things must somehow be different afterwards. But nothing had changed. Of course nothing had changed. He stared at his reflection in the mirror for a moment, then switched off the light.

When the letter from the bank came two days later, Larry wondered if perhaps the storm had changed things after all. Rosemary had taken the children to buy new school shoes and he was alone in the house. He stood in the hall and read the letter three times, looking for a different meaning in the words. But it was always the same. The bank had cancelled his overdraft and called in his loan.

He sat at the kitchen table, then went upstairs to the bathroom where he was sick twice in the lavatory. It did no good though, the awful clenching and unclenching in his stomach continued. He filled the sink with cold water and lowered his face into it, opening his eyes enough to see a chip in the porcelain he'd never noticed before. Pulling up from the sink, he felt dizzy for a moment. If I fell and hit my head, it could all be over, he thought. The edge of the bath would do, or one of the taps if it was at the right angle. He turned the cold tap on and off. There was drowning too, of course.

Shouts came from outside the window, just children playing in the street, but the noise brought him out of his thoughts. He couldn't do it, not once he'd thought about it. That kind of thing had to be done in an instant or not at all. He dried his face and went downstairs. The letter lay where he'd left it on the table, and he felt sick again just seeing it there. It was tempting, so very tempting, to rip it up and pretend he hadn't received it. But he would still know, and he would still have to face what had to be done. He could sell the house and they could rent somewhere, but that wouldn't come near to covering the loan; something else was going to have to go.

He went out to the garden and lit a cigarette. All the heat of the last few weeks had disappeared with the storm and it was a cool, overcast day. The garden looked straggly and worn out, as if it had had enough of putting on a show. He dead-headed a few geraniums, rubbing the fuzzy leaves to bring up the scent, dropping the stalks on the compost heap. When he turned back towards the house, Rosemary was standing on the back step, holding the letter in her hand.

He went slowly towards her. The anger and disdain he expected were replaced by a new expression. Her hand shook as he took the letter from her.

'What now?' she said, sinking down onto the step. 'What do we do now?'

'It's bad, I know.' He ignored the cramp that was clutching at his stomach. 'But something will come up. We'll muddle through.'

She looked at him and he realised that the expression on her face was defeat. She started to cry. 'I've coped with so much, coped with everything you've thrown at me, and it's got me nowhere.' A loud sob burst out of her. 'Bloody nowhere.'

Larry turned his cigarette packet over and over between his fingers. He was chilly now, and wanting to get indoors. He needed a whisky and a bit of peace and quiet to think things over. 'I'll go and talk to the bank manager on Monday,' he said. 'See what can be done.' He attempted a smile. 'Buck up, Rosemary, do.'

She stayed hunched up on the step, staring at the ground. Her hair flicked in the breeze and he noticed how much grey was mixed in with the brown.

'We won't lose the house, will we?' she asked.

He didn't answer straight away. A couple of sparrows had landed on the fence and he watched them dart and flutter down to the grass and back up again. When he lifted his hand to light another cigarette, they flew up, chattering, and disappeared into the next-door garden. 'I don't know, Rosemary. It might have to be the business or maybe the house. I just don't know.'

'I see.' She stood up and wiped her eyes. 'Well,' she said dully, 'at least it'll be the end of all that nonsense with the pub. That's something.' She blew her nose and went inside.

Larry fought the urge to cry. He could feel The Dolphin slipping away from him, slipping away when he'd only just caught it, only just understood what it meant to him. The thought of going back to the way he'd lived before – so bleak, so narrow – made him afraid. He couldn't live that way again.

They went together to see the bank manager on the Monday. Larry would much rather have gone alone, but when he suggested it, Rosemary glared at him. 'A fine job you've done of it so far.'

In the wood-panelled office, Larry felt as if he'd been sent to see the headmaster at school. There was the same intimidating desk, the same hush of disapproval, the same anxious knots in his stomach. He and Rosemary waited on hard wooden chairs as the bank manager looked over Larry's records and made notes on a jotter. He kept them waiting, then looked up and said, 'It seems things have gone from bad to worse, Mr Lambert.'

'It's just been a bit slow for the last month or two, Mr Pierce. People aren't planning anything new with things the way they are in Europe. It'll settle down again soon.'

'You think so?'

'Well...'

Rosemary cut in. 'All we ask, Mr Pierce, is that you extend the overdraft again temporarily and give us some time to pay back the loan. The pub will go up for sale straight away and once it's been sold, we can repay the loan and the overdraft.'

Larry felt his heart beat faster. It couldn't end as abruptly as this, could it?

'Well, Mrs Lambert, I've been looking at the various possibilities and I'm afraid I've reached a rather different conclusion.' Mr Pierce patted some of the paperwork on his desk. 'The bank must of course be prudent at all times and the state of your finances doesn't allow me much leeway. However, we aren't without humanity here.'

He smiled and Larry's heart beat faster still, waiting for the axe to fall.

'I've looked at the value of your assets, the building business, the pub and your house. It seems to me that the best way to cover everything you owe would be to sell both the building business and the house and retain the pub. I understand that it does have living accommodation?' He screwed the top back on his fountain pen and looked over at them. 'So you'll have both a viable business and a home. Some security for your children at least.'

Larry dared a glance at Rosemary.

Her eyes were fixed on Mr Pierce and her cheeks were flushed. Her mouth had fallen open slightly. 'But surely,' she began, 'surely the pub would be better off sold.'

Mr Pierce pushed a sheet of paper across the desk. 'I'm sorry, Mrs Lambert, but I simply can't recommend it. The figures here show that the sale of the pub is unlikely to achieve the required figure, not even if the house is sold as well. The building business is well established with a lot of goodwill attached to it and frankly put, it's a better bet for a sale than a new and let's say, somewhat unusual, public house which would have a rather limited appeal.'

Larry let out a long sigh. It felt like the first time he'd exhaled since the letter came. He leaned back in his chair and gazed up at the ceiling. Not the end after all.

That night he went up to The Dolphin and got drunk. He opened a bottle of whisky, sat at the end of the bar and bought round after round for customers and staff. By closing time, he was woozy, the lights shifting in front of his eyes as if he was looking through water.

Malcolm cleaned up until only Larry's glass was left on the bar.

'Join me, Malcolm,' Larry said. 'Have a celebration drink with me.'

'I was wondering what the occasion was,' Malcolm said.

Larry lifted his glass. 'The occasion is the saving of The Dolphin!' he shouted, and poured the whisky into his mouth from high up. It splashed and caught in his throat and he coughed most of it out onto the floor.

Malcolm held onto him and slapped his back. 'All right, Larry, all right now.'

Larry leaned in against Malcolm's jacket, the cloth cool against his face. He wanted to stay there forever.

'What about a cup of tea?' Malcolm asked and Larry nodded.

He felt himself being placed in a chair and heard Malcolm go into the little kitchen behind the bar. His head spun gently as he waited for him to come back, listening to the quiet sounds The Dolphin made when it was empty. A tap dripping, a floorboard settling, a window giving a little in the wind. He closed his eyes.

When he opened them again a cup of tea was in front of him. Malcolm sat opposite, drinking a glass of water and staring at Larry over the rim. 'Drink up,' he said.

The milky steam in Larry's face made him feel sick. He pushed the cup away. 'Maybe just some water.' Malcolm obliged, and Larry drank it down. He felt he had to explain things.

'You see, I thought I was going to have to sell The Dolphin. Trouble with the finances.' He took a breath. 'But I don't, it's safe.'

'Well, that's good news, really good news.'

'The other business has to go, and the house. That's not good news. Bad news for Rosemary.' He leaned forward. 'Rosemary doesn't like pubs, doesn't approve of pubs. And now she's going to have to live in one!'

'How do you mean?'

'We're coming to live here too, Malcolm. The Lamberts are taking up residence at The Dolphin.'

'Really?' Malcolm looked anxious. 'Does that mean I won't be able to live here?'

'No, no, of course not. You'll be here with us.' He felt a surge of joy. 'We'll all be here together. One big happy family.'

Chapter 11

Joanie
July 1949

Joanie took the scarf from its brown paper wrapping and laid it over her arm. The thick grey silk was cool against her skin, slippery as oil. She rubbed it against her cheek one last time then folded it into a square and wrapped it in the blue crêpe paper she'd saved from a case of brandy. The effect was shabbier than she'd hoped so she smoothed out an old hair ribbon and tied it round the package in a bow.

Patrick was due to arrive in twenty minutes and she wasn't ready. She took Betty's black silk dress from its hanger on the wardrobe door and slipped off her dressing gown. She had tried to refuse when Betty offered to lend it to her, but Betty had insisted.

'I'm not likely to be needing it, am I?' she'd said.

Since the disastrous dinner with Frank, there had been no more boyfriends and she spent most of her free time alone in her room. Joanie wondered what she did there, but she felt she couldn't ask.

She stepped into the dress and pulled it over her shoulders. It was surprisingly heavy, and chilly where it touched bare skin. She shivered slightly and zipped it up. The waist was a little tight and the bust definitely loose but the skirt hung in great, shimmering pleats and when she twirled, it lifted and floated the same as it did for Betty. She tucked little wads of cotton wool into her bra, patted them into shape, and went over to the mirror.

How womanly she looked, a grown-up woman with a proper figure. There was something else too, an elusive impression that Rosemary's features lay behind her own, waiting to surface. She applied lipstick and a dab of rouge – Rosemary never wore make-up – and her face became her own again.

She had no shoes good enough for the dress, and Betty's feet were smaller so it was the old, battered black pair again, and she felt like crying as she put them on. She remembered those green lizard-skin sandals. How lovely to slip on shoes like that. How wonderful to have some irresistible perfume too, but instead, she rubbed her wrists and throat with the lavender bag from her drawer, hoping it still had some scent.

Betty knocked and came in. She gave Joanie a long, appraising look. 'Not bad,' she said. 'You're almost there. Now if we just ....' She tugged the dress until it sat just right, then fluffed up Joanie's hair and smoothed down her eyebrows. Stepping back, she let out a laugh. 'God, you'll scare him to death!'

'Why? What's wrong with me?' Joanie spun round to stare at herself again in the mirror.

'Nothing, nothing, don't worry. There's just a lot more to you than usual – no shrinking violet in a tweed skirt tonight. He certainly won't forget you.'

'He'll be here any minute. Are you ready?'

Betty nodded. 'Just shout to your mum that you're opening up as usual. Then you can scarper.'

'I'm going down now, Mum. I'll bring the takings up later,' Joanie shouted from the landing, then ran downstairs before Rosemary could come out of her room and see her.

She slipped the crêpe paper package into the pocket of her coat as she put it on. Betty had unlocked the outer doors and was opening the gate outside. The van was already there, with Patrick leaning out of the window, chatting to her. Joanie felt a stab of jealousy. On this, his last evening, every word was precious and she wanted all of them for herself. She hurried towards them.

'Look after yourself,' Betty was saying. 'Hope the barracks isn't too bad.' She turned towards Joanie as she approached. 'And have a good time.'

'I'll be back by quarter past ten,' Joanie said. 'Then I can cash up as normal. If Mum comes down just say I'm...' She couldn't think of a good excuse.

'She won't come down. You know she never does. You get off now. See you later.'

Patrick jumped out to open the door for Joanie and as she settled into the seat, he brushed her cheek with his fingers. 'You look like a million dollars,' he whispered.

They drove without speaking, heading towards the town. The sky was full of cloud, a flat grey blanket that pressed its dreariness on the buildings and roads. A dreariness that would be everywhere once Patrick had gone.

'Where do you want to go first?' he asked. 'The Royal?'

They had planned to have a drink somewhere smart and then go dancing, but now Joanie couldn't bear to go somewhere crowded and noisy and share Patrick with other people. 'If you want, though I'd rather just go somewhere on our own.'

'I want to show you off,' he said. 'You can't waste all that effort on me.'

She was both pleased and disappointed. 'All right, let's go to The Royal,' she agreed.

He made her take her coat off before they went in. 'Make an entrance, Joanie. You deserve it. Every man in the room is going to wish he was me.'

She did as he asked, but felt self-conscious and awkward as they went through the revolving door. Patrick held her arm and steered her towards an empty table, confident and happy.

'What do you want to drink?' he asked, then laughed. 'Isn't it strange that we've never done this before? Come out for a drink together. I don't even know what you like.'

Joanie smiled. 'I'll have a gin and lemon, please.'

All their meetings had been under the cloak of driving lessons. Once or twice, Rosemary had been there when Patrick arrived and had given him a pitying look, hurrying them out of the door. 'No need to linger. Get her to pass the test quickly, won't you?'

It was the only thing they argued about.

'Why can't you tell her you're seeing me?' Patrick asked.

'It would make things difficult. Anyway, she thinks you're interested in Betty. It's easier that way.'

'She can't be that bad. Surely she wants you to be happy.'

'Not as much as she wants me to be respectable.'

'What isn't respectable about me?'

'It isn't you, it's anyone. She doesn't want me to go out with anyone.'

'But she went out with your dad once, didn't she? Wasn't that respectable?'

'I suppose they must have done, but she's never talked about it. Neither did he.' She realised that she simply didn't know. 'I wonder what they did together.'

She thought about it now as she watched Patrick ordering their drinks. Why did her parents get married? She couldn't imagine Larry and Rosemary courting, kissing, holding hands. There were no signs of affection between them and they were barely on speaking terms towards the end of Larry's life. Rosemary was impossible to live with, of course, but what an awful life for both of them, stuck together and rubbing each other up the wrong way, day in, day out. Nothing would make Rosemary happy, that was clear to Joanie. Larry was different though. She remembered him playing the fool with Malcolm, the two of them making her and Roy laugh. He could have been happy, in other circumstances. For a moment, she felt wistful. For all of them.

'Here you are, Joanie.' Patrick put down the drinks and raised his glass, 'To the most beautiful girl in the room.'

'And the handsomest man.'

She sipped her drink, and the alcohol soon gave a glow to the surroundings. They nestled into the red velvet seats, holding hands underneath the table. She watched Patrick's face as he took a sip of beer, noticing the way his eyes had turned colourless again, noticing everything about him as if she could save it for another time.

'I wonder what I'll be doing this time tomorrow. Getting kitted out, I expect, and finding my way round.'

She tried to imagine him in uniform. 'I hope it's not too spartan. Can you have photos, do you think?'

'I'll take one of you whether they're allowed or not.' His hand squeezed hers.

Joanie couldn't think of anything to say. Everything that came to her was either too big or too trivial to say out loud. Then she remembered the scarf. 'Oh, I almost forgot. I got you something.' She pulled the package from her coat pocket. 'I don't know when you'll get a chance to wear it.'

He untied the ribbon and pulled the paper apart. The scarf gleamed seal-grey as he lifted it out and draped it round his neck, one end flung over his shoulder.

'I don't think I can do it justice. I should be going to the opera.'

'Don't you like it?' She should have known she'd get it wrong.

'Of course I do. Thank you. I'm going to take it everywhere. I'll be the most debonair squaddie they've ever had.'

She briefly rested her forehead against his, closed her eyes and breathed in the smell of him. All she wanted was for them to be alone together.

Then Patrick was on the move, and laughing. 'My God! What are you doing here?'

He was shaking the hand of a dark, stocky man, both of them grinning like fools.

'Just here for a drink with the lads,' the man was saying, pointing towards a boisterous crowd across the room. 'You'll know most of them. Come over and join us.'

Patrick shook his head. 'Another time. I've been called up. Leaving tomorrow. Early start and all that.'

'Bloody bad luck.' The man let go of Patrick's hand and turned towards Joanie. 'And this is?'

Patrick laughed again. 'Sorry, bloody rude of me. Joanie, this is John Burton. We went to school together. John, this is Joanie Lambert.'

She hated him instantly, but managed to smile and offered her hand. 'Hello, there.'

'Delighted. A pleasure to meet you, Miss Lambert.' He turned back to Patrick. 'Sure you won't come and have a drink? And the lovely Miss Lambert too of course.'

For a moment she thought Patrick was going to accept.

He glanced across at John's crowd, eagerly, Joanie thought. 'Not tonight, John. I'll look you up when I'm back on leave though.'

'Cheerio then, Paddy. Don't let the buggers get you down.'

They clapped each other on the shoulder and parted company.

'Well, what a coincidence,' Patrick said. 'He's a decent chap, John, great footballer. I remember he once scored four times...'

'Patrick, please can we go now?' She started to gather up her things.

'Already? We've only just got here. Don't you want another drink?'

Everything she wanted from the evening was slipping away. 'I'd really like to go.'

'Where to? Not home, surely not yet. We were going to make a night of it, remember?' His tone was almost harsh.

Close to tears, she stood. 'Please.'

He finished his beer and stood too. 'Come on then.'

She wept quietly as they walked back to the van. Patrick passed her his handkerchief, and she wiped her face and blew her nose.

'Feeling better?' he asked.

'A little.'

'Not in the mood for dancing then?'

'I'd rather not.' She heard him sigh. 'Sorry.'

At the van, he opened the door for her, but stayed leaning against the bonnet for a while, smoking. She watched how his fingers held the cigarette and how he took each puff almost as a luxury, tipping back his head and blowing the smoke high in the air. She couldn't see his expression in the gloom. She climbed back out.

'I'm sorry if I spoiled the evening.'

He nodded slowly and looked at the ground. 'Well, never mind now.'

'I just didn't like it in there, too busy and noisy.' She touched his arm, then withdrew her hand, unsure.

'That's exactly what I wanted though, busy and noisy. A big night out I can remember when I'm stuck in some God-forsaken barracks for months on end.'

How had it turned so sour? She looked down at her dress. It too was drooping, and her lips felt rough and dry, the lipstick gone. Her drab, ordinary life was returning, even before Patrick had left.

'I just wanted to have you to myself,' she said. 'I didn't want to share you.'

'It's all right,' he said, his voice softer now.

They stood as the light deepened and became shadow. A black river of starlings wheeled and twisted above them. Everything was all right before, Joanie thought, when it was the two of them in the van on Sunday afternoons. She heard Patrick sigh, then felt his hand touch hers. He kissed her hair.

'It's getting cold,' he said. 'Let's get in, shall we?'

The starlings had found their roost on the ledges of a bomb-damaged building and the sky was empty again. She nodded and got into the van.

They drove out of town, back towards The Dolphin. Patrick kept turning to smile at her and she smiled back, but she felt a sadness that was nothing to do with him leaving.

They went through the estate that Larry had built and turned off into the narrow lane.

'What time is it?' he asked.

She checked her watch. 'Nine o'clock. I don't have to be back for over an hour.'

He slowed the van. 'Let's stop somewhere then.'

Near the ford at the bottom of the hill, he turned onto a track that led through the woods, and parked a little way along. He turned off the engine and in the silence, Joanie registered the bustle of birds settling down for the night and the mutter of the stream. A faint grey light was visible through the blackness of the trees. She wondered if anyone else was out there.

Patrick moved close and touched her cheek. 'You look lovely tonight.'

'I'm sorry I...'

'Don't be sorry. It's as much my fault as yours.'

He was stroking her neck, then his hand was inside the front of her dress. He was kissing her and murmuring, 'You're so lovely,' and moving his other hand up her thigh. It started to rain, big drops stuttering on the roof of the cab. He pulled her towards him, pushing aside the silky folds of the dress. She held him close. He was the only good thing in her life. He was going away. She couldn't bear it.

The rain lessened. Patrick groaned and buried his face in her neck. She stroked his hair, then reached behind to wind down the window and let in a few raindrops and the smell of damp ferns.

October 1949

She was so tired. The alarm clock was ringing, but she simply couldn't move her hand to turn it off. Back she went into the comfort of her dreams. In the end, her bladder woke her. She banged a hand on the clock, then hurried to the bathroom.

When she came out, she paused on the landing. Roy was home on weekend leave and had spent the previous night getting drunk with some friends in the bar. They had stayed over. She could hear loud snoring coming from his room. They wouldn't be up for hours. Rosemary must have known about the carousing – they'd made a lot of noise coming up the stairs – but she'd done nothing about it. She seemed to accept Roy's boorish behaviour, behaviour she would utterly condemn in anyone else. Joanie couldn't understand it.

She fetched her dressing gown and went into the kitchen, sighing when she saw the state of it. Half-drunk glasses of beer littered the table and a saucer had been used as an inadequate ashtray. The room smelled of smoke and stale beer and it made her queasy to breathe.

She cleared the debris and opened the window, letting in a sharp wind, but that was better than the stink inside. Leaning on the window sill, she shivered and gazed out. What was Patrick doing? Polishing his boots? Cleaning his kit? There seemed to be an awful lot of that kind of thing. She would write to him later and ask. Then she could picture him every Sunday morning.

Outside, the sky hung low and dark, promising rain. She turned away and put the kettle on, warming her hands at the flame. An unhurried breakfast, by herself, was a treat. In the larder, there were eggs and a new loaf, even a couple of sausages left from the day before, but looking at them made her feel queasy again. What a waste, she thought. In the end, she made herself a cup of tea and took it back to her room.

On Sundays, there was no possibility of a letter from Patrick. Partly she was relieved not to be waiting for the first post, and then for the second, but without those milestones, the hours stretched out blank and empty. She sat on the bed and wrapped the eiderdown round her shoulders. He'd been gone for eighty-three days, each as meaningless as the next. When a letter came from him, she briefly felt alive again; reading it, remembering it, reading it again. But once she knew it by heart and had put it in the box under her bed, she had to wrench herself back to ordinary life. Sometimes she thought it would be easier to stay there.

She pulled the box from under the bed now, then curled up and leafed through the envelopes inside. His letters were short, informative, increasingly full of army jargon she didn't understand. There was always an affectionate sentence or two at the end and these she treasured, like jewels. When she wrote to him, she tried to pretend it was a conversation, as if he was still there with her. She asked him dozens of questions – most of which he never answered – and recounted the small dramas of her days in a light-hearted tone. But by the time she finished each letter, she felt in a bleak mood and many of them were spotted with tears.

It was another six weeks before he would be home on leave, still too far away to be a reality. She thought about bringing him to The Dolphin, even introducing him to Rosemary, but whether it would actually happen, whether she would have the nerve, she didn't know. Rosemary knew nothing of course; he was just the man who gave her driving lessons and had left before Joanie passed her test.

'Well, that's left us high and dry, hasn't it?' she'd said. 'No licence to show for all those lessons. It's been a complete waste of time.'

'Perhaps I could carry on,' Joanie had suggested. 'A few more lessons and I'm sure I'd be ready for the test.' And then I can get away sometimes, she thought, maybe even visit Patrick.

Rosemary had considered this and finally agreed. Joanie's Tuesday afternoons were now given over to a brusque ex-army captain whom she loathed for not being Patrick. She told herself it would be worth it in the end.

She finished her tea and put the box back under the bed. There was still half an hour or so before she had to go downstairs. Was there time to start a letter now? Perhaps later would be better, once lunch was over. It was so tempting to lie down and drift back into the comfort of sleep. She closed her eyes for a moment.

'Joanie, Joanie, get up!' She was woken by Rosemary shaking her shoulder. 'It's nearly ten o'clock, for heaven's sake.'

'Oh dear.' Joanie struggled to gather her thoughts. 'I fell asleep again. Didn't mean to. Sorry.'

'What's wrong with you lately? You've been drooping about all over the place.'

'I'm just a bit under the weather.' She thought she'd put up a good appearance since Patrick left but it obviously wasn't as convincing as she'd hoped.

'You need a tonic. Phosferine'll buck you up. I'll get some when I'm next in town. We can't afford for you to be ill, Joanie. There's too much to do.'

'I know, I know. I won't be ill.' How marvellous to be just a little bit ill, she thought. Bad enough to stay in bed all day but well enough to appreciate it. A week of that would do her no end of good. She stood up and stretched. 'I'll get on then.'

All day she felt slow and thick-headed. Twice she gave out the wrong change and by the end of lunchtime, she could have fallen asleep standing up. As soon as all the customers had gone, she poured herself a glass of soda water and sat down at one of the tables. The waistband of her skirt had been chafing all day and she unzipped it with a sigh of relief. She was hungry now, but too tired to go upstairs yet. It must be my monthlies, she thought. She tried to work out if her period was due, counting back to the last one. They'd been erratic recently, but when was it exactly? She'd had one not long before Patrick left – she remembered worrying that if it came at the wrong time, it would spoil their last evening together – and then...

There hadn't been another. Nothing since the night of rain and love in the cab of the brewery van.

Her hand shook as she picked up her glass. Everyone knew that you couldn't get pregnant the first time. She didn't know much, but that was common knowledge, wasn't it? And if her period was late, surely that was the stress of Patrick leaving and her being overworked. Anything else was unthinkable. She put the glass down again. There was the constant tiredness though, and the clothes getting a little tight. She'd put the nausea down to missing Patrick so much. That seemed naive now. She sat very still, staring at the tabletop.

The door at the top of the stairs banged and she heard Betty call out as she came downstairs. 'Joanie? Are you coming up?' She appeared at the entrance to the Circular Bar and came towards her. 'Your mum's got lunch ready.'

Joanie nodded, stood up and felt dizzy. She mustn't betray anything. 'Yes, I'm coming. I'll just go and lock the gate.'

Betty put a hand on her shoulder. 'You look white as anything. Are you poorly?'

Joanie took a deep breath, not sure she could answer

without crying. 'I'm all right.' She picked up the keys and went to the door. The wind was lifting and tumbling the fallen leaves in the yard and they batted her legs as she crossed to the gate. She pulled it closed and locked it, then paused for a moment, not wanting to go back inside. But where else was there? Slowly, she walked back and closed the door behind her.

They went upstairs together, a pungent smell of stewing offal growing stronger with every step. Betty made a face. 'Hearts again. Surely they must have something else at the butcher's. That's twice this week.' She sighed. 'I'd give anything for proper roast beef. Or a nice leg of lamb.'

'Oh, don't,' Joanie said. 'It'll taste even worse now.'

She was so hungry she ate the heart anyway and had second helpings of cabbage. Roy's friends had all left – she'd watched them troop out through the bar earlier, pale and subdued – and he sat at the end of the table looking bilious. Now and again, he stared intently at Betty. Rosemary spooned extra boiled potatoes onto his plate. 'Eat up, Roy. You'll need it for the train later.'

He pushed the plate away and stood up. 'I'm not really hungry. Think I'll go for a lie-down.'

Joanie speared one of his potatoes with her fork and ate it quickly.

'Manners, Joanie!' Rosemary snapped. 'You'd think you didn't know how to behave.' Joanie watched her chew each mouthful the requisite fifteen times while discreetly removing bits of gristle to the side of her plate. What if she knew Joanie was pregnant? Joanie felt her cheeks redden.

Betty leaned back in her chair. 'What are you doing this afternoon, Joanie? Fancy going to the pictures?' she asked.

'The pictures? Oh, no...I mean, sorry, but I don't really

feel up to it.' She spoke as evenly as she could but longed to be by herself in her room. 'I haven't been sleeping very well lately. I'll rest a bit, I think.'

'You did look awfully peaky earlier,' Betty said.

Joanie stood up and began to clear the table. 'Finished, Mum?'

Rosemary nodded and sighed. 'Well, some of us have work to do this afternoon. I'll be in my room with the banking. Joanie, bring me a cup of tea when you've washed up, will you?' She heaved herself to her feet and went out.

Joanie piled the plates by the sink and wiped down the table. A hard, sleety rain had begun, beating against the steamed-up glass.

Betty lit a cigarette and put the kettle on. 'I'll make the tea,' she said.

'Thanks, Betty.'

While Joanie washed a saucepan, she wondered what Betty would say if she knew. She wanted desperately to tell someone, to share the unbearable secret, and Betty was the only person she could think of who, perhaps, wouldn't be appalled. But how could she tell anyone when not even Patrick knew? She would have to tell him. She would have to take a sheet of her blue writing paper, pick up a pen and form the words, 'I am having a baby'. She would have to seal the envelope and stick on a stamp and walk to the letterbox. And once sent, her words couldn't be taken back.

'Are you sure you're all right?' Betty asked. 'You've gone all pale again.'

'I just need to lie down. I'm going for a rest.'

She hurried to her room and closed the door. The pad of writing paper lay on her bedside table, her pen next to it. She sat down and stared at them. How to even start?

174

Whatever she wrote, this letter would change things forever.

She lay back on the pillow and closed her eyes. What if they got married? She tried to imagine Patrick as her husband, as a father, but all that came were questions. Where would they live? What would they live on? Did she even want to marry him?

What else, what else was there, what else could she do? She turned on her side and covered her face with her hands. Have the baby adopted. That was the only other option. To go through the whole nine months, slowly swelling in full view of the world. To be judged. To be shamed. For nothing.

Her mother would never allow that, her living at The Dolphin pregnant and unmarried! Oh, the humiliation for Rosemary! She began to giggle. The utter, utter humiliation! The giggles became uncontrollable, then turned to sobs. She wiped her face on the eiderdown. There was simply no way out.

She drifted into a sleep full of fleeting, anxious dreams, and when she woke up, it was dark and the room was cold. Rain still battered the window, rattling it in its frame, and a gusty draught blew across her neck. She lay exactly as she was, hoping that time had somehow ceased and that, if she didn't move, an answer would reveal itself.

But no answer came. She tentatively reached under her blouse and placed her hand on her belly. No discernible difference. No beating heart beneath the skin. No lump. But she knew it was there, growing like a bulb in the winter earth, getting ready to push its way out. She ran her hands over her body, kneading the skin, jabbing and poking, unsure exactly where it was rooted, but hoping she could maybe dislodge it.

A door opened across the landing and she heard footsteps

and another door closing. She stopped pummelling herself. Rosemary called out, telling Roy to hurry up. She lay for a few minutes longer, knowing she ought to get up and say goodbye. Apart from his drunken presence in the bar on Saturday night, she had barely seen him. With an effort, she threw off the eiderdown and stood up.

Roy was in the kitchen doorway, drinking a glass of milk and putting on his coat.

'There you are,' he said. 'I thought I was going to have to come and get you.'

'Sorry, I fell asleep.'

'You look awful, you know.'

'Thanks very much.' She thought of saying he didn't look so good either, but actually, she thought he looked extremely well. He had a healthy colour to his face and he was bigger and more muscular. National Service suited him.

'Are you glad to be going back then?' she asked.

He shrugged. 'It's all right, I suppose. Plenty of pals there now. We have a laugh. And I might be sent over to Cyprus soon.'

'Really? What does Mum think about that?' How wonderful that would be, she thought. To be sent to a warm, distant island where nobody knew her and she could tell them anything she wanted about herself.

'Let's say she's getting used to the idea.' He drained his glass and gave her a long, critical look. 'So what's been happening here? Have you passed your driving test yet?'

She clenched her fists and dug her nails into her palms. 'Not yet. Patrick...remember him from the brewery?...was giving me lessons, but he's been called up too.'

'Oh, it was Patrick, was it? Mr Dreamboat himself. Mum didn't tell me that.' Roy smiled a sly smile. 'I bet you got up to all sorts while you were meant to be having a lesson.'

Joanie felt her face flush scarlet, the heat spreading all the way down her neck. 'Oh, for goodness' sake, Roy. Grow up, will you?'

The door to Rosemary's room opened and she came out, wearing her hat and coat. 'Are you ready yet, Roy? It's time we were going.'

He hoisted his kit bag onto his shoulder. 'Bye then, Joanie. See you at Christmas.' He followed Rosemary down the landing then stopped at the top of the stairs and pulled an envelope from his pocket. 'Here, give this to Betty, will you?'

'Can't you do it? I think she's in her room.'

'I've got to go. Make sure she gets it.' He sprinted down the stairs.

Joanie went into the kitchen and put on a pan of milk, wishing she had a sister she could confide in, rather than a piggish brother. What would he think of her if he knew? It almost made her smile to imagine his stupefied face. But after the shock, Roy wouldn't be forgiving, she knew that. He might pity her, but he would despise her too. She couldn't expect any help from him.

She sat at the table, turning Roy's envelope over and over. For a moment she wished that she could talk to Malcolm. Whatever she'd done, he would be kind. He was always kind. But Malcolm had disappeared, scared off by Rosemary's mysterious threats. The letters she'd written to him had been returned, 'Not known at this address.'

The milk began to sizzle. She got up and stood by the stove, watching the white froth that rose suddenly to the rim, taking it away only when it was about to boil over. She'd forgotten what she meant to do with it. Betty came in as she stirred a spoon round and round the pan.

'Making cocoa?'

'Oh, yes, of course, cocoa,' Joanie said.

Betty sat down. 'Feeling better?'

'Not really. I'm just going to make this and go to bed. And Roy left this for you.' She pushed the envelope across the table.

Betty frowned as she read the letter. 'For heaven's sake,' she muttered. When she'd finished, she crumpled it into a ball. 'He thinks he's in love with me.'

'Does he?' Joanie remembered what Betty had done with Roy before he went away in February. 'Because of that time you...?'

'Mmm.' Betty lit a cigarette and sighed. 'It's never the right one, is it? The ones you want don't want you and the ones who want you are not worth bothering with. Bloody men.' She blew out a stream of smoke. 'Or maybe it's just my bad luck. You and Patrick are doing fine, aren't you? When's he coming back?'

Joanie had often wished for cosy chats about boyfriends with Betty, talking like equals about their little foibles, their maddening habits, their silly maleness. But not today. 'He's back at the end of November, just for a weekend.' She fetched a cup from the cupboard. 'Do you want some cocoa?'

'No, ta. So is he enjoying the army?' Betty had her feet on the table and leant back in her chair. She looked as if she wanted to talk.

'Oh, you know, it's early days. Look, I'm going to...'

'Must be awful in those barracks. No home comforts, terrible food. Though I bet he doesn't get hearts every other blinking day!' Betty laughed at her own joke.

It was too much. Joanie felt tears massing. 'Betty, I've got a splitting headache. I just have to go to bed. I'll see you in the morning.' She turned round quickly, spilling her drink as she headed for the door. She saw the look of surprise on Betty's face.

Monday morning. Joanie did not want to open her eyes. The day – the week, the future – pressed in on her like a fog to be navigated. There seemed to be no way forward but she knew that somehow, she would have to move.

Pretend it's an ordinary day, she told herself. Just get on with it.

Nobody else was up, but she hurried down to the bar anyway to be sure of being by herself. There was always a lot to do on a Monday and she set to work polishing the metalwork and the floors until they glittered like sunlight on ice.

She kept busy all day, serving customers, collecting glasses, washing up and wiping down. Talking enough to appear to be her ordinary self. Betty gave her the occasional odd look, but seemed happy to have more time for chatting and flirting with customers.

Once, she caught sight of herself in a mirror. She was pale and her hair hung lank around her face. Her eyes seemed huge. She turned away quickly.

It was the same all week. Keeping busy, making herself too tired to think, avoiding Betty and her mother as much as possible. Avoiding the pad of writing paper on the bedside table, clean as a pale blue sky.

When John Burton came into the bar on the Thursday night, she recognised him straight away. She was wiping tables and watched him stroll up to the bar, lean one elbow on it and imperiously survey the room. He wore a smart blue suit but still managed to look like a thug. An arrogant thug. Betty went over to serve him and they exchanged a few words, Betty giving the unconvincing laugh she used on ugly men. He sipped his drink and looked round the room again. Joanie bent her head and wiped the table furiously, but a moment later she saw a pair of shoes – very black, very shiny – come to rest by the table leg.

'Miss Lambert, what a surprise to see you here,' he said.

She straightened up. 'Hello, Mr Burton. What a surprise to see you too.'

'I wish Paddy had mentioned you worked here. I would have come in sooner.' He smiled and she saw he had very small teeth, dozens of them pegged into his jaw. 'Only dropped in for a swift one. I'm on my way down to Birmingham. Very important business meeting tomorrow.' He clearly thought she should be impressed.

'Oh, I see,' she said. 'Well, I must get on.' She moved to the next table.

'Don't run off. Have a drink with me. It's Joanie, isn't it?' He showed his teeth again. 'Come on, Joanie.'

The cheek of him, she thought. And he's meant to be Patrick's friend. 'I'm really much too busy, Mr Burton.'

'Just one drink.' He sat down and put his hands flat on the table she was clearing. His fingers were thick and white, tufted with black hairs. 'A lovely girl like you shouldn't be on her own and now Patrick's gone...' He trailed off.

It took Joanie a few moments to understand what he'd said. 'Sorry?'

His smile turned to a leer. 'I mean, now that Paddy's not around, perhaps you and I could have a nice time together.'

He thought she'd go behind Patrick's back while he was away! 'I really don't think so, Mr Burton. Patrick will be back on leave very soon and I wouldn't like to be in your shoes if he finds out you propositioned me.'

His expression changed, first to annoyance, then to amusement. 'Oh, God, you don't even know, do you?' He moved his hands across the table towards her, like some kind of creeping sea creatures. 'Your Patrick was back on leave last week. Didn't he tell you? Oh no, he wouldn't though, would he? Seeing as he was out with a rather nice brunette. Very friendly they looked.'

'No,' she said. 'That's not right. He doesn't get leave for another five weeks.' She turned to walk away with the stack of glasses, her hands trembling.

His voice followed her. 'He's got a bit of a reputation for the ladies, our Paddy, but you probably don't know that either. Stuck out here, I expect you don't get to know much at all.'

She kept walking towards the bar, the glasses quaking and clattering in her arms.

'Joanie?' Betty took the glasses from her. 'You're shaking like a leaf. Has something happened?'

If she spoke, it would make it true. She shook her head. Somebody came up behind her and she heard John Burton say, 'Goodnight then, Miss Lambert.'

She kept very still.

'Was it him?' Betty whispered. 'Did he say something?'

She didn't move.

'Good night, sir,' Betty said, somewhere to her right.

She heard his footsteps retreating, then the squeak and slam of the door opening and closing. She sighed, and began to cry.

'Oh no, don't cry,' Betty said. 'Go and sit in the Circular Bar. It's nearly closing time anyway. I'll finish up.'

Joanie walked slowly to the Circular Bar. Already closed for the winter, it was unlit and unheated and she shivered as she sat down on the window seat.

How easy it had been for Patrick, she thought. She was stuck at The Dolphin, tethered like a goat. He could do whatever he liked without risk of being caught. Apart from Sunday afternoons, he'd had the whole week to himself, to see anyone else he wanted. She remembered the few affectionate lines at the end of his letters and wondered how many other girls had read the same words and thought they were the only ones.

The last customers left and Betty came over with a glass of brandy.

'Don't tell your mum,' she said.

Joanie smiled weakly and took a sip.

'Come on then. Is it something to do with that man in the bar? Is he something to do with Patrick?'

Joanie nodded and took a deep breath. 'He says...he says Patrick's been back on leave already. He says...that he was out with someone else.' Her voice sank into tears again. 'He's been two-timing me.'

Betty rubbed her shoulder. 'Poor old Joanie. Who'd do a mean thing like that to a soft thing like you, eh? Do you think he's telling the truth, Patrick's friend?'

'I think so. The way he said it, it sounded true.' She struggled to hold back another sob. 'Like I should have realised already.'

'Well, time to move on then,' Betty said. 'They're not worth crying over. Don't waste your tears on him.'

The sob burst from her ribcage. 'Oh God, Betty, what am I going to do?'

'You'll get over it, Joanie. Believe me, you will.'

She couldn't lift her head, couldn't stop crying, couldn't speak. She leaned against Betty's cardigan with its faint scent of lavender and sweat.

'There's nothing else, is there?' Betty asked.

It was so hard to say the words. She tried three times before they finally emerged in a wavering whisper. 'I'm pregnant.'

Betty said nothing for a minute then let out a long, sad sigh. 'Oh, Joanie, how did you let that happen?'

'It was just the once, before he went away. I couldn't say no.'

'Did he hurt you?' Betty gripped her hand.

'No, he didn't hurt me. I wanted to. That makes it even worse. And now...' She couldn't say any more.

'Does Patrick know?'

She shook her head and thought of the writing paper upstairs. 'I can't tell him now.'

'You ought to, Joanie. It isn't fair for you to face this by yourself.'

'But I can't, I just can't. It would have been bad enough before, but now I know about him, I can't.'

They sat silently for a while. Outside, the darkness was absolute, like a blindfold wrapped tight around the building. How can I ever escape? Joanie thought. I can't stay here and I can't go anywhere else. I can't have a baby and I can't not. I can't marry Patrick and...well, that's all. I can't marry Patrick now.

Betty cleared her throat. 'Look, Joanie, you go up to bed and get a good night's sleep. You can't make any decisions tonight. I'll do the takings...'

'Mum won't like that. She'll get suspicious.'

'All right, I'll tell her you did them, but you were really

tired so I just brought them upstairs. Okey dokey?'

Joanie nodded and stood up. 'Sorry, Betty,' she said, fiddling with her cuff. 'I didn't mean to come out with it all like that. It's really nothing to do with you.'

Betty took a sip from the brandy glass. 'If there's one thing I know, it's that you can't keep a secret like that for very long. You've got to do something, Joanie. Whatever you decide, you've got to do something.'

Betty didn't say anything until Saturday. They were clearing up at the end of the night when she suddenly announced, 'The way I see it, you've only got three choices.'

Joanie put down the glass she was drying.

'You tell Patrick you're pregnant and make him marry you. What do you think?' Betty raised her eyebrows questioningly. 'Recipe for disaster, if you ask me.'

Fleetingly Joanie saw a cosy family of three, fragmenting almost instantly into John Burton's leer. 'What are the others?'

'You go through with the whole thing then have it adopted. Though what your mum would say I don't know.'

'She'd throw me out if she even thought I was pregnant,' Joanie said.

'Then the only other choice is to get rid of it before she finds out.'

Joanie stared at her. 'But that's against the law.'

'Well, it shouldn't be.'

'And it's horrible. A horrible thing to do.'

Betty gave her a pitying look. 'It'd sort out your little problem though, wouldn't it?'

Joanie started putting glasses back on the shelf so she didn't have to look at Betty. It was disgusting to think of

184

some dirty old woman interfering with her, poking about in a part of her body that she couldn't even name out loud. She didn't know how it worked, but she imagined something being pulled from inside her, something red and mangled, and she shuddered.

'Look, I know it isn't very pleasant, but I'm right, Joanie. Those are your only choices. Unless you want to keep it and bring up a little bastard on your own.'

Joanie flinched at the word.

Betty came and stood very close to her. 'I know someone,' she said in a low voice. 'If that's what you want to do, I know someone.'

Before she went to bed that night, Joanie stood naked in the bathroom. In the mirror, she examined herself from all angles. Belly, breasts, arms, legs, buttocks. It was cold and her nipples were jutting out and her skin pimpled all over. There were bruises on her shins from hauling crates up from the cellar and a burn on one wrist from a hot roasting tin. A vein forked the length of one thigh. She hardly ever looked at her body. What was the point? It did what she needed it to do. Now she stuck out her belly and put her hands around it, imagining it swelling, imagining it growing huge and fleshy. A wave of nausea hit her and she sat down on the side of the bath. Betty was right. She had to make a choice.

The address was in a part of town she had never been to before and she felt horribly conspicuous as she got off the bus, as if every other passenger knew where she was going. The houses were old and tired-looking, some with sagging window sills and door frames, and there were occasional gaps where bomb sites interrupted the terraces. She peered at the directions Betty had written down and began to walk.

The afternoon light was dimming, but she wished she'd come even later, when it was fully dark and no one would see her. Whenever she passed someone on the pavement, she ducked her head and walked faster, then worried that maybe that made her more, not less, noticeable.

She turned right onto a narrower road lined with cherry trees. A few leaves still hung on the branches, as limp and faded as old bunting. There were no pedestrians here, no cars or bikes, and her footsteps rang out too loudly. She slowed and lightened her step, almost to a tip-toe. The directions said the house was at the end of the road, just before the park gates, number forty-seven.

She checked her watch. She was too early but she couldn't walk any slower and she could hardly stand outside the house and wait. Number forty-seven was in sight now. There was nothing significant about it, nothing to set it apart from the other houses in the street. It looked reasonably well kept and there was a winter jasmine in bloom in the small front garden, starry with yellow flowers. For a moment she thought she might not be able to face it and her heart beat loudly, almost painfully, as she came level with the gate and then walked past. The entrance to the park was straight ahead and she saw with relief that the gates were still open and that there was a bench a few yards inside. She could sit there for ten minutes and wait.

She was suddenly very tired. All of her will power had gone into getting herself there, to that street, that house; now it was spent. Where would she find the energy to get up and walk the few steps to the front door, to ring the bell and give the false name she'd prepared, to go through with the whole thing? If only it was already done, she thought, and I could just go home.

It was very quiet, only the sound of a leaf falling and landing on another dry leaf. A car passing on the main road made a faint hum. She could almost hear the bristle of frost forming on twigs and grass stalks. To be quiet and alone like this felt like a kind of luxury. Except for what she had to do next.

She closed her eyes. And sitting there on the freezing bench, she imagined what it would be like to have a child of her own. To be a mother. A real mother full of love who expected the child to be just that; a child. A mother who wasn't Rosemary.

She continued to sit even though it was time to go. The daylight had completely gone and a paring of moon gleamed in the sky. Through the gates, she watched a cat spring silently from a wall and cross the road. This is not what I want, she thought, the certainty growing the longer she sat there. And then, with a clarity that surprised her, she knew exactly what she was going to do.

Chapter 12

Lottie
September 1972

Dan was in the greenhouse. Lottie watched him from the kitchen window as she washed up, her hands deep in soapy water.

He was bent over the bench that ran the length of the greenhouse, pouring compost into flower pots. Every now and then he paused to mime a drum roll in the air and she knew he had the radio on loud. Dusk was gathering at the edges of the garden, the bushes turning dark green, then black, and the lit greenhouse dazzled. When he wiped his hands, she thought he was on his way back to the house, so she opened the porch door ready for him, but he headed for the shed and dragged a heavy hessian sack back to the greenhouse. It must be snowdrop time. She knew there were hundreds of tiny bulbs in the sack, waiting to be planted. It was Dan's only successful line.

She made him a coffee and took it outside. The air was sharp, full of the promise of autumn, and she warmed her hands on the mug as she went across the lawn.

Dan didn't notice her come in. The Strawbs were playing on the radio, blasting *Lay Me Down* into every corner. Dan was picking bulbs from the sack, shaking them free of sand, examining them and placing five in each pot, all in time to the music. She reached under the bench and turned the music down.

'Oh, hi, love. Didn't know you were there. That for me? Thanks.'

She put the mug down next to him. 'Want any help?'

'You can start covering them with compost if you want. Like this, look.' He scooped compost up and let it filter through his fingers to cover the bulbs. 'About this deep. OK?'

'OK.'

They worked in silence, the radio playing quietly. Lottie wondered if there was any point in planting the snowdrops. She looked at Dan, nestling bulbs into pots, taking time to arrange them evenly. The bulb business just wasn't working. Orders came in fitfully, most of them small, and she wondered how he could keep up his enthusiasm. The business cost almost as much as it made yet on he went, nurturing the bulbs, posting them off when an order came in, whooping happily when a cheque arrived. She sighed.

'What are we potting up anyway?' she asked.

'*Galanthus nivalis*. The ordinary ones.' He fetched a pot from the other end of the bench. 'Look at this one though. Don't know what's happened but it's come through early.'

Lottie took it from him and looked at the sheaf of thin stems that ended in three stiff white petals. 'Not petals, tepals,' Dan always corrected her. These enclosed other petals, smaller and marked in green with an upside-down heart shape.

'*Galanthus reginae olgae,*' Dan said. 'Shouldn't be flowering for another month. I forgot about that one, haven't watered it, haven't fed it and look at the little beauty now.' He smiled. 'That's what I love about snowdrops. You don't even know they're there, but it's all happening underground. Then one day, even though it's still winter and they could freeze and die, out they come. You can't stop them.'

She trickled compost into a pot and tapped it down lightly. He was so sure he was doing the right thing, that everything would work out. She just couldn't see it.

'You all right, Lottie?' he asked.

'Sorry?'

'Only you've been standing there like that for a while.'

Lottie sighed. 'Oh, I'm fine. Just thinking about the future, I suppose. Where we'll end up. What we'll do.'

Dan held up one of the bulbs in a theatrical gesture. 'We'll be rich! Rich, I tell you!'

'I don't think so.' She couldn't even force a smile.

'We'll be fine, Lottie. Things will get better. Or I'll come up with another idea. A really brilliant one.'

She reached for another pot and added the compost. His optimism and confidence were beginning to feel like blindness. She remembered how on a walk during his parents' visit, his father had insisted on taking a path that led them miles out of their way. He hadn't apologised, or even admitted it was a mistake. He just kept going, ignoring any opportunity to turn back. Perhaps that's where he gets it from, Lottie thought.

Dan reached into the hessian sack. 'Actually, I have been thinking about something,' he said.

She pushed the finished pot to the end of the bench and waited.

'We could move to Kenya.'

'What?'

'If you want a future, let's go to Kenya. There's so much we could do out there, Lottie. We wouldn't have to stay with Mum and Dad for long. We could buy some land and build our own place.'

Lottie ran her fingers round the rim of a flower pot and avoided looking at him.

When Dan's parents came to stay, it had been their first holiday in fifteen years. They spent all their time, energy and money on their farm – breeding cattle, rearing cattle, slaughtering cattle, selling cattle. It was all they did. The papers had been full of photos of Kenya when Prince Charles and Princess Anne visited earlier in the year. People in exotic dress featured widely, as well as exotic animals and exotic beaches, but there seemed to be no connection to the hard, arid life of Dan's parents.

And there was no doubt that it was a hard life. Any vague thoughts Lottie had about cocktail parties and colonial glamour were quickly crushed when Dan's father told her, 'We're usually in bed by eight, unless there's calving. Nothing much to stay up for. And it saves the generator.'

She had stared at their photographs, horrified at their bleak bungalow and parched landscape. There was a picture of Dan, aged seven, amongst them.

'Oh, look, there's the sofa before the leg fell off it,' Dan's mother had cried out. 'We've still got that,' she told Lottie. 'It's propped up on a pile of books now.'

It was fifteen miles to the nearest neighbour, twenty-five to the nearest town. It would be just the four of them on the farm, day in, day out. No one else to talk to. Nowhere else to go. Nothing would persuade her to move there.

'But how on earth would we support ourselves? We couldn't live off your parents.'

Dan laughed. 'There are thousands of things we could do out there, Lottie. They're crying out for people like us to come and develop the place.'

'I couldn't leave Mum. It wouldn't be fair.'

'She's the one who wanted you to go and do something different, isn't she? That's what you told me.'

'Yes, but she'd be all on her own now.' It wasn't just leaving Joanie either, it was the thought of leaving Bill too. Everywhere she went – the cafe, the pier, the whole town – had some connection to him. To move away would be to lose that forever.

'Well, give it some thought, Lottie. I don't mean we go next week or anything. But just keep it in mind, eh?'

December 1972

For the first time ever, they closed the cafe between Christmas and New Year. It felt like they were betraying Bill, but even Lottie had to admit that with so few customers, it made no sense to stay open. She'd longed for time off but she couldn't relax. Dan kept talking about Kenya, saying 'when' instead of 'if' and she had to remind him often that she'd not agreed to go. Thinking about it made her jittery, as if she'd drunk too much coffee, and by lunchtime on New Year's Eve, she was desperate for something to do. Dan was tidying up in the greenhouse and she went out to help.

The greenhouse had a comforting smell of humus and hessian sacking which made her want to curl up and go to sleep there. Dan was at the bench, nodding along to the radio, and labelling a package of bulbs.

'Need a hand with anything?'

'Not really. I'm pretty much done. I'll just go and post this then I thought I might go to the pub for a bit, see the lads.'

'Can I come?'

He looked uncomfortable. 'It's more of a men-only thing... you know. Sorry.'

'Oh, OK.'

'I'll meet you at the beach for the fireworks tonight.'

She sighed. 'All right.'

'Why don't you go and see your mum?'

'Maybe.'

'Come on, love. You've been moping about since Christmas. You need to get out and do something.' He picked up his parcel and went out.

It was a twenty-minute walk to her mother's house, up to the top of the hill and almost to the edge of town. The higher she went the stronger the wind blew, making her eyes water and numbing her ears, and by the time she rang the bell, she felt cold to her bones. There was no answer. She had her key, of course, but there was no point going in if her mother wasn't there so she turned and walked back down the hill, continuing on towards the sea. The cafe it is then, she said to herself. I can find something to get on with there.

From the pier, she watched the preparations being made on the beach for the New Year. A huge bonfire of driftwood was being constructed and pits dug to hold fireworks. She sighed as she approached the cafe, unable to summon up any enthusiasm for the evening. Maybe I'll feel better if I have a good go at cleaning the fridges, she thought. She took out her keys to unlock the door and was surprised to find it already open.

Her mother was leaning on the counter, a copy of *The Caterer & Hotelkeeper* open in front of her.

'Hello, Mum,' she said.

Joanie looked up, startled. 'Oh, hello, love.'

'Didn't expect to see you here.'

'I was at a bit of a loose end so I came down to do some

tidying up.' The magazine was open at the property section.

'Not thinking of buying something else, are you?' Lottie laughed. 'We've got enough on our plates already.'

Joanie didn't answer. Lottie went to look over her shoulder and saw a full-page ad for a pub, a white building on the top of a hill, poorly photographed. It had a tower full of windows built into one side and a terrace with a pool on the other. It looked shabby and forlorn. She read the text: *Public house for sale with full planning permission to demolish the existing building and construct two detached houses. Excellent location close to all amenities. Half acre of grounds. All fixtures and fittings included. Enquiries to Humphries Estate Agents.*

'Looks a bit like a ship,' Lottie said. 'One that's about to sink though.'

When Lottie looked up, she saw tears in her mother's eyes.

'Mum? What is it?'

Joanie shook her head, eyes squeezed shut.

'What's wrong?'

'Nothing. It's fine.'

'Are you ill? You're shaking.'

'No.' Joanie straightened and dabbed at her eyes. 'I'll make us a cup of tea. Then I thought I might give the windows a proper clean. They need it.' She closed the magazine and put it in her bag.

They worked silently. Lottie glanced at her mother now and then, but there was nothing to see, no way of knowing what had upset her. She sneaked another look at the magazine when Joanie went outside to clean the windows but it offered no clues. The photo was too grainy to see much detail, only that the building was of an unusual design and in poor condition. She watched her mother rubbing a chamois cloth over the glass and wondered what she wasn't saying.

By four o'clock it was almost dark and the cafe was gleaming. Lottie had cleaned every shelf and drawer in the fridges and the windows were so clear they were almost not there. The thickening dusk looked like it could come right in.

She looked at the Christmas lights strung along the pier and then at the bigger, gaudier displays along the Esplanade. 'Well, that's it then,' she said. 'Almost the new year.'

'You'd better go and get yourself ready for tonight. I'll lock up.'

'It's OK, Mum. I'll wait for you.'

They pulled down the window blinds, turned off all the switches and went outside. Lottie leaned against the balustrade while her mother locked the door, and stared down at the water glittering blackly below. It seemed to be sucking at the pier supports as it swirled round them and she imagined the metal giving way, slowly crumpling towards the seabed, bringing down the cafe and all the other pier buildings. For the first time ever, she felt vulnerable out there.

They walked along the pier towards the Esplanade. Fog blended with dusk, blurring the Christmas lights. The air was dank.

'I'll give you a lift,' Joanie said when they reached her car.

'Thanks. Don't fancy that walk tonight.'

The streets were empty as they drove up the hill. Joanie was silent. Lottie wondered what she was thinking about.

'Do you want me to come over tonight?' she asked. 'I'm not really bothered about seeing the fireworks.'

'No, it's fine.'

'You don't want to see the new year in by yourself though, do you? I'll come round.'

'Margaret next door invited me for drinks. I expect I'll pop in there.'

Lottie didn't believe her.

When they stopped at the end of her road she leaned over and kissed Joanie's cheek. 'Happy new year then.'

'Happy new year, Lottie. Here's to 1973.'

February 1973

It was the usual Tuesday arrangement. Lottie drove up to her mother's house early and they went to the cash and carry together to stock up for the week. Dan could cope by himself for an hour or two.

On the way back to the cafe, they stopped to drop off the few things Joanie had bought for herself. The phone was ringing in the hall as Lottie opened the front door.

'I'll get it,' she called.

'Is that Mrs Lennox?' The voice sounded northern.

'I'll just get her. Who's speaking please?'

'It's Humphries Estate Agents.'

Lottie handed Joanie the phone and continued into the kitchen. She put down the bags and tiptoed to the door to listen. Why on earth was her mother speaking to an estate agent? What was she selling? Or buying? She remembered that Humphries was the name on the advert in *The Caterer & Hotelkeeper* and felt uneasy.

Joanie's voice was muffled but loud enough for Lottie to hear most of what she said.

'Well, what would be a reasonable offer?'

A pause.

'And when?'

Another pause.

'I see. All right. I'll phone you back later.'

There was something else that Lottie couldn't hear, and then the click of the phone on its cradle. She hurried to unpack the bags.

It was a moment or two before Joanie came into the kitchen. Lottie had meant to be subtle, but she couldn't contain herself. 'What was that, Mum? What's going on?'

Joanie sat down at the table and rubbed her temples.

'Mum!'

'It's not important. It's nothing.'

Lottie was suddenly furious. 'How can it be nothing? That's the estate agent who's selling that wreck of a pub, isn't it? Why would you even think about buying it?'

The light in the kitchen had dimmed and now rain was beating against the window. Lottie stared at her mother, hunched and grey in the gloom.

'It's a very long story, Lottie. And I can't really explain it all to you.'

'But you are trying to buy that place?'

Joanie nodded.

'But why? Why, Mum?'

Joanie gave a deep sigh, then closed her eyes. 'Because my father built it. I lived there from when I was twelve until I came here. And I don't want it to be demolished. That's why.'

Lottie leaned back in her chair, her head full of questions she couldn't put into words. 'How much do they want for it?'

'A lot. Eight thousand.'

'Eight thousand! Where are you going to get eight thousand from?'

Joanie didn't reply.

The answer surfaced as if she'd known along. 'You're selling the house.'

Joanie spoke very faintly. 'It's not worth enough on its own.'

'But then how are you...?' Another realisation. 'And the cafe too?'

Joanie nodded.

Lottie stood up and went to the sink, filled a glass of water from the tap and took a gulp. It was too much to take in. She drank more water, but it felt like swallowing lead. 'And you weren't going to tell us?' she said.

'Of course I was going to tell you.'

Lottie stared at her, angry. 'When?'

Joanie bent her head. 'I know I should have said something sooner. It might not have come off though and then, well, nothing would have changed and I'd have upset you about nothing.'

'But didn't you think we should know? Didn't you think we should discuss it?' First Dan wanted her to go to Kenya, and now this. Nobody seemed to care what she wanted. 'Look, I can't do this now. I have to go to work.'

She hurried to the door, then ran to the car. In the rear mirror, she could see Joanie on the doorstep, pale and small, diminishing further as she drove away.

By the time she turned the corner at the end of the road, she was shaking so much that she had to pull in. She leaned her head against the steering wheel. How could things have changed just like that? Her job, her mother, her whole life. Nothing seemed solid any more. Everything was just cards flung in the air.

And then there were those words. 'My father built it and

I lived there from when I was twelve.' A whole past that Lottie knew nothing about, that Joanie had barely hinted at. How much more didn't she know?

Dan was making sandwiches when she walked into the cafe. 'Hi, love,' he said. 'Need a hand bringing it in?'

She'd forgotten about the supplies in the boot. 'In a minute. Dan, listen, something's happened.'

He looked up, concerned.

'Mum's selling the cafe.'

'What?'

When she'd finished telling him, he let out a long sigh. 'Christ, that's a bloody big spanner in the works, isn't it?'

'I don't know what to do. I don't want her to sell the cafe. What shall we do, Dan?'

'Well, Kenya's looking like an even better prospect now. What do you think, Lottie?'

She couldn't answer him.

When they got home, Joanie was standing on the doorstep. Lottie was tempted to walk straight past her and shut the door in her face, but Dan brought her inside and offered her a cup of tea.

'Actually, Dan, I'll have a gin if you've got it.'

Dan looked surprised, but managed a smile. 'Of course.'

They went into the living room, Joanie sinking into the armchair by the fireplace. She was clutching a large brown envelope.

'Do you want tonic with that?' Dan asked.

'Please, Dan.'

'We don't have any ice, sorry.'

Lottie watched her mother take a gulp of her drink, then put the glass down on the hearth. The room was cold and she thought she should probably light the gas fire, but she stayed where she was on the arm of the sofa, unwilling to make things any more comfortable. She waited for someone to say something.

Dan started first. 'Lottie mentioned your plans.' His words petered out into silence.

Joanie opened the envelope, and pulled out a wad of documents. Lottie saw that the advert from *The Caterer and Hotelkeeper* was stapled to the back.

'I know I haven't gone about this in the right way.'

Lottie refused to look at her.

'I'm sorry you found out like this,' Joanie said. 'I didn't mean it to be such a shock.'

'I think you selling the cafe would be a shock, Mum, no matter how you told us.' Lottie's anger rose again.

'It's just that it's been very hard to tell you because... because there are some things you don't know about.'

'What things?'

Joanie didn't reply. She pulled out the advert from the pile of papers and passed it to Dan. 'My father was called Larry Lambert. He built this pub, The Dolphin, in 1938 and we went to live there, my parents and my brother Roy and I, in 1939. I know you can't see from the photo, but it was a really wonderful place. Not like anything else I've ever seen.' She took another gulp of gin.

'Where is it?' Dan asked.

'It's in the middle of nowhere, north of here. It's a long way inland but somehow my father made it all about the sea.'

Dan peered at the photo. 'I can see it must have been a pretty unusual building.'

'It was his pride and joy. My parents weren't very happy

in their marriage – my mother was a very difficult woman – and I think it was an escape for my father. Though less so, I suppose, once we were all living there.'

'Well, fine, Mum, but you don't have to sell the cafe! Anyway, it's not just yours, it's ours, mine, Dad's.' It's where I learned about the sea, she wanted to say, it's where I waited for the mermaids. 'It's where you and Dad met.'

Joanie looked down at her lap.

'Lottie,' Dan said quietly. 'Just let your mum finish, eh?'

'My father died during the war,' Joanie continued. 'And then things got harder. My mother hated the place, wouldn't set foot in the bar, so as soon as I was old enough, I had to run it. It wasn't much fun, but nobody else cared about it. I was the only one who knew what it meant to my father.'

Lottie couldn't contain herself anymore. 'Then why did you leave? If it was so important, why didn't you stay there when your mum died?'

Joanie continued as if Lottie hadn't spoken. 'So if I don't do something to save it, it's gone forever. And I can't let that happen.'

Dan cleared his throat again. 'If you don't mind me asking, how far has this gone?'

'They accepted my offer this afternoon. I've instructed the estate agents here to put the cafe and the house up for sale.'

It was unbearable. Lottie stood up and went to the kitchen. They were behaving as if her mother was acting reasonably, as if the demolition of Lottie's livelihood didn't matter. And Dan was going along with it! She kicked the pantry door in frustration.

Intermittently, their voices reached her from the living room. 'Copper reliefs,' she heard Joanie say. 'And dolphins everywhere, of course.' Dan murmured something and her

201

mother laughed. 'Well, most pubs were, but we had the Ladies Lounge, you see. Terribly genteel.'

Lottie stood listening, arms folded, her face a stubborn pout, as if she was a child again, sulking at not getting her own way. Her mother hadn't answered any of her questions, had simply carried on, justifying what she'd done. Lottie couldn't let her get away with it.

When she went back into the living room, Joanie had spread a floor plan across the sofa and she and Dan were bent over it. 'The Circular Bar's here,' she was saying. 'Just off the main bar. Windows and window seats all the way round so you could see for miles in every direction. The surveyor's report says it's very dilapidated though.'

Dan picked up one of the documents. 'Let's see what it says about the Circular Bar.' He ran a finger down the page. 'Ah, here we are. *Much of the interior is damp as a result of damage to the roof and windows. It will require extensive work, particularly if the unusual architectural features are to be restored and/or preserved.* Sounds expensive.'

Lottie recognised the eagerness in his voice. It had been there when he decided to change the food at the cafe, when he told her about starting the bulb business, when he talked about Kenya. The new thing was always the most exciting. She watched him as he went over other sections of the report, cross-checking them with the floor plan and asking Joanie about the interior decoration. He was in his element.

She suddenly felt immensely sad. The cafe was sliding out of her hands, as surely as if the pier had collapsed and tipped everything into the sea. She pictured it, veiled in greenish water and sinking slowly out of sight, tables and chairs crowding against the windows, plastic sauce bottles bobbing like useless buoys.

'What else don't I know about?' she said loudly.

Joanie didn't look up. 'Look at this, Dan,' she said. 'It says the mezzanine – that's the Ladies Lounge – is in reasonable condition. The roof damage must have missed it.'

Dan looked uncomfortable now. 'I think Lottie needs a word, Mrs L.,' he said. 'I'll just go and check the greenhouse.'

'You said there were things I didn't know about,' Lottie repeated when Dan had gone.

'Yes.' Joanie was pushing her wedding ring up to the knuckle and back. 'Maybe I shouldn't have said that. It's all so long ago, it can't make much difference now.'

'You're selling everything I love. You should tell me if there's something I don't know.'

'Me and your dad decided that it was best you didn't know. Not yet.'

It was like a bell ringing. 'The dates don't add up,' Lottie blurted. 'Between you meeting Dad and me being born. I only realised when I saw your wedding photo.'

Joanie looked horrified. 'Oh God, so you know. You've worked it out.'

Lottie stared at her, almost afraid to say more. 'You have to tell me, Mum.'

Joanie nodded and kept on nodding. 'I know I do.' Still fussing with her ring, she paced the length of the sofa and back, mouthing something, but not speaking.

The glass on the hearth was full again. Lottie wondered if it was her second or third gin.

'He was called Patrick,' Joanie said eventually and Lottie felt a painful unravelling begin inside her. 'I thought I loved him.'

Lottie gazed at the floor, trying not to hear. The past, her past, her history, was suddenly as unreliable as the future.

'When I found out I was pregnant, I had to run away. My mother would have thrown me out otherwise.'

'But your mum was dead.'

'No.' Joanie's voice was low and clear. 'I came to this place to get away from her. She was a mean, spiteful woman. And then I met your dad, just the way we always told you.'

Lottie felt a sadness as heavy as wet wool draped across her shoulders. She picked up a photo of her parents from the mantelpiece. They were at a Christmas party, laughing, flushed, a bit tipsy. Bill's arm was round Joanie's shoulders and he looked the way he'd always looked, completely at ease with himself and the world. Lottie touched his face and wished fiercely that he was here and she could ask him what to do.

Joanie touched her arm. 'Your dad was one of the best. He knew I was having someone else's baby and he married me anyway. Loved me anyway. And as soon as you were born, he loved you too, Lottie. More than anything.'

'But it's Dad's name on my birth certificate. I've seen it.'

Joanie turned away. 'We lied,' she said, sounding tired now. 'We lied about it.'

Lottie woke up on the sofa, cold and disorientated. She pulled back a curtain. The street was dark and empty. There was a blanket on the floor which Dan must have brought. She wrapped it around herself while she went into the kitchen.

The clock showed a quarter to five. Only an hour or two before it got light and she had to get dressed. Only an hour or two before everything that had been said became real.

She ran water into the kettle, wishing the night could go on forever.

As she turned off the tap, she looked at her hand. The long fingers, the broad palms. Were Patrick's hands like this? Did her chin or her cheek bones come from him? She'd never looked like Bill but it hadn't mattered. No one expects girls to look like their fathers, and anyway, everyone said she took after her mother. She had Joanie's dark, spaniel hair, the same slight build. But how sad it was, how unbearably sad, that she had nothing of Bill's.

She switched on the kettle, took a cup from the cupboard and dropped in a teabag, surprised at her ability to do something so normal. But that was the strangest thing – everything was so normal and yet she felt as lost as an unmoored boat.

Upstairs, the bed creaked and she heard faint sounds of snoring. She thought of the warm blankets and the soft mattress, of fitting herself against Dan's sleeping body and closing her eyes.

But she wasn't going to do that. She might never do that again.

When Joanie had left the night before, Dan had come back into the living room. 'I thought you probably needed to talk to her by yourself, love. Thrash things out, let off some steam. You OK now?'

Lottie was curled up in a corner of the sofa. She wondered how she was going to tell him what she knew. She didn't reply.

'The thing is, Lottie,' Dan continued, 'I was thinking while I was in the greenhouse.' He began to walk around the room. 'See, I don't think your mum can do this by herself. I mean, the amount of work that place needs is massive and it'll be expensive too. The surveyor's report makes that very clear.'

He came over and sat beside Lottie. 'So I thought, why don't we go too?'

'What do you mean?'

'I mean we could sell this house and move to The Dolphin too. The bulb business can come with us, no problem. It'll be a bit of income until things get going properly. And I think the change would be really good for us, Lottie. I think it would make all the difference.'

She stared at him. 'But the cafe's my place, Dad's place. And this is our house.'

'Lottie, your mum's put the cafe up for sale,' Dan said gently. 'It's going. And you're the one who's been worrying about the future and where we're going to end up. This could be our future.'

'What about Kenya? I thought you were dead set on going there?'

'I know, but this could be brilliant. I've got all sorts of ideas already.'

She took a deep breath and then told him about Patrick.

'God,' he said and she thought he looked almost disappointed. 'I never expected that. Are you OK?'

She shrugged.

He jumped up and strode around the room again. 'But, you know, it makes even more sense now. If we go to The Dolphin, you'll be able to find out more.'

'I don't want to find out anything. I just want my dad to be my dad.'

'I know.' He was tactful enough to pause. 'But we haven't got many options, love, and if you think about it, going with your mum does make sense.'

She'd started shouting at him then, accusing him of

selfishness, of not listening to what she wanted. Eventually, he'd gone to bed and she'd stayed on the sofa.

She made tea, warming her hands on the cup and inhaling the steam. Through the window, the greenhouse glimmered in the streetlights and she thought about the pots of snowdrops lined up on the bench. In every one, a cluster of green stems was pushing up through the compost, thin and fragile, but doggedly alive.

Chapter 13

Larry
October 1939

The day before they moved, Larry went to The Dolphin to check that everything was ready. He and Malcolm had brought some furniture from the house and with the help of the barmen, they had pushed and pulled it up the circular stairs and into the rooms above.

Larry looked at it and hated the way the heavy wooden pieces blocked the light and filled the rooms with the drabness and tedium of life in the old house. He wanted new furniture, modern furniture that was bright and clean. No fussy details. No dark wood.

He wandered from room to room, frowning. It wasn't just the furniture. Until now, he'd been able to keep the real world away from The Dolphin, leaving his anxieties about the war at the bottom of the hill. It had begun to creep up though, in ways he couldn't ignore – the blackout curtains, the gas mask that bumped against his hip, the dwindling supply of barmen as they enlisted.

He sighed, wondering when the rest of it would catch up with him and what he would do when it was his time to go.

Malcolm emerged from his room as Larry came out of the kitchen. 'Got everything sorted then?'

'I think so,' Larry said. 'Rosemary's bound to want things

moved around so I may as well leave it as it is. No point doing it twice.'

He peered behind Malcolm and saw that his room looked neat and light. 'No more peace and quiet for you, I'm afraid. Roy and Joanie can be rather boisterous.'

Malcolm laughed. 'Oh, I don't think they'll trouble me.' He cleared his throat. 'And how is Mrs Lambert? Is she looking forward to moving in?'

Rosemary had been out when they had moved the furniture; the two had yet to meet. 'Oh, you know how attached women get to a house,' Larry said. 'And there's been all the extra work packing, of course.'

He said nothing about Rosemary's violent fury the previous night. They had been in the sitting room, the last room to be packed, boxing up the ornaments from the cabinet. When they were all neatly wrapped in newspaper and placed in the tea chest, she had looked around the room and started to cry. Larry bent further to his task of tapping the lid on with panel pins, pretending he didn't hear.

Suddenly she came at him with her fists, shouting, calling him names he didn't even know she knew. He tried to push her back, but she kept on at him. 'This is all your fault.' Her face was crimson, her breathing ragged. 'You don't even care what you've done to me.'

He grabbed hold of her arms. 'Stop it, Rosemary, stop now!'

She thrashed about, trying to free herself. 'I should never have married you. You're common. And you're a fool. A fool about money. A fool of a husband.'

'Calm yourself! You'll wake the children.'

She quietened then and Larry let go of her. In that instant, she drew back her hand and slapped him across the face. He fought the urge to slap her back. Then she leaned in close. He shut his eyes and smelled her sour breath, the faint lavender of her clothes. 'You aren't a real man,' she had hissed. 'I don't know what you are, but you aren't a real man.'

Back in the present with Malcolm at his side, Larry sighed. 'Well, there's a war on, isn't there?' he said. 'We all have to make sacrifices.'

The next day he packed up the Austin with everything that was left. It was so full that there was barely room for Roy and Joanie.

'I'll wait here,' Joanie said, as they stood on the pavement outside the old house. 'You can come back for me later.'

Larry rearranged things in the van yet again. 'I'm sure we can squeeze you in if I can just shove this case over here.'

'I don't mind, Dad. I'll be fine on my own for half an hour or so.'

Larry glanced at her, twirling round a lamppost on her tiptoes. She could get up to anything in half an hour. He gave the case a final push. 'There, it's shifted. You can fit in now.'

She looked disappointed as she climbed in. Roy was already there, wedged into a corner and holding his school satchel on his knee.

'All right in there, son?' Larry asked. Roy nodded without enthusiasm and Larry sighed as he closed the back doors and got in. This wasn't going to be easy.

Rosemary sat very upright in the passenger seat, wearing her best grey suit and the pearl necklace her mother had left her. She hadn't spoken to him since their row two days before and she didn't acknowledge him now as he started the engine.

'Well, I think that's it,' he said. 'I think we're ready to go.'

They were all quiet as they drove away from the house. Larry had wondered how he would feel when it came to actually leaving; it was the only place he had ever lived and all his memories of childhood and his parents were contained in it. And yet, when he hit the road out of town, he felt that a tether had snapped. The house, the town, the past all fell away as the van climbed the hill, lifting him – despite Rosemary, despite the war – into the sun.

At The Dolphin, Malcolm was there to welcome them. He opened the door for Rosemary and offered his hand. 'Mrs Lambert. Very pleased to meet you at last. I'm Malcolm Gardiner.'

Larry knew he had made an effort. The creases in his trousers were sharp as knives and his shirt was dazzling white. Rosemary looked up at him. What would she make of him, Larry wondered.

'Mr Gardiner,' she said, ignoring his hand and heaving herself out of the van. Malcolm grimaced and glanced over at Larry. Larry grimaced back. He went to help Roy and Joanie out, keeping an eye on Rosemary as he unloaded the bags. She stood for a moment, fussing with her gloves and holding her head so high that he could see the tendons stretch in her neck. Then she walked up the steps and into The Dolphin. Larry followed her, carrying two suitcases, bracing himself for her reaction.

There was none. She took a few steps into the lounge bar and then turned to him. 'Which way is it?'

She was standing stiff and grey on the turquoise carpet. Dolphins and seaweed twisted on the walls behind her head and the bar curved around her like a wave. But she didn't see it, he thought. Her face was closed, blank.

'This way,' he said.

He let her go up the stairs in front of him, Roy and Joanie behind. They were both subdued, even Joanie, and they didn't respond when Malcolm, bringing up the rear with more cases, tried to make them laugh. Larry sighed again; Rosemary made it so hard for them. In silence, they filed past the Ladies Lounge and up again to the living quarters on the top floor.

On the landing, Rosemary paused and Larry put down the cases. 'Our room's at the end there,' he said. 'And here's the kitchen. Look, the cupboards are all fitted.' He opened the door to show her, but Rosemary had already pushed past. Her footsteps rang loudly on the floorboards as she walked to the end of the corridor, went into their bedroom and closed the door.

He turned to the children wearing the brightest smile he could muster. 'Mummy's very tired after all that packing. Shall we let her have a rest while we sort out your bedrooms?'

Joanie rolled her eyes. Roy nodded. They took his things in first. His room was small, overlooking the terrace and the lawn beyond. He went in and sat on the bed, his face anxious.

'You're next door to me, Roy,' Malcolm told him. 'So no rowdy behaviour and keeping me up at night, eh? I need my beauty sleep.'

Roy managed a small smile.

Joanie's room was bigger, with a view down the hillside and across the flat land below. She crossed to the window and leaned on the sill while Larry brought in her cases.

'How long do we have to stay here?' she asked.

'What do you mean, love? We're not going anywhere else, this is where we live now.'

'But when things change…when the war's over…we'll move back into a house again, won't we?'

Larry stood beside her and looked out over the October landscape. The colour had leached into a pale mist and, apart from a stand of yellow birch trees, there was only brown and grey. 'I thought you liked The Dolphin.'

'I do, but not to live here all the time. What about my friends? How am I going to see them when I'm stuck out here? There's nowhere to go.'

'Well,' Larry began, but couldn't come up with any satisfactory answers. 'Things are different for everyone now that there's a war on.'

She fiddled with the window catch and spoke in a low voice. 'But we didn't come here because of the war.'

Larry took out his cigarettes and lit one, taking his time about it. He'd been vague with the children, hoping that they wouldn't question him too closely when he said he was giving up building work. Rosemary had refused to discuss it with the children. 'So now that I don't have to go to mucky old building sites anymore,' he had said. 'I can spend more time at The Dolphin. We thought it might be a good idea for us to go and live there.' He had prayed that Rosemary wasn't listening.

Joanie had been excited at first, asking him which room she could have and whether she could help at the bar sometimes. But she'd spoken of it less and less and now she was here, she seemed as miserable as Roy.

Larry was suddenly angry. They were here now and there was no choice in the matter. But none of them seemed willing to make the best of it. He remembered standing on the hill top that first time with Rosemary and the children, when Rosemary talked about him building houses there. Well, The Dolphin had put an end to that but now, even without the houses, all the petty clutter of his life had followed him here. His earlier optimism evaporated. How could The Dolphin withstand boiled potatoes, liver salts and carbolic soap? Bickering, sulking and seething silences? How could he hold on to that vision of a boat cresting a green wave, pure and beautiful, when Rosemary lived here?

He opened the window and flicked out the finished cigarette. Joanie had started to unpack, arranging the contents of her sponge bag on the dressing table. Comb, mirror, toothbrush, white tin of talcum powder.

'Look, Joanie,' he said. 'Like it or not, we're here. We're lucky we had The Dolphin to come to and we weren't out on the streets. Think of all those evacuees who've had to leave their homes and have nowhere to go. There's nothing any of us can do about it.'

She didn't answer.

He went in to see Roy. The boy was still sitting on the bed, his hands between his knees, his legs looking thin and cold beneath his shorts. 'Not unpacked yet, Roy?'

Roy said nothing. Larry sat down next to him, patting his knee. 'I know it's all a bit peculiar at the moment, but you'll get used to it.'

Roy flung himself back on the bed. 'I hate it here!' he shouted. 'I don't want to live in a pub. I want to go home!' He thumped his fist against the wall.

'All right now, enough of that!' Larry felt his anger rising again. Roy was thrashing about, kicking his legs and knocking Larry's arm.

Larry caught hold of him and held him down. 'Enough! Don't be such a baby.'

Roy pulled free and turned away, his shoulders heaving as he moved to the other end of the bed.

Larry stood. It took an effort not to pick up Roy's satchel and throw it at the wall. In the corridor, he took a few steps towards the room at the end, then turned back. He couldn't deal with Rosemary yet.

Malcolm was setting up the Ladies Lounge as he came down the stairs. A lemony autumn sun broke through the mist and lit up the chrome on the bar. The room shimmered with spots of light. Malcolm was lit up too, his black hair glossy as a sea bird as he stood behind the bar, polishing a glass. Larry sat down on one of the armchairs and rubbed his eyes.

'Kicking up a stink, are they?' Malcolm poured him a glass of soda water. 'I heard Roy shouting. He'll get over it in a week or two.'

'I don't know, I just don't know. Joanie's furious with me, Roy's furious with me, Rosemary's shut herself in our room. Hasn't said a word.' But then Rosemary had been furious with him for years. His hand trembled as he picked up the glass.

Malcolm sat down opposite him. 'Can I do anything? Perhaps I could have a chat with them. The children anyway.' He smiled. 'I don't think wives are really my department.'

Larry smiled too, but there was still a rage inside him. Their arrival at The Dolphin could have been – should have been – different. Rosemary should have understood that it was much more than a pub. The children should have been grateful. Larry should have been allowed some satisfaction in having done the right thing. He stood up, needing to be active. 'I'll just go and check the cellar. Thanks for the offer, Malcolm, but there's no need. They'll settle down, like you say.'

Down in the cellar, he welcomed the physical effort of changing the beer barrels and rolling the empties out into the yard. When he'd brought out the last one, he sat on top of it and lit a cigarette. The yard was a dank, gloomy spot, the only part of The Dolphin he didn't like, but it suited him today. He sat while his anger subsided and watched a spider knit a web across a mossy corner. When the web was done, the spider crept into the centre and stayed there, waiting. Larry didn't miss the similarity with Rosemary in the room upstairs. What was she doing? What was she thinking? What was she waiting for?

When it was too cold to stay outside, he went back through the cellar and slowly climbed the stairs. There were sounds of talking from the kitchen and when he looked in, he saw Roy and Joanie sitting at the table eating sandwiches. Malcolm was pouring glasses of orange squash and telling them a joke about an elephant. He slipped past without any of them noticing him. At the end of the corridor, he paused, feeling as if he should knock, then opened the door. Rosemary was standing with her back to the window, arms folded, her face in shadow. Waiting for me, Larry thought.

'What are the children doing?' she asked.

'Just having some lunch. Are you hungry?'

She shook her head.

'Cup of tea?'

'No.'

He didn't know what else to say so he sat on the bed and was quiet. Rosemary turned her back and looked out of the window.

'You can see for miles,' Larry said. 'I say it's the finest view in the county.'

'Don't expect me to ever appear in the pub,' Rosemary

said, her words clearly rehearsed. 'I will not be setting foot downstairs and neither will the children.'

'But you'll have to go through the place, Rosemary, just to get in and out.'

'You mean that staircase is the only one?'

'Yes. It goes past the Ladies Lounge though and the Circular Bar. It's not like you'll have to go through anywhere rough.'

'The Ladies Lounge! As if any real lady would think of entering it.' She sniffed. 'And I will not have any of the staff coming up here.'

'Malcolm lives here too remember.'

She turned to face him. 'This must make you so happy.'

'It doesn't, Rosemary, not at all.'

'You've got exactly what you wanted, haven't you?' Her mouth was set in a sneer. 'Right about The Dolphin all along.'

Larry leaned against the bedpost and stared at the floor, trying not to hear. The rose-patterned rug from their old bedroom was much too small for this room and a wide expanse of bare floorboards surrounded it. A draught was blowing up through the gaps. Must seal those, Larry thought, and varnish the wood. That would look smart. He kept his eyes on the floor. She would stop soon and then he could go back downstairs and get on. Malcolm would need a hand after helping with the children. But the bitter voice continued.

'Well, that's it, Larry. You've thrown away every ounce of respectability this family had. If it wasn't for the war, I'd throw you out too. Anyway, I don't want you here, not in this room.'

Larry looked up.

'You can go and share with Roy.'

He stared at her, not sure if he had heard her right. 'Roy's room is too small.'

'Share with Malcolm then. Or you can sleep in the bar for all I care.'

'Well, I don't know about that.' He stood up.

She was unpacking and hanging up clothes in the wardrobe. Sparks of hate flew off her with every movement.

'I'd better go and help Malcolm then. Roy and Joanie might need something.'

'I know what my children need, thank you.'

He went to the door. 'Right then.'

His head churned with possibilities and impossibilities for the rest of the afternoon. The lightness and freedom he had felt as they left the old house had become something uncomfortable, a sense of loss. While he was serving in the Ladies Lounge, he could hear footsteps above and Roy shouting. Everything was different now.

When they closed after lunch, he went upstairs. Rosemary and the children were in the kitchen, unpacking tea chests of china and cutlery. Discarded newspapers lay all over the floor.

'Everybody all right?' he asked, sounding too jaunty even to himself.

At the sink, washing a stack of plates, Joanie gave him a resentful look. 'Mum says we can't go down to the bar.'

He looked across at Rosemary. 'Oh, well, not when it's open of course, but maybe between shifts. What do you think, Rosemary?'

She didn't look up from unwrapping the kitchen knives. 'They will not be going into the bar.'

'Oh, Mum,' Joanie whined, 'if we're going to live here,

you could at least let us downstairs. We can't be stuck up here all the time.'

'Like prisoners!' Roy exclaimed. 'And if the Germans bomb us and we die up here, you'll be sorry.'

'Roy! Don't talk to your mother like that.'

'See?' Rosemary said, crumpling newspaper into a ball. 'They're already being influenced by the place.'

'That's a bit strong, Rosemary. We've only just arrived.'

She shrugged her shoulders. 'They're beyond my control now. It's your place. You make the rules.'

The children had paused in their tasks and were looking at him with hopeful faces. Larry felt another flash of anger. She was making him responsible for everything. Whatever happened would be his fault. Well, he would do what he wanted then.

'I say you can come down when the pub's closed, but only with me or Malcolm, mind.'

Rosemary's face was white with fury but she said nothing.

Amongst the noise and bustle of Saturday evening, as he served drinks and chatted to customers, Rosemary's words played over and over again. 'Share with Malcolm then.' It was a simple solution. There were other possibilities of course, but each had drawbacks. Roy's room was far too small to lie full length on the floor. Joanie's would have been fine, but it wasn't right to share with her, not now that she was growing up. It seemed that sharing with Malcolm was the best solution by far.

By the end of the night, he had worked out the details so carefully that he felt it was all arranged. There was plenty of space for a camp bed and the wardrobe was big enough for their clothes.

'See you in the morning,' Malcolm said and went upstairs on his own.

'Good night,' Larry called back. It was too late to say anything now. He turned off the lights and went into the Circular Bar.

Pulling aside the blackout curtains, he stared into the darkness. He hated the blackout, the way the night pushed right up to the windows, the way it smothered any sense of life outside. He would almost have welcomed the sight of German planes flying over. At least there would be a purpose to the blackout then.

He sat in one of the armchairs. There was nowhere else to go. He took off his jacket and shoes and pulled up another chair for his feet, shuffling to find a comfortable position, but he was cold and his back hurt, so he fetched cushions and a tablecloth to cover himself. It wasn't very satisfactory, but it was something.

He woke into blackness. It was too dark to see his watch, but he felt he hadn't been asleep for long. His breath was scratchy in the silence. He wondered if everyone else was asleep upstairs.

He tucked the tablecloth more tightly to ward off a cold draft that was blowing across his legs. His joints were aching and he longed for a comfortable bed, but he felt a small buzz of excitement. He was free of Rosemary's resentful back on the other side of the mattress, free of her bony feet bumping his in the night. And he was free at last of her silent face beneath him when his need for someone had been too strong to ignore.

He shifted position again but trying to get comfortable was hopeless. He switched on a wall lamp. The shadows behind him were huge in the circle of light and when he struck a match they shuddered. He lay there, enjoying the luxury of a smoke in the middle of the night, and thinking about the countless hours he'd spent lying next to Rosemary and wishing he was anywhere else. Well, he was somewhere else now and he was glad, very glad, to be by himself.

What was it like for her, alone on the other side of the mattress, he wondered. And then he asked himself, for the first time, what her body had wanted while it accommodated his, while he gripped her hips and pretended she wasn't Rosemary. Did she have any desires? Any feelings? He had no idea.

All those years ago, when he had turned up to build the sun porch, she hadn't fallen in love with him. After their first outing, there was never any pretence of romance. She had wanted a husband. Her mother had wanted her to have a husband. And he was there, chosen for opportunity and convenience. He watched the smoke tangle and curl in the air, trying to remember why he had let it happen. Rosemary had seemed more sympathetic then, bent under the iron rule of her mother and it would have been cruel to refuse her. And anyway, marriage was what people did, for all kinds of reasons. Was there any other choice? I did what was expected of me, he thought, did what everyone else does and now look where we are. The smoke disappeared into the shadows. He stubbed out his cigarette and switched off the light, feeling cold again and empty.

After a week of sleeping in the bar, Larry was exhausted and his body ached. He had to do something. Sharing with Malcolm had seemed logical, inevitable even, but now he found it impossible to say anything to him. During his long, uncomfortable nights in the armchair, he had imagined the conversations, the camaraderie, the closeness, and now it was unbearable to think it might not happen.

There was a send-off and a sing-song on Friday night for Ted, the latest barman to enlist. Larry supervised the jollity from behind the bar, supplying beer, and watched as the young man's expression changed from defiant triumph to bleak melancholy. When he slumped, pale-faced, to the floor, Larry dragged him to the van and took him home.

They had to stop on the way for him to be sick. Larry helped him onto the verge and held him while he vomited.

'Sorry, Mr Lambert, very, very sorry,' Ted slurred as he stumbled back to the van. 'You're a kind man, so kind.'

'Don't worry about it, son. We've all had nights like this. God knows you deserve one tonight.' He settled him back in the front seat and opened the window. 'There, bit of fresh air for you.'

They set off again, Larry straining to see the road in the dimmed beams of the headlights. Ted's breathing slowed to a light snoring. 'You sleep on, lad,' he said. 'Get all the sleep you can.'

When they reached the outskirts of the town, he shook Ted awake. 'Which way is it? Which road?'

Ted mumbled his address and Larry drove slowly through the darkened streets. Bad as the blackout was at The Dolphin, it was worse here in town. The pubs and dance halls that had shone out so gaily were almost invisible. There were very few people out on the streets, just one or two gloomy shapes making their way by torchlight. At Ted's house, Larry helped him out and half-dragged him up the garden path. He propped him against the wall and as he rang the doorbell, he realised Ted was crying. Out of breath with the effort of getting him there, Larry leaned against the wall beside him and waited.

'Come on now, you don't want your mum seeing you like this.'

Ted's voice came suddenly, high-pitched like a child's. 'I'm scared, Mr Lambert, I'm so fucking scared.'

Larry closed his eyes. He rested a hand on Ted's shoulder. There was a noise from inside and the door creaked open. An anxious-looking woman exclaimed in horror and pulled Ted inside, closing the door behind her.

Larry took his time going back to the van as waves of tiredness washed over him. For a while he sat there, watching the moon dip behind a bank of clouds and then reappear. It was the only bright thing in the night.

At The Dolphin, all the lights were off and the rooms were cold. He poured himself a whisky and went into the Circular Bar. More than anything he wanted to lie down in a proper bed, with smooth sheets and a feather pillow. His limbs ached just thinking about it. He sipped at the whisky, but it wasn't what he needed. There were sounds from the upper rooms, then footsteps, and then the door at the top of the stairs opening. The stair lights went on and there was Malcolm, peering at him over the rail.

'Is that you, Larry? I heard someone come in. God, you look awful. Was Ted in a bad way?' He came down and sat across the table, his dressing gown gaping open over his bare chest.

Larry stared hard at his whisky and nodded. 'Poor bugger, scared to death. I couldn't give him any comfort, couldn't think what to say.'

Malcolm put his hand on Larry's arm. 'There isn't much you could say, not truthfully. You got him home anyway.'

He paused. 'Listen, Larry, tell me to mind my own business, but I can't help noticing that things aren't very happy between you and Mrs Lambert.'

'Yes, well, you're right of course.' Malcolm's hand was still on his arm. He could feel its warmth through his sleeve. 'It's all quite difficult.'

'Of course.'

They were silent. Larry began to shiver. Malcolm looked cold too, holding his dressing gown up to his throat with one hand. Larry watched him fidget with the cord.

Malcolm put his cigarettes down and cleared his throat. 'Look,' he said. 'If you need somewhere to sleep, there's always my room.'

'Oh, you don't have to do that.' Larry flushed. There was colour in Malcolm's cheeks too. Larry felt his heart jump. 'But if you're sure it's all right.' He began to laugh. 'Another week on this chair could cripple me.'

Malcolm laughed too. 'Well, that's that then. We need all the able-bodied staff we can get.'

'There's a camp bed upstairs somewhere. I'll go and get it out.' Larry jumped up, his heart thumping, his legs trembling like a new-born lamb's.

April 1941

Larry wheeled his bicycle out of the shed and propped it against the wall while he snapped bicycle clips around his trouser legs. Malcolm's letter crackled in his breast pocket as he bent down. It was a mild afternoon with a bright patch in the clouds where the sun had almost burned through. He knew he would be sweating and uncomfortable by the time he reached the town. He undid the top button of his tunic and ran a finger round the inside of the collar.

The air felt new and lithe, as if spring was finally established, and as he pedalled slowly through the gate and onto the road, he felt relief. Whatever else happened, it wouldn't be cold anymore.

The road down to the ford was always an exhilarating ride and he freewheeled recklessly. The landscape streaked past in pennants of green. At the bottom, he rolled through the shallow water with a pleasing hiss and began the uphill climb. This was where he missed the van the most, but petrol was so scarce these days that he only used it when it was really necessary. Home Guard drill didn't warrant the expense. He'd brought Malcolm's letter to read when he reached the top of the hill. That would be his reward.

The steepest stretch was in the middle and once over that, it was a manageable ride to the top. Still, he was out of breath and hot by the time he came out of the lane and onto the main road. He flung the bicycle onto the verge and sat down next to it. Bees nosed in the hawthorn hedge behind him and a wood pigeon cooed from a nearby oak as he took the letter out of his pocket and smoothed it flat on his knee. Rosemary had interrupted him when he'd tried to read it earlier, banging around the kitchen and turning the volume up on the wireless. He'd been conscious of it in his pocket ever since.

Dear Larry, Hope all is well at the Dolphin and you're managing to keep it afloat without me (ha ha).

It was a short letter, only a side and a half of notepaper. There wasn't much news, just a few anecdotes about the lads and boozing at the local pub. *Not a patch on The Dolphin*, Malcolm wrote, *and they'd knock your teeth out if you suggested a Ladies Lounge.*

Anyone could have written the words. They were matey, jokey, a message from a former employee. But Malcolm's handwriting – small, thick, black – conveyed an intense intimacy. His hand had formed each letter, had made the pen's indent on the paper. His tongue had licked the seal on the envelope and moistened the stamp. Larry stroked the paper gently with his thumb.

The last line had smudged a little and was difficult to read. *We're off tomorrow – will write again when I get back.* There was a small ink blot then it was signed, *Yours ever, Malcolm.*

We're off tomorrow. Malcolm had been on a submarine for six months. Larry pictured it slipping into the water, burrowing deep to where it was dark and cold. Surely he would be safe there, tucked into a fold of the ocean, like dust in a pocket. A submarine was a speck, no more than a fish scale in all that water. *We're off tomorrow.* He looked up from the letter. A kestrel was hovering in the air above the road, swooping lower, then hovering again. But Malcolm's submarine wasn't hiding, of course. It was a hunter, and would be hunted in turn.

He stood up, startling the kestrel into flight. The bicycle had been lying on a clump of daisies and buttercups, and when he lifted it, the scent of their crushed stalks filled the air. He brushed grass from his uniform and set off towards the town, thinking that Malcolm would have had no fresh air for days and none for many days to come. How could he bear it, he wondered.

After drill, Larry was on fire-watching duty until midnight. From the walkway round the cupola on top of the town hall, he scanned the sky for planes, waiting for something to happen. So far, there had been nothing. The radio and

226

newspapers were full of the Blitz, but for Larry, it was happening in a different country. The war had only made his life, and the life of everyone he knew, more difficult and more tedious, without any compensatory drama or excitement. Or pain, he thought, or loss. He was grateful for that.

He shared his shift with Arthur, a retired teacher, each patrolling one side of the dome. Larry faced north. As dusk gathered, he reread Malcolm's letter in the last of the light and shared a flask of tea with Arthur. The sky deepened and turned black. Through gaps in the clouds, he watched the North Star shine.

By eleven, it was hard to stay awake. Arthur was humming under his breath, soothing as a lullaby. Larry shifted on his camping stool, leaned his head on his hand, and his eyelids closed.

Suddenly Arthur was shouting, 'Larry, listen!'

Larry jumped up. He could hear a faint hum. 'What is it?'

'Planes, you stupid bugger, planes!'

They gazed at the sky, with binoculars and then without, but there was nothing to see in any direction. The hum turned to a low rumble.

Larry crouched by the parapet, feeling exposed and vulnerable. There was a squawk and the air raid siren started up. 'Where are they?' he shouted.

'There, look!' Arthur shouted back. There was a black shape in the sky, almost not there but growing more solid as they watched. Then came a dozen more, crawling across the clouds, heading north.

'Bloody hell,' Larry whispered.

It took an age for them to pass. He kept waiting for them to break formation and dive towards him, or for bombs to rain down, but nothing happened. The rumble faded, night folded over them and they were gone.

'My God, I felt as if I could reach up and touch them,' Arthur said.

Larry took out his cigarettes, offered one to Arthur, and they stood and smoked. His heart was still racing and Arthur's hand trembled as he held his cigarette. Then the all-clear sounded and people poured back into the street below. Larry's heart raced with a jittery euphoria, whether because the bombers had gone or because they had been there in the first place, he did not know.

Roy and Joanie listened open-mouthed as he told them about it at breakfast. Even Rosemary, who hadn't spoken to him that morning, stopped washing up and listened.

'Did they drop any bombs?' Roy asked.

'Not here. I think they must have been heading for Sheffield or Manchester. I feel sorry for the poor blighters who got it.'

'Was it scary, Dad? Were you frightened?' Joanie asked. She was clutching her glass of milk tightly and looked ready to cry.

'There was nothing to be scared of, love,' he said. 'They weren't coming for us.' It wasn't the full story, but there was no more to be said.

'But will they come back?' she asked. 'Will they come for us another time?'

He sipped his tea, wondering if he should tell her that he simply didn't know. 'There's no reason for them to bomb us, Joanie. There's nothing here for them, no airfield, no shipyard, no steel works. If they bomb us, it'll be by accident.'

Rosemary began to clear the table. 'Enough now, time to get ready for school.'

Roy ran from the kitchen, flinging out his arms and making ak-ak noises. Joanie went to follow him but loitered in the doorway. 'But what if they do make a mistake?' she asked. 'What if they think we're important?'

'Like I said, there isn't anything here to attack. They'd be able to see that. And we'd hear the warning first anyway.'

Rosemary interrupted sharply. 'Just get yourself ready for school and stop going on about it.' Then she turned to Larry. 'As if you know what you're talking about. As if you know anything.'

'She was scared. I was just trying to reassure her.'

'As if you know anything,' Rosemary repeated.

Despite what he said, throughout the day he found himself listening out for noises. The sound of a car climbing the hill. The whine of the hot water running through the pipes. He had to stop what he was doing and make sure it wasn't more planes.

That night, in the bar, everyone was talking about it, speculating on the narrowness of their near miss, and whether they would be a target another time. The mood was nervous and giddy.

By closing time, he was tired of feeling anxious and tired of all the chatter. For once, he had no appetite for whisky. Tea would be just the job, he thought, and then a long, restful sleep. He climbed the stairs wearily, noticing a bar of light under Rosemary's door. It was unusual for that time of night, but he thought nothing of it and went into the kitchen.

When she came in, he was standing by the cooker, waiting for the kettle to boil and wondering what Malcolm was doing at that exact moment. He hoped he was sleeping. The sound of a chair scraping on the floor startled him and he turned to see Rosemary sitting at the table.

'Well then,' she said, 'what about a cup of tea?'

She was wearing the pink and blue paisley dressing gown she'd had for years, faded now almost to white. Her hair was pulled back in a plait and her face was shiny with cold cream. In the bright light of the kitchen, she looked faded too and as if she belonged in the old house, down in the town.

'All right,' Larry said, getting another cup from the cupboard and spooning more tea leaves into the pot. He wondered what she wanted.

The kettle boiled and he busied himself with pouring and stirring, taking his time. Milk spilled over the counter and he rinsed out a cloth and wiped it up.

'Quite the little housewife, aren't you?' Rosemary said.

Larry carried her cup over to the table. 'Just keeping things ship-shape.'

She sipped at the tea, nodding. 'Yes, very domestic.'

Larry stood by the sink. She sat facing him, with her back to the door

'You're up late tonight,' he said. 'I wouldn't be surprised if the children can't sleep either. Those planes have unsettled everyone. They couldn't talk about anything else in the bar.'

She didn't reply and he carried on talking. 'I hope Roy doesn't start with his nightmares again. Though he seems more excited than anything else.'

She said nothing, just tapped her fingers on her cup.

Larry couldn't think of anything else to say. He was too tired to face whatever grievance Rosemary had tonight. 'Well, I think I'll turn in,' he said.

'I see you had a letter from Mr Gardiner then.'

'Sorry?'

'You had a letter from Malcolm, didn't you?'

230

He looked at her. She stared back at him.

'Yes, I did. He's fine.'

'He's such a good friend, isn't he?' Her voice was thick with sarcasm.

'Of course he's a friend.'

'Such a very close friend.'

He wiped a cloth round and round his cup and stared at the water whirling round the plug hole. He felt heavy and couldn't move.

Rosemary's voice grew louder. 'I saw you with his letter. You were all over it like a lovesick girl.'

He switched off the tap and turned to face her. She was standing, fists bunched tight on the tabletop. 'And the two of you, together in his room all those months. It makes me sick to think of it.'

Larry saw the words form in her mouth. Gnarled and ugly, they fell from her lips and dropped onto the table like squat toads. Soon there was a heap of them, wheezing, crawling, oozing poison. He looked at Rosemary and she was ugly too.

'Well, your fun's over now, isn't it?' she said. 'It's a short life on a submarine, I've heard, and a nasty way to go.'

'Don't say those things.'

She made a face of mock concern. 'Ah, poor dear. Are you worried about your darling Malcolm?'

'Stop it, Rosemary. You're making a fool of yourself.'

She laughed a forced, hard laugh. 'I don't think I need to worry about making a fool of myself. Not me.'

With a huge effort, Larry pushed himself away from the sink. He walked past her and out of the kitchen, crossing the landing to Malcolm's room. Rosemary's voice followed him

'This kind of news spreads fast, you know. I expect the Home Guard will want to know about it. Nobody wants to do drill with a pervert, do they? And there's the police too, of course.' The same hard laugh. 'Then you're in trouble, Larry Lambert. Then you're in trouble.'

Closing the door behind him, he went over to the bed. He'd been sleeping there since Malcolm was called up, settling himself each night into the faint indentation that Malcolm's body had made in the mattress. He straightened the eiderdown and went to sit on the camp bed.

How many hours had he spent lying there in the dark, unable to sleep, every nerve cell alive to Malcolm's body a few feet away? How many days had begun with him awake, waiting for dawn, watching as the light slowly picked out Malcolm's face, his arm flung across the pillow, sometimes a leg thrust out from beneath the covers?

And now here were Rosemary's squalid accusations that were wrong and cheap and filthy. And all the more powerful because he wanted them to be true. Even as he thought this, he felt himself grow hard, almost painfully so. With a sob, he flung himself on the bed, rubbing and pulling until he was done, then falling into a dead sleep.

He kept busy the next day, swallowing down nausea whenever he remembered Rosemary's words. He buffed the copper reliefs in the main bar until they shone like red gold. When he had finished there, he went out to the terrace to tidy up the edging plants. The air was soft and warm, full of gauzy spring sunshine, and he took off his jacket, lit a cigarette and stood facing the breeze blowing from the south. He closed his eyes, the better to feel it. If only everything was different, he thought.

A door banged and there was Rosemary leaving the building and striding towards the road. She was wearing her smartest hat and carrying a shopping basket, her walk purposeful and determined. Larry felt his stomach lurch and he vomited into the shrubbery by the steps. When he had finished, he wiped his mouth with his sleeve and sat down on the bottom step.

She could just be going shopping, he told himself. Or maybe to the cinema; she often did that on weekday afternoons. He looked at his watch – it was half past eleven. His stomach clenched again, but there was nothing left to bring up. 'Oh God,' he said aloud.

She hadn't returned by the time he closed up after lunch and Roy and Joanie were back from school.

'Where's Mum?' Joanie asked.

'She had to go into town for some shopping,' Larry said. 'The queues must be extra long today.' He was wiping the same beer pump over and over and Joanie was watching him. 'Come on, drink up. I've got a lot to do this afternoon and there's drill tonight.' He paused. How could he possibly go to drill? 'Upstairs, the two of you. Time for homework.'

'I haven't got any homework. Can't I stay in the bar?' Roy asked.

'No, you can't stay here, Roy. Read a book if you've nothing else to do.'

Roy made a face. 'Books are boring.'

'Just go upstairs and find something to do.'

'But there's nothing to do.'

Larry slapped his cheek. Roy's eyes widened and he lifted his hand to touch the sore spot. An angry weal bloomed beneath his fingers.

'Upstairs now, please,' Larry said, turning away.

'Come on, Roy,' Joanie said.

Larry heard them go up and close the door at the top. He tried to change the gin bottle on the optic but his hands shook so much he gave up.

Rosemary came back just before five o'clock. Larry was in Malcolm's room when he heard footsteps on the stairs, then her voice in the kitchen. He leaned against the door, straining to hear, but the words were too muffled. Then Roy and Joanie started up, high-pitched and agitated, and he knew they were telling her what he'd done.

If he was going to go to drill, it was time to leave. His uniform lay on the chair and he put it on slowly, fumbling with the buttons, his fingers thick and useless. When he was ready, he looked at himself in the mirror. The collar was crooked, but he made no move to straighten it. He couldn't go. A cannonball thundered into his stomach when he thought of facing the others in the church hall, not knowing what they knew. The police could be waiting to arrest him. But he couldn't stay either, not with Rosemary there. He stared at himself in the mirror, seeing someone much older than he had expected. Older and weaker, too weak to bear this.

He slipped out of the room. The kitchen door was slightly ajar and the side of Joanie's head was just visible. He hurried past and went down the stairs.

For an hour he cycled around narrow lanes and roadways, stopping often to sit on a gate or stile and stare across the landscape. The sky was as clear and richly blue as he had ever seen it. When it was too late to go to drill, he headed into town for fire watching duty, keeping to the side streets and looking out for policemen.

Arthur was already there, fussing with his cushions and flask of tea. Larry felt safer now he was high up above the town and away from everyone. Rosemary didn't know Arthur and couldn't have told him anything. He accepted a cup of tea and settled onto his camp stool.

Arthur chatted inconsequentially as dusk fell. Larry half-listened, only paying attention when Arthur began talking about the call-up.

'So it'll be June then for you, Larry.'

'What?'

'It goes by age, doesn't it? So forty-year-olds will be June, won't they?'

It was a moment before Larry could answer. 'Yes, I suppose so.'

He leaned back and looked up at the sky, thick with stars and smudges of light. He wished himself lifted up there, absorbed forever into its pattern.

'Sorry, Larry, thought you would have realised. I'm just glad I'm out of it.'

For once, Larry had no trouble keeping awake. He paced the walkway, smoking, thinking of plan after plan that could somehow change his fate. By eleven o'clock his cigarette pack was empty and he'd run out of ideas. There were just the two alternatives – a humiliating trial or, if Rosemary hadn't actually done anything by then, the call-up. He flicked away his last cigarette stub, watching the dot of red vanish into the dark. Arthur's voice came suddenly from the south side of the cupola.

'Oh Christ, Larry, they're back again.'

It was the same hum as before and Larry grabbed his binoculars, straining to see the planes. The hum grew louder and there they were, so low this time that Larry thought he could see moonlight reflected off their wings. The air raid siren started up and there were running footsteps and panicked voices in the street below. Out of the corner of his eye, somewhere to the right, he registered a flash of light. Seconds later, there was another and this time he heard it too. Then they were everywhere, until the dark was studded with fire and the air was burnt and smoky. A crash came, close by, and bright orange blossomed in the top window of the office building opposite.

Arthur appeared beside him. 'I'll telephone the Fire Brigade, though God knows who they'll be able to send,' he shouted.

'They won't have anyone spare. Look, you phone and I'll go across and see if I can do anything before it gets out of hand.'

Together they ran down the stairs. Larry left Arthur to use the telephone in one of the offices and hurried to fetch the stirrup pump and water bucket. He carried them down the wide front steps and across the road, cursing the weight of the bucket and the hose that kept unwinding as he ran. A few others had gathered outside the building and someone was breaking down the front door with an axe. The wood cracked and gave and Larry helped to push a way through into the lobby.

Inside was complete darkness and he bumped awkwardly into what must have been the reception desk and chair. Someone produced a torch and the room filled with a gloomy light that was almost as dense as the dark. The stairs loomed in the torch's beam and Larry started up them, following two others who had gone ahead.

He climbed through layers of smoke, each thicker than the last. The air was unbearably heavy and hot. There were only three storeys, but in the dark, it seemed hours before he reached the top floor. As he came onto the landing, one of the men in front of him was shouting, 'It's a bloody furnace up here.'

The fire had taken a vicious hold, breaking out of the offices and advancing along the corridor. There was a background roar and cracks and crashes as windows broke and furniture collapsed. The other two had set up their pumps and were aiming an ineffectual flow of water at the blazing floor. Larry did the same, but in minutes the water buckets were almost empty and the fire had crept closer. Larry kept pumping until the man next to him shook his elbow. 'It's not going to work,' he shouted. 'We need to get out.'

Larry nodded, but carried on, arms aching, until his water had completely gone. The others were at the top of the stairs, beckoning him to leave it, to run. He took a step towards them, but a sudden pain shot through his arm. The sleeve of his tunic was on fire. The last few drops of water from the hose did no good. Swatting at his sleeve, he flung himself down on the floor and rolled over and over until the flames were doused. He stayed there, out of breath.

A second later everything changed. In front of him, the two men came forwards to help him up. Behind him, he heard the sound of rushing air. Then came a brilliant glow that lit the scene in minute detail. He could see specks of dust on the skirting board and a dead bluebottle on the lino. The two men backed away down the stairs, shouting something he couldn't hear. Flames shot over his head. Then smoke ballooned around him and it was dark again.

On his elbows, he crawled slowly towards the stairs. If I get out, he thought, if I get out...And then he saw Rosemary in front of him, scornful, hateful, ugly with her toad-like words. Then Malcolm, his clear, beautiful face so close that Larry began to cry. There was a crash behind him and the floor shuddered as something big fell. Images came to him of Malcolm and himself in the courtroom, in a prison cell, their names in newsprint. Of Roy and Joanie with loathing in their eyes. He moved forward another few inches until his fingertips felt the curve of the top stair. His escape route. Fire surrounded him now and he could smell his singed hair. He shuffled a little further. How could he let Malcolm go through all that? Rosemary was intent on making him, Larry Lambert, suffer. He wouldn't make Malcolm part of it.

The floor shifted beneath him. Larry closed his eyes. Too weak to bear it, he thought, too old and too weak. There was a buckling and rippling as one of the walls gave way and for a moment Larry felt he was riding a wave, galloping with white horses towards the shore, before everything around him fell and he fell too.

Chapter 14

Joanie
July 1952

The sun was almost too hot, although it wasn't yet noon. Light bounced off the sea and the sand, sharp as diamonds, dazzling her as she watched an oystercatcher strut along the shoreline. Lottie slept beside her on the rug, curled protectively around her doll and sucking her thumb.

Bill shifted in his deckchair and held out his tin mug. 'Any tea left in that flask, dear?'

Joanie unscrewed the cap and poured what was left. 'That's your lot. We can always walk up to the cafe and get some more.'

Bill grunted. 'Not on your life. Soon as we set foot in there, we'll get caught up in it all and we'll never get away. This is my day off and I don't want to see the place again until tomorrow.'

'All right,' Joanie said. 'There's some water if we get thirsty anyway.'

She stood up and stretched. They had come down to the beach early, before it got too busy, so that Lottie could run around safely. It was beginning to fill up now, the sounds of shrieking children louder than the quiet shh and pat of low waves and the wailing of gulls.

She headed for the sea, pausing to pick up a mussel shell, then walked on until the water slid over her feet and skimmed her ankles. Hitching up her skirt, she went further, to where the waves bubbled round her calves and sucked the sand from under her feet as they retreated. Then the cold was too much and she splashed back out again. It was such a simple thing to do, in fact, it was rather childish, yet she never tired of paddling in the sea. And on a day like this, with the sun already drying her legs as she walked back towards Bill and Lottie, she couldn't imagine how she had ever lived without it.

Lottie was awake when she reached the rug. She reached for the shell and stroked its pearly inside and cooed over it.

Bill looked up at her. 'Water too cold?'

'It is, but it's lovely,' Joanie said, turning to look back at the sea.

'You should get some swimming lessons, you know. Wouldn't that be grand? To be able to dive right in?'

Joanie laughed. 'Well, maybe one day. When I've got a bit more time on my hands.' She knelt in front of Lottie. 'You like that, don't you, sweetie?'

Lottie was running her thumb back and forth around the inner curve of the shell. Joanie stroked her hair, untangled a knot with her fingers and pushed a strand out of the child's eyes. 'Want a little drink, darling?'

Lottie raised her head and nodded, gazing at Joanie with eyes that were almost colourless in a certain light. Joanie searched in the beach bag for the beaker, settled Lottie on her knee and held the beaker to her lips. And this, she thought, how did I ever live without this? The weight of my child on my lap, the clean smell of her skin, the way her hand seeks mine.

The breeze strengthened and the rug was flapping at the edges, tipping a nearly empty packet of biscuits into the sand. Bill stretched out his good arm and picked them up. 'Ready to go soon?' he asked. 'It's getting too busy for me.'

Joanie looked around the beach. It wasn't so crowded, but Bill couldn't take too many tourists. 'I get enough of them in the cafe,' he liked to say. 'Don't want to be rubbing up against them everywhere else too.'

'I'll start packing up,' she said.

It didn't take long to throw everything back in the bag and shake out the rug. Bill heaved himself out of the deckchair and began to fold it. 'Here, I'll do that,' Joanie said, taking hold of one side.

'It's all right,' Bill said, shaking her off. 'I'll do it.'

Joanie watched him lay it down on the sand and laboriously fold wood over canvas, his limp arm swinging uselessly by his side. Eventually, it was done and the three of them walked back towards the car.

It was a long way for Lottie to walk and she tripped and grazed her knee as they climbed the steps up to the road. She started to cry. Joanie put down the beach bag and the rug she was carrying and tried to soothe her, but the crying went on.

Bill bent over the wailing child. 'What about a lift on Daddy's shoulders?' he whispered. 'Joanie, put her on.'

Joanie picked up the child and placed her on his shoulders. Lottie stopped crying and gripped his hair, leaning forward with a shout of 'Daddy Horsey!'

Bill held her legs with his good hand and looked at the deckchair he'd been carrying. 'Oh, I forgot about that. Can you manage, love?'

Joanie stuffed the rug on top of the beach bag and picked both up as well as the deck chair. 'I'll manage.' She smiled and leaned her head against his chest for a moment. 'You be Horsey.'

Bill and Lottie both fell asleep in the car. Joanie watched them in the mirror, Bill with his head flung back against the seat, Lottie lying with her head in his lap. She took a long route home so they wouldn't wake. There was noise and bustle everywhere. Tourists drifted over the pavements and across the road in unseeing crowds, as if they had the right of way, and ice cream vans blasted out their tinny tunes.

At the end of the esplanade, she turned away from the beach and headed for home. The streets were quieter here and she relaxed a little.

'Are we home yet?' Bill mumbled from the back seat.

'No, not yet,' Joanie said. 'You go back to sleep.'

She drove on slowly. Bill napped like this only when he was overtired and she wanted to let him rest as long as possible. July and August were hard going at the cafe and they were lucky to get away for the day. Although he complained about the long hours, she still marvelled at how much time she had for herself, even in their busiest periods. The cafe closed at six and then she was free until the next morning. No late nights, no drunks, no stink of beer on her clothes. It was almost luxurious.

They began to climb uphill and she saw the end of their road, and then their house with its pointed wooden porch and heavy Victorian carving around the front window. There were hundreds like it in the town, something she found comforting. So many people living their lives within the same rooms, the same dimensions, and all of us, she liked to think, finding our own way through, making whatever we can of whatever we've got. Sometimes though, when she'd heard the next-door neighbours arguing through the thin party wall or found herself in a conversation about the woman at number nineteen who was no better than she should be, she ached for the space and loneliness of The Dolphin.

She came to a stop in front of the house but didn't turn off the engine. There was lunch to prepare and housework to do, but she didn't want to be inside yet. It wouldn't matter if things were a little late today and anyway, Bill and Lottie were still sleeping; they wouldn't notice if she went for a drive. She put the engine back in gear and set off.

The town ended quite abruptly not far from the house. A road of big Edwardian villas became a lane through rabbit-cropped grass verges and ended in a windy cliff-top car park. She parked near the barrier that stopped people driving over the edge. When they first came up there together, Bill had told her that it was a notorious suicide spot. 'Of course, the barrier doesn't stop them if they're on foot,' he said. 'And sometimes they just park their car and jump anyway.'

She got out of the car. The wind was rushing up over the cliff edge, snatching at her skirt and hair, and she laughed out loud as she struggled to a bench set back from the edge. The grass was white with daisies, opened up fully to the sun, and she leaned back on the seat and did the same. How could you want to kill yourself up here, she thought? She looked out over the miles and miles of sea, then down along the line of the cliffs towards the town, feeling as if she owned it all. This is what makes life good.

A memory came back of driving with Larry in the old Austin van, finding the spot where he would build The Dolphin, and leaning over a fence into the wind. She remembered how bitterly cold it was and how her coat had been blown almost off her shoulders, leaving her shivering but exhilarated. How long ago that day was, and how far away.

She closed her eyes and wondered what they were doing at The Dolphin at that exact moment. Just opening up, she guessed, straightening the chairs and maybe setting out tables on the terrace if it was a nice day there too. Betty – if by any chance she was still there – would be having a quick smoke before it got busy. Perhaps Roy was in charge now. And Rosemary...

Joanie could hardly bear to think about her mother. When she did appear, unbidden, in her thoughts, she could feel Rosemary's poison seep into the present, tainting everything she did and everything she had.

Today though, high up in the sunshine and happy, she felt safe to go back and remember it all. What came back to her now, insistent, was the way she'd left and the last time she saw her mother.

When she had got back to The Dolphin after her decision in the park, she went straight to her room and started to pack. It didn't take long to fill her suitcase with the few decent clothes she possessed. Then she put on her coat – too tight to button now – and the beautiful hat and sat down on the bed to wait.

When a door opened along the landing, she stiffened and gripped the handle of the case. Then there was a quiet knock and Betty's voice, 'Joanie? Are you all right?'

Joanie opened the door and pulled Betty in. 'Shh! Don't let Mum come in.'

Betty stared at her coat and the suitcase. 'Oh God,' she said. 'You didn't go through with it, did you?'

Joanie shook her head and looked down at the floor. 'No. I couldn't, Betty.'

Betty sighed and rubbed her forehead. 'Are you going somewhere then?'

'I don't know where I'm going. Just somewhere else.'

'It'll be hard on you, Joanie. Not many people put out the welcome mat for an unmarried mother. Are you sure you can take it?'

'I don't have much choice, do I? Mum'll throw me out once she knows, so what's the difference? At least this way I won't have a blazing row with her. Anyway, where is she?'

'She's in her room. Listen, you could slip away now. She won't know you've gone. I'll keep a look out for her, delay her in the kitchen if I need to.'

'Not yet. I have to get something before I go. I need to pop into her room for a minute.'

Betty looked at her curiously. 'Well, how on earth are you going to do that?'

'I'll do it when she goes into the bathroom. She always has a bath on a Sunday night.' She sat on the bed again and put the suitcase on her knee. 'I'll just wait until then.'

Betty sat on the dressing table stool and lit a cigarette. 'She won't have a clue what to do without you here.'

'Maybe she'll have to go and work behind the bar!' Joanie laughed. 'I've always wanted to see that. See what a hash she makes of it.'

'Oh God, please not!' Betty laughed too, then looked more serious. 'Will you be all right, Joanie? I never thought you'd be doing something like this.'

Joanie stared down at her hands. 'No, well, neither did I.'

Betty took a long drag on her cigarette and they gave each other tight little smiles. Then they heard Rosemary's door open. Her footsteps passed Joanie's door and continued to the bathroom. There was the sound of the bath running.

Joanie stood up. 'Right then.'

Betty stood too. 'I'll wait just inside my door,' she whispered. 'If I hear her come out, I'll do something to stop her.'

They slipped out of the room and Joanie tiptoed to Rosemary's door, praying it wasn't locked. She turned the handle slowly, felt the catch click, and opened it.

The bedside lamp was on, casting a pink light over the bed and leaving the rest of the room in shadow. She hurried to the dressing table, fleetingly thinking that this was the last time she would see this room, then opened the drawer and searched under the petticoats for the key to the safe.

The safe door creaked horribly as it swung open and Joanie held her breath as she pulled out the hessian bag of takings. It was impossible to tell how much was in there but she extracted some notes and a handful of coins and shoved the bag to the back of the safe again. Then she clanged the door shut – loud as a gunshot! – locked it and put the key back in the drawer.

It had taken no more than a minute but she felt exhausted as she emerged from the room and crept back to her own. She stuffed the notes and coins into her handbag and picked up the suitcase.

But she couldn't go just yet. She went over to the window and gazed out into the dark. There was the same thin moon that had hung over her in the park, cold and pale and far away. She would never see it again from this precise spot. Never lean on the window sill in the summer and watch the house martins fly higher, faster, higher, then swoop unerringly back towards their nest in the eaves. Never again be anywhere that connected her to her father.

The realisation came with a jolt – there was no one left who understood the place. Rosemary would never run her fingers over the brass dolphin window fastenings, or feel the sleek metal of their bodies. She wouldn't follow the trails of copper seaweed or imagine them undulating in a warm coral sea. Not in a thousand years would she sit in the dust of the Ladies Lounge and remember how it used to sparkle like a case of jewels when the sun shone. Worst of all, when she left, no one would remember how much The Dolphin meant to Larry and no one would care about that at all.

There was a sound at the door. Lost in her thoughts, she didn't know if Rosemary had come out of the bathroom or not. Then Betty's voice came very quietly, 'Are you there, Joanie?' The door opened and Betty's face appeared.

'Oh, I am glad,' she said. 'I was listening to the wireless and when I turned it off, everything was quiet. I thought for a minute you must have left without saying goodbye. Are you ready then?'

'Yes, I suppose so.' She tightened her grip on the suitcase. 'Is Mum still in the bathroom?'

Betty looked dismayed. 'I think so. I don't know. Like I said, the wireless was on.'

Joanie quashed a quiver of alarm. 'Oh, she can't be out yet surely. It's much too soon.' She squared her shoulders and looked at Betty, feeling terribly young. 'Will you come downstairs with me?' she whispered.

Betty nodded and opened the door a crack. 'I'll go past the bathroom first,' she said, sidling into the corridor. Joanie took a last look around her room and followed.

With the bathroom door closed it was hard to tell if anyone was inside. Joanie hurried past to the top of the stairs where Betty was waiting and they went down together.

Rosemary was on the bottom step, in her dressing gown, holding a bottle of soda water. 'Oh, there you are,' she said, glancing up. 'The indigestion's terrible tonight. I just came down for some soda water.' She began to slowly climb the stairs.

Joanie had frozen where she was, at the entrance to the Ladies Lounge, and she watched, mesmerised, as her mother climbed towards her. At the mezzanine, Rosemary raised her head and Joanie saw her surprise at the coat and suitcase.

'What's this?'

Joanie couldn't speak. She felt Betty's hand grasp her shoulder.

'Are you running off somewhere? What's going on?'

Joanie tried to button her coat across her belly.

'Well?'

'I'm leaving.' It was a huge effort to whisper the words.

Rosemary frowned, then tutted, 'What silly idea have you got now? Where on earth do you think you're going?'

'I don't know.'

'Then why all this?' She came closer.

Joanie instinctively put her hand on her belly, but Rosemary batted it away and stared hard at her.

'Oh, so that's it, is it? You're pregnant.'

'Yes, Mum.'

Rosemary breathed in sharply, drew back her hand and slapped Joanie's cheek.

'Hey!' Betty said, pushing Rosemary away.

'You stay out of this! Don't think I don't know where she's got this behaviour from.' Rosemary turned to Joanie, her face warped with disgust. 'I should have known you'd end up this way. Ever since we came here, this place has been corrupting this family. First your father, now you.' She sneered at Joanie's puzzled expression. 'Oh, yes, he wasn't the saint you think he is. The filthy, wicked things he did. Him and that Malcolm. If he wasn't dead, he'd be in prison.'

Joanie began to cry. 'Don't say such a horrible thing, Mum. You don't know anything. About him or about me.'

'I know he was a pervert, that he did horrible perverted things with Malcolm. And you?' She looked Joanie up and down. 'You're just a tart. Get out then.'

Joanie ran down the stairs. She heard Betty coming after her and together they raced through the Circular Lounge and across the main bar. The windows were feathered in frost.

'It's freezing tonight,' Betty said. 'You aren't going to walk, are you?'

Joanie pulled out the key to the van. 'No, I'm going to drive.'

Betty grinned. 'Come on then.'

They pushed the doors open and stepped into the dark. It was bitterly cold in the yard. Joanie opened the van door and flung her case inside.

Betty hugged her. 'Good luck, Joanie. Write and tell me where you are.'

'I don't think I can, because Mum might open it. I'm taking something else as well as the van, you see.'

Betty began to laugh. 'Aren't you full of surprises tonight? Try and get in touch, somehow, won't you?'

'I will. Listen, will you be all right? After all that with Mum, are you going to stay?'

Betty shrugged. 'I don't know. We'll see. I'll be fine, one way or another.'

They looked at each other and smiled.

'Bye then, Betty.'

'Bye, Joanie.'

Joanie got into the van and reversed slowly out of the yard, hoping that the sound of the engine couldn't be heard from inside. She waved as Betty disappeared into the darkness, then drove through the gate and away from The Dolphin.

A seagull landed on the grass near the bench. Joanie watched it hop closer, hoping for food, its feathers ruffling in the wind. After a few moments, it lumbered away across the daisies and launched itself into the air again.

That cold night seemed so long ago now. And as if it had happened to someone else. Yet she remembered the fear she'd felt driving down the hill in a stolen van, with stolen money in her bag and no driving licence. Rosemary's words echoed in her head until she thought she'd be sick and she had to stop the van to compose herself. And then she'd driven on, out of that world and towards this one, though she didn't know it at the time.

A car door slammed and she heard Bill calling, 'Hello over there.'

She turned to see him standing by the car and waving. He was smiling, squinting into the sun, the wind plucking at his hair the same way it had the first time she saw him.

When the train pulled into the station that early morning, the guard calling out, 'All change,' she stayed in her seat. As soon as she stepped onto the platform, it would be real and she would have to decide what to do and how to live. Or perhaps she could just keep travelling instead.

But the guard came round then and insisted on helping her with her bag. She found herself walking out of the station onto an unknown street in an unknown town. For a few minutes she stood there, trying to choose which direction to take. In the end, she turned left, walking slowly past closed shops until she reached the end of the road and hesitated again.

'Come on, Joanie, pull yourself together,' she said aloud and turned right.

The sun had come up and as she walked, she noticed a brightness ahead. Seagulls wheeling in the sky. She turned a corner and the road opened onto a wide promenade, a beach, a pier, waves washing on the sand.

It was so unexpected she stopped. When the van broke down, she'd walked until she found a train station, hauling her bag, shivering with cold. Then she'd taken the first train that came, the destination not known but hopefully far enough away for Rosemary never to find her. And now here she was by the sea.

She carried on, crossed the promenade, passed between two turreted pavilions and stepped onto the wooden boards of the pier. The weak winter sun touched her cheek as she walked towards the building at the end. In the doorway, a man was lifting bottles from a crate, one at a time. His left arm hung loosely at his side and as she approached, she could hear him swearing. The bottles were the same brand of lemonade they sold at The Dolphin and she smiled at the familiarity.

'Can I help?' she said, putting down her bag.

He looked up and grinned. 'Well, if you like, Miss.' He held a bottle towards her.

She ignored it and picked up the crate, squeezing past him to take it inside. Behind her, she heard him laugh. 'Well, I never! I could use a strong girl like you. Want to come and work for me?'

Inside the cafe, everything was soft green, lit by the palest of sunshine. Through the windows the sea glittered, stretching away until it merged with the sky. She had come as far as she could.

She turned back and nodded. 'Yes. I'll work for you.'

With an effort, she pulled herself back to the present.

'Hello,' she called to Bill, the wind whipping the word away as soon as she said it. He gestured at his watch and shouted something she couldn't hear. It must be lunchtime, she thought, probably long past lunchtime, in fact. She stood and walked towards the car, towards Bill, towards Lottie still sleeping on the back seat, towards home.

Chapter 15

Lottie
May 1973

Dan planned their route on a road map he'd bought especially. He drew a red line along the roads they were to follow and marked the start and finish points with a heavily inked X.

The night before, Lottie opened the map and traced the red line with her finger, watching it veer away from the sea and run far inland. She counted the squares as the route crossed them; it was about ninety miles. Dan had estimated the journey would take about three hours. They were leaving early to arrive in good time, though in good time for what, Lottie didn't know.

It was a warm evening and all the windows were open. From her seat at the kitchen table, she caught the scent of the early honeysuckle by the fence. Dan was in the greenhouse, finishing his tidy-up, and she thought she probably ought to go out and help. But she stayed where she was, thinking instead about what she'd be doing the following evening.

Dan and Joanie had visited The Dolphin over the past few months, but she'd refused to go. Her stand was pointless, she knew, but it made her feel better, less disloyal to Bill, to take no interest. Dan had returned subdued from his first visit and admitted to Lottie that they might have taken on too much. Briefly, she had felt triumphant until she realised that she was stuck with it anyway.

She folded the map and put it on top of the bag she'd prepared for the journey. They planned to stop for a picnic on the way so earlier Joanie had brought crisps and pork pies, more animated than Lottie had ever seen her.

'Pick me up at eight and we'll miss the rush hour,' she'd said, tucking the food down the side of the bag. 'And don't pack away the picnic rug. We'll need it for when we stop.'

She'd gone over the map with Dan, nodding as he explained the route. 'I think that's the way I came before. I drove as far as Sleaford, then I got the train.' She smiled. 'That was a miserable night waiting in the station. Freezing cold and no idea where I was going to end up.'

Lottie turned away. As their departure grew closer, Joanie had become quite talkative about The Dolphin. Lottie couldn't bear to listen, but Dan would sit patiently and ask questions as another story unfolded. 'It sounds pretty incredible,' he told Lottie. 'I know the building work is a bit daunting, but I think we're really going to love it there.'

Now, she picked up the bag and put it in the hallway ready for the morning, doubting very much she would love The Dolphin.

A delicate spring dusk had started to gather, deepening the shadows, furring the rooflines of the houses opposite, and she was suddenly gripped by panic. This might be the last time she would ever see this street, this view. The last time she would ever see the cafe. She went to the back door and called out, 'I'm going for a walk, Dan. Won't be too long.' Inside the greenhouse, he looked up and cupped his hand to his ear, but she pretended she hadn't seen and hurried on out.

It was nearly ten o'clock and the hill was alive with the sounds and scents of late evening – baths running, roses, the last few children still playing out, sausages cooking, televisions. When she reached the Esplanade, she noted the drop of waves onto the beach and the smell of damp seaweed.

She walked slowly along the pier. The arcades and candy floss stands were still open and crowds sauntered between them. There was a mood of pleasure at such a beautiful evening so early in the year, and a determination to make the most of it. Lottie drifted, feeling out of place and lonely. She stopped before she reached the cafe and leaned on the balustrade to take her last look.

The new owners were halfway through painting it, the old green colour only visible in a few places. From the ground up it was a harsh acid yellow, jarring even in the soft twilight. Inside, the old Formica tables were piled in the middle of the room, waiting, she supposed, to be thrown out and replaced.

It wasn't hers anymore. It may as well have fallen into the sea, as she'd sometimes imagined. It was gone.

Road works delayed them and a heavy shower meant they had the picnic in the car. By the time they drove through a nondescript town and up a hill through a 1930s estate, Lottie felt stale and irritable. She wound down the window to breathe fresh air.

'Here's the turning, Dan, remember. Left here,' Joanie said, and twisted around to talk to Lottie in the back. 'When I first came here with my father, this was a tiny country lane. You could practically touch the verges on both sides. Now look at it.'

New houses, some of them still unfinished, lined the road.

They looked smart, Lottie thought, with their big picture windows and built-in garages. How lovely to come home to one of these, to pull up in a nice car on one of those smooth driveways, unlock the glass front door, slip inside, kick off her shoes and walk barefoot on a fluffy rug. She sighed.

The road dipped and the houses came to an end, replaced by scruffy woodland. At the bottom of the hill, an ugly concrete bridge spanned a trickle of a stream. 'It used to be a ford,' Joanie said, gazing into the trees. 'That bridge is new.'

They went up again, past land that looked uncared for, not farmed, not built on. Then at the top of the hill, Lottie spotted The Dolphin.

Dan turned into the car park and stopped the car. Joanie was out of the door before the hand brake was on, striding towards the steps of the decrepit building with the keys in her hand.

Dan stretched and yawned. 'Well, then,' he said, looking at Lottie in the rear-view mirror, 'Home sweet home. Shall we go in?' He got out, stretched again, then opened her door.

Very slowly, she got out. The car park, the steps, the terrace were all covered in weeds. Clumps of rosebay willow herb swayed in the gutters of the building and the walls were patterned with faded graffiti. It must have been empty for years.

She climbed the steps and paused at the top. Sun warmed the back of her neck. A swallow scooped flies from the air. Behind her, Dan grunted as he unloaded the bags from the car. Inside, Joanie was humming, opening windows, moving things. A smell of old, smoky damp and dirt came through the front door and Lottie glimpsed a large room with peeling wallpaper and broken floorboards. This was where she came from, where the messy, painful past was made. She took a breath and crossed the threshold.

September 1973

When she was ready to scream, the view saved her. On the window seat in the Circular Bar, she would hug her knees and stare across the landscape. The tiny cars creeping along wire-thin roads, the dinky houses and toy trains all gave her hope. Other lives existed, other things were possible. The Dolphin wasn't everything.

Today, fog obscured the view. Lottie shivered as she gazed at the depthless white beyond the grassy edge of the cliff. With all the glass in the curving tower and no proper heating installed yet, the window seat was cold and draughty, but she didn't move. She was grateful that at least the roof had been fixed and the damp was beginning to dry.

Sounds reached her from the Ladies Lounge on the mezzanine. Dan was attempting to re-silver the most badly spotted mirrors, but it was a difficult job and he was making slow progress. She could hear him now, coaxing the silver backing to take, swearing when it went wrong. They should have found a professional to do it but there was no money for that, no money for anything. Dan had taken it on, as he'd taken on so many things.

Lottie yawned. She ought to be packing bulbs in the outhouse, but it was an unappealing job and she'd been putting it off all morning. The outhouse was even colder than the Circular Bar and inhabited by large spiders. There would be a movement, then one would cross the workbench in front of her in a horrible urgent scuttle. She had learned not to shriek, but they still revolted her.

There were footsteps on the stairs. 'Hi,' Dan said, wiping his hands on his trousers. 'I thought you were doing that order.'

'In a minute,' Lottie said, standing up. 'Want a cup of coffee?'

'OK.'

The fog brightened everything, creating whiteness at every window, and she felt exposed as she went upstairs to the kitchen. She switched on the kettle, thinking how much she hated this room. It was cramped and mean, always dirty even though she and Dan had scrubbed it down with sugar soap. The cooker was ancient and the sink was chipped. When she washed up, she imagined germs breeding in the water. The cupboards smelt stale and when she reached for the cups, she tried not to inhale.

There had been no fridge when they arrived. A new one gleamed quietly in its corner, satisfyingly white and clean. She gave it a little pat when she opened it to get the milk. How on earth had anyone managed without a fridge? 'We had the pantry, of course,' her mother had told her. 'That kept things cool enough. And we didn't mind so much in those days. If something was beginning to go off, we ate it anyway.'

Life at The Dolphin twenty or thirty years before disgusted her. She imagined it as grubby and uncomfortable, perpetually difficult. Joanie had laughed when Lottie said as much. 'This kitchen, this whole place, was the bee's knees when we moved in. All mod cons.' She ran her hand along the roughened edge of the sink. 'Dad built it like that.'

But Joanie talked less and less about the past, about anything at all. She went out on unexplained errands and sat silently at meals, barely present. It was as if she had used up her energy getting to The Dolphin and, now that they were here, she had nothing left to make anything of it. Lottie stirred the coffee and wondered where she was now. She had gone out soon after breakfast and still wasn't back, though it was nearly lunchtime.

Dan was back at one of the mirrors when Lottie took the coffee down. He had taken it off the wall and laid it across two tables, leaving a fan-shaped patch of palest green behind. She ran over the outline with her fingers.

'That green is the original colour, I think,' Dan said. 'Eau-de-nil, your mum called it. Must have looked incredible in here when it was new.'

For a moment, Lottie saw the room in its heyday, a dazzling box of light. She shook her head, determined to find nothing good about it, now or then.

'I'll go and pack up that order,' she said.

The plan had been to restore The Dolphin to its 1930s splendour and open it in November. 'We'll catch the Christmas trade then,' Joanie had said. 'Make a bit of a splash. There'll be nowhere else like it.'

The trouble was that very little of its splendour remained. Lottie wondered what her mother had actually seen when she came on those visits, before they moved in. Blinded by nostalgia perhaps, she thought, and unable to see that the main bar was battered plywood and bare walls and that the Circular Bar had been stripped of everything except the window seat. The mirrors in the Ladies Lounge were the only hint of The Dolphin's opulent past.

When the bank statement came at the end of the month, Lottie opened it anxiously. There wasn't much left. The only regular income was Joanie's widow's pension, with a few pounds now and then from the bulbs. The expenditure column was crowded with figures.

She passed it to Dan and watched him wince as he read it.

'Not very cheerful reading, is it?' he said. 'We'd better get this place open and some cash coming in.'

Lottie sighed. 'Or we could give up the whole stupid idea and go home again.'

Dan laughed. 'You're joking, yeah? We've gone much too far for that.'

'Who says we've gone too far? If we cut our losses while there's still some money in the bank, it won't be too late.'

'But your mum's so desperate to make it work.'

'Yes, I know Mum's obsessed with this place, but she's living in cloud cuckoo land. There's hardly anything left of what it was before. It's just a wreck, an ugly wreck.'

'She can't do it on her own.'

'I know she can't so she needs to drop the whole thing and we can get back to normal and carry on with our lives.'

Dan frowned. 'Lottie, don't be ridiculous. The cafe's gone, remember? We can't go back to how we were. It doesn't exist anymore.'

She couldn't bear to hear it said out loud. As long as it wasn't voiced, the possibility – the very slight, fragile possibility – of somehow going back was still there. She picked up the bank statement and waved it at Dan. 'We can't exist here either. These figures say it all, Dan. We're barely surviving.'

'Look, Lottie, I know you don't want to be here and

there's all this stuff about your real dad, but don't you want some kind of future?' He sighed. 'If you could just make a bit more effort maybe it could work. It's like you've given up before you've even tried.'

'Are you saying I'm not pulling my weight?'

'It's just that...'

'Who do you think has been doing all the bloody bulbs? I've spent God knows how many hours in that poky shed with the spiders.'

'We need to get down to work on The Dolphin. All of us.'

'I'll stop potting up any of the bulbs then.'

'I didn't mean that.'

'I can't do both.'

'No, neither can I!' He flung up his arms and for a second she thought he was going to hit her. 'Forget the fucking bulbs for now then,' he shouted. 'In fact, let's forget them altogether.' He stormed out, and from the window, she saw him striding towards the outhouse.

She felt like screaming, but instead filled a bucket with soapy water and began to scrub angrily at the shelves behind the bar. The chant in her head piped up. Hate it here, hate it here, hate it here.

The suds turned black as she worked, loosening decades of dirt and smoke from the painted wood. Underneath the foam was a grittiness that set her teeth on edge and she wished she'd thought to wear rubber gloves. See, she told Dan silently, I'm not shirking. I can do the mucky jobs.

When the water was too dirty to do any good, she went outside to empty the bucket. Dan was digging at the far end of the garden, a sack beside him on the grass. For a minute she watched him stab the spade into the earth and hurl shovelfuls of soil to the side. He still looked angry.

It took more than an hour and numerous buckets of water to get all the shelves clean. Every time she went outside to empty the bucket, Dan was digging or crouched on the ground by the sack, always with his back towards her.

The cleaned shelves made a bright spot in the gloom of the main bar and, pleased with the result, she looked around for the next job. The bar itself was covered in rubbish, things the builders had left behind when they came to repair the floor and other bits and pieces that had accumulated there. She found an empty packing case and started to throw it all in. As she worked, she remembered how excited Joanie had been about the bar when they first arrived. 'There was a copper relief along the front of it, waves and dolphins. And look, it's the still same shape, that curve round the room so it must be underneath somewhere.' But when they prised off a section of the plywood panelling there was only plasterwork beneath. 'How could they?' Joanie muttered. 'How could anyone destroy something so beautiful?'

Lottie heaved the full packing case out of the way, catching a corner of it on the exposed plaster. A chunk fell away which she swept up. She brushed the crumbled edges and more disintegrated as she brushed. It's damp, she thought. We're going to have to redo it. Then a larger lump broke off and a dark surface appeared behind. Reaching in, she ran her fingers over something cold and metallic. Rippled waves and the backs of dolphins? She pulled at another bigger lump. More waves, more dolphins and something else. Perhaps mermaids.

Joanie had chipped at the plaster when they first removed the plywood, but she just hadn't gone far enough. It was only where the plaster was damp that it came away easily. The rest held fast to its secret.

She knelt down on the floor to get a better look. It was hard to see any detail, but where the light caught, she could make out curves and loops that could be dolphins' tails or mermaids' hair. Curves and loops that, even in the tiny, dark portion that was exposed, were intricately and beautifully designed.

She sat back on her heels. This was what Joanie meant, the spark that set The Dolphin apart. For an instant, she felt like she did in the cafe long ago, when it was full of strange and exotic possibilities. Was that what her grandfather had wanted when he built it? The feeling that anything could happen there? She leaned in again and smoothed her hand over the metal, glad that he had.

It was very quiet in the bar. Dan was still in the garden and Joanie was upstairs making lunch. If she covered up the relief, neither of them would know anything about it and she could carry on wearing down Dan's resistance, persuading him that it was all a lost cause. She might even win in the end.

Or she could show them what she'd found and see what came of it. She could help restore its strange beauty.

For a minute or two she stayed where she was, staring at the dark space in the plaster, then she stood up.

'Mum!' she called. 'Mum, come and see!' She went to the Circular Bar and shouted again. 'Mum, you have to see this.'

She grabbed Joanie's hand as she came downstairs and dragged her into the main bar. 'Look,' she whispered and watched her face as she took in the broken plaster and the dark gleam behind.

Joanie reached in just as Lottie had. And smiled.

In half an hour they had uncovered a patch of copper about two feet square. Joanie rubbed a tea towel over a small section until it shone auburn. 'Dad spent hours and hours polishing this. It was like the sunset when it was all done. It lit up the whole room. Have you told Dan yet? Where is he?'

'He's outside.'

'Go and tell him, Lottie. I'll carry on.'

Dan was sitting on the terrace steps, his face smudged with dirt, his eyes closed. She sat down beside him.

'Finished what you were doing?'

He nodded.

'What were you doing anyway?'

'Just some gardening.'

'We've found the copper panel in the bar.'

'Have you? I thought you didn't care about any of that.'

'It's beautiful, looks just like Mum said.'

He glanced at her then turned away again.

'Come and see, Dan. You'll be amazed.'

'So you're all excited about it now?' He picked up a pebble and threw it hard down the garden. 'Earlier on you were desperate to get away from the place. What about tomorrow, what'll you want to do then?'

Lottie rubbed away a patch of moss from the step and didn't answer.

'I can't live like this, Lottie. Your mum's been in a daze ever since we arrived, you've been moping about like the world's ended. We burnt our bridges when we came here, but no one else seems to have noticed. If this doesn't work there's nothing else to fall back on.'

'What about Kenya?'

'We couldn't afford the plane ticket now, let alone any land.'

'The bulbs?' she said hesitantly. 'Maybe if we worked on them properly.'

'Too late.'

'What do you mean?'

'None left.' He swept his arm across the garden to the newly turned earth in all the borders. 'They're all gone.'

That afternoon, Lottie and Joanie pulled away the rest of the plywood and loosened the damp patches of plaster. They soaked the dry sections with water and chivvied away at the edges with a screwdriver and chisel. 'Don't scratch it,' Joanie warned. 'Whatever you do, don't scratch it.' By the end of the day, about a third of the panel was visible.

They stepped back to look at it. Dolphins leapt out of the stylised waves, mermaids swam within them. Seaweed borders trailed along the top and bottom.

'I don't know where it all came from,' Joanie said. 'Dad only ever went to the seaside once that I know of. And then he built this place. But have you noticed how the hills roundabout are like waves? He seemed to come alive here. With us he was, I don't know, ordinary. When he was here, he was a different person. It would kill him to see it like this.' Joanie smoothed her hand across a polished patch of copper. 'But we'll get it right. It'll be beautiful again.'

Lottie watched a rabbit hop cautiously across the ragged lawn. 'Dan's planted all the snowdrops, you know. There's no bulb business anymore.'

'Has he? Why's he done that?'

Lottie shrugged, not wanting to admit she might have pushed him to it. 'So it's all or nothing now I suppose. Like Dan says, there's nothing else to fall back on.' She immediately wished she hadn't said it. She saw the three of them standing on the edge of the rocks, facing The Dolphin and leaning back, further and further, until they fell into nothing.

'Well,' Joanie said. 'The Dolphin will be all right.'

That night, Lottie couldn't sleep. She rolled over and stared at Dan's silent outline, the slight movements as he breathed. They had barely spoken all evening. It took a lot to make Dan really angry. It must have been building for weeks, months even.

He grunted and his legs twitched under the blankets. She gave up on sleep, got out of bed and started downstairs. The treads were rough under her feet, gritty with dirt and dust.

A full moon lit the Ladies Lounge. The mirrored walls reflected it back, silver and black, like the negative of a photograph. Lottie continued on down. The Circular Bar looked bare and cold. The main bar hunched in shadow, the light not penetrating here. She pulled out a chair from a pile in a corner and sat down.

She had to give in now. She had to accept that this was what she had and this was where they were and that she had to get on with it. If he was here, Bill would know what to do, how to make it all right. But he was gone and he wasn't even hers anyway.

At the window, she looked out at the car park. There was something else she had to do, something that had been gnawing at her. She had to decide whether to try and find Patrick.

A cloud passed over the moon, deepening the shadows. How lonely it must have been up here, she thought. If she looked in the direction of the new houses, she could see a few street lights, hear a car in the distance but when The Dolphin was first built, it was far away from the rest of the world.

The moon reappeared and at the same time a car drove

past. Its headlights streamed over the bar and were gone. So this was what life had been like for her mother – boredom, drudgery, frustration and no other choices. Patrick must have been a godsend.

Had it all started in this room? She went to stand behind the bar. Perhaps Joanie was here and Patrick was leaning there, drinking what? Beer? Cider? Whisky? Chatting easily or awkwardly? Each trying to read the other. Hoping for something to come of it.

And I came of it, she thought. Even if it all went wrong – and it obviously had – that's what happened and I can't pretend otherwise.

Would it make things better or worse if she knew? There was no way of knowing unless she tracked him down; she didn't know if she could face that.

The next day Joanie went out early and didn't come back until nearly three o'clock. Lottie was attempting to weed the terrace when she saw the car turn in at the gate. Joanie got out stiffly, as if she'd been driving for a long time, then stood very still.

Lottie thought how tired she looked. But then they all looked tired. 'Hi, Mum,' she called.

'Hello, love. Getting somewhere with the weeds?'

'Not really. It's going to take forever. Have you had a good day?'

Joanie sat on the terrace wall. 'I did something that maybe I shouldn't have done.' She gave a bleak little smile. 'I went to see my brother.'

'What?'

'He works down in the town. Never moved away. He's with the council.' She bent to pull a weed from the crack between the paving stones. 'Funny that he's been here all along. And hasn't done anything about The Dolphin. Just let it go to rack and ruin.'

'What was he like?' Lottie said, struggling with too many questions.

'Oh, he wouldn't see me; wouldn't even come out of his office. He sent a note. Look.' Joanie took a piece of paper from her pocket.

Joanie, you have a real nerve turning up at my office like this. I have no wish to see you today or any other time. Your sins are neither forgotten nor forgiven and you can be certain that Mother went to her grave feeling exactly the same way. Please do not visit me again. It was signed, *Roy Lambert,* in pen strokes that had almost gone through the paper.

'Oh, Mum,' Lottie sighed.

'So after that I went to the Registry Office,' Joanie said. 'To see about Mum.' She paused to blow her nose. 'And they let me see her death certificate. 1957 she went. Sixteen years ago. I could have come back sixteen years ago.'

Lottie sat down next to her. It was a grey, chilly afternoon. Everything was still and quiet, as if the place had been waiting for news like this. Waiting to know what to do next. She picked at a loose bit of mortar. 'What about...' It was hard to say it out loud. 'Did you find out about Patrick?'

Joanie looked at the ground. 'I think it would have to be you who does that. If you decide that's what you want to do.'

They sat in silence.

'We'd better go in,' Lottie said, noticing it had started to drizzle.

Joanie nodded, but they both stayed where they were until the rain grew heavier.

November 1973

At five o'clock, Lottie went outside to open the gate. She was used to it now, the way it had to be hitched up so it didn't catch on the ground and pushed hard to reach the hook on the wall. When it was done, she climbed onto the top bar and gazed at The Dolphin.

Against a darkening sky and with the lights on in the bar, it glimmered gold and amber. Inside, every surface was polished, every carpet was swept, every glass was stacked in a perfect pyramid on the shelves behind the bar. She'd been scrupulous about that every night since they had opened. Everything had to be right. How else would she know what was possible?

She shivered as a gust of wind caught her back and rattled the dry leaves collected by the wall. There always seemed to be a wind here. It chased over the grass in the field opposite, then blew straight at The Dolphin, streaming past the tower and into the empty air above the rocks. At night she heard it butt against the walls and windows and felt as if the whole building might actually be flying.

She jumped off the gate when she heard a car coming slowly up the hill and smoothed her skirt. It was surprising how many customers turned up early. Best to be ready.

She went back inside to make one last check, then switched on the tape player. Joanie disapproved of the tape player on the grounds there had been no music in the past, but Dan and Lottie had installed one anyway.

'You need to create the right atmosphere,' Dan said. 'Make it seem authentic 1930s.'

'Having no music would be authentic,' Joanie said.

'Yes, but the music makes it *seem* authentic.'

Pennies from Heaven started up. A car turned in at the gate. Lottie put on her welcoming face and stood behind the bar.

A middle-aged woman came in, took a few steps, then paused and stared at the copper reliefs, the wall panels, the sheer extravagance and beauty. She smiled.

'Evening,' Lottie said. 'What can I get you?'

'I heard the place had been done up. Looks marvellous. I just wondered, is there someone called Joanie here?' She tapped a packet of Silk Cut on the bar and drew out a cigarette. 'A Joanie Lambert?'

Lottie stared. She had a silky blonde chignon and a smart camel coat with a fur collar. She was a similar age to her mother, but she was infinitely more glamorous. How come Joanie knew anyone like this?

'I'll just go and find her. Can I get you a drink while you're waiting?'

'Campari-soda please, dear.'

Lottie made the drink then went to the Circular Bar and called up the stairs, 'Mum, there's someone here to see you.'

Joanie's voice came down from the Ladies Lounge. 'Two minutes. I'm just finishing the stock take. Who is it?'

'I don't know.'

When she returned, she felt the woman watching her.

'Did I hear you shout for your mum? Is Joanie your mum?'

'Yes. She won't be long.'

'Well, bloody hell.' The woman smiled, apparently delighted. 'That is a surprise.' She blew out smoke and leaned across the bar to get a good look at Lottie. 'You're the spit of your mum when she was your age. I should have known.'

Lottie busied herself with slicing lemons, unsure how to respond.

'What's your name, dear?'

'Lottie.'

'That's cute. I guessed it wouldn't be Rosemary!' She gave a sharp laugh.

'Betty?'

When Lottie looked up, her mother was at the end of the bar, staring at them both with a look of disbelief. Joanie took a step forward. 'Good God, is that really you?'

The woman smiled the same delighted smile as before. 'Well, Joanie Lambert. Look at you, you clever old thing.'

The two women embraced, Joanie with tears in her eyes. 'I so wanted to write. But it was too risky, Betty. Did you understand?'

'Once I heard how you'd taken the money I did.' Betty laughed again. 'Oh, Joanie, what you did to your mum!' She collected herself and gestured towards Lottie. 'And is this?'

Joanie nodded and reached over to squeeze Lottie's arm. 'This is Lottie. Lottie, this is Betty. She worked here with me for a long time after the war. Actually, she lived here too.' Joanie's eyes were shining and her face was flushed. 'We went through a lot together.'

Lottie was unsure what to think. She smelled smoke and a rich, heavy perfume when Betty leaned forwards. 'Never underestimate your mum,' Betty said. 'She's stronger than she looks.'

That's what Dad said too, Lottie thought. And it's true. Here I am cutting lemons behind the bar at The Dolphin because she wanted to come.

Joanie had made herself a drink and was sitting on a bar stool next to Betty, looking livelier than Lottie had ever seen her. Lottie watched the wide smile, the animated expression, the gestures around the room as she pointed out the work they'd done. She realised how rarely she saw her mother like this, relaxed and open, and she understood how much Joanie had hidden, how much she couldn't say. How much she had needed to come back to The Dolphin.

She tried to listen to the conversation, but more customers arrived and only snatches reached her.

'So how long did you stay afterwards?' Joanie asked.

'Only a few weeks,' Betty said. 'And it certainly wasn't pleasant.'

Lottie fetched ice from the machine and missed the rest. Tuning in again, the topic had changed.

'God, no, not Frank!' Betty laughed. 'Geoff's much nicer. And he's never minded about my... you know... past.'

'Then we both found someone good,' Joanie said. She glanced at Lottie and leaned in closer towards Betty. Lottie strained to hear.

'Do you know what happened to him?'

She bent down, pretending to count the mixers in the fridge. Did they mean Patrick?

'I heard he married an Irish girl and emigrated. Canada? Australia? I don't know.'

When she looked up, Joanie was gazing down at her, her face full of love and worry. And now she knew. Patrick was out of her reach, too far away to find. Lottie pictured him running to catch the boat, dragging his bride behind him, desperate to get away before she – Lottie – snagged him in a tangle of nappies and crying and prams and baby talk. That was, if he even knew about her.

Joanie was asking her something. 'Lottie? Are you OK?'

He had done nothing for her. Never held her hand, dried her tears, kissed her cheek. Bill had done all that and more.

He'd taken her on and made her his daughter. She didn't need anyone else. Patrick was just a name.

'Lottie? Are you OK?'

'I'm fine, Mum, absolutely fine.' And she found that she was.

February 1974

Joanie was at the table when Lottie came into the kitchen. The kettle was boiling on the little camping stove they had been using during the power cuts.

'Tea?' Joanie asked.

'Please'

Lottie sat down and held her hands to the stove to warm them. It was a cold morning and she could see nubs of ice on the windows. 'Another day in paradise.'

'It's like being up here during the war all over again,' Joanie said. 'And then all those years of rationing afterwards. It's no more fun this time round.' She passed Lottie a mug of tea.

'We're going to get some wood for the fire in the bar this morning,' Lottie said. 'At least it'll be warm down there.'

They freewheeled down the hill to save petrol and parked at the bridge. A grainy light came through the trees and underfoot the ground was soggy with a winter's worth of fallen leaves. Veering off the path, they began to climb uphill, looking for wood that wasn't too damp.

They found a huge dead limb from a beech tree lying on the ground. Dan inspected it to see if it was dry enough to chop up.

'I don't think it's too bad,' he said. 'If we hack off these branches here, we can drag them back to the car and chop them into firewood at home.'

They set to work. The wood was dense and it was hard to make any impression on it. Lottie's axe kept slipping off. It took ages to make the pile of cut branches, and three slow, awkward journeys to drag them to the car. When they were all loaded in the boot Lottie gave a sigh of relief. 'Thank God for that. It'd better bloody burn!'

She stood on the bridge. The stream was muddy and sluggish, clotted with leaves. 'I wish it was still a ford here, like Mum said it used to be. Then when it rained it would be like a moat around The Dolphin and no one could come and disturb us.'

Dan joined her. 'We'd starve.'

'Oh, we'd manage somehow. We'd have to shoot pigeons or rooks or something. Mum said they were cut off in 1947 when it snowed. They managed.'

She tried to imagine what it must have been like, trapped in The Dolphin in that freezing winter. But then Joanie had been trapped there anyway, with Roy and Betty and the difficult mother that she didn't talk about. Trapped by circumstance and convention and duty. The snow wasn't really necessary. She threw a stick into the water and watched it spin in the current. Yet Joanie had returned. The Dolphin had pulled her back, hauled her in like a fish in a net, even though she'd been so unhappy there.

'Let's get going,' Dan said. 'I'm freezing.'

With the cargo of heavy wood, the engine struggled to get up the hill and by the time they reached the top, Lottie could smell hot oil. A weak sun came through the grey sky and the light lifted a little as they drove slowly into the car park. The copper roof of the tower gleamed a bright, almost summery, green.

They unloaded the wood by the outhouse and Dan went inside to change his clothes. Lottie took the mat from the car boot and went to shake out the leaves and twigs over the compost heap in the garden. As she crossed the terrace, she stopped to look in the pool. The dark blue tiles seemed to disappear into themselves. She stared into its depths and imagined the mermaids she'd dreamed about at the cafe suddenly swimming up into the cold water.

Joanie waved from inside the bar and came out to stand beside her. 'Did you get some firewood?' she asked.

Lottie nodded.

Joanie peered over the edge of the pool. 'It looks as if it goes on forever, doesn't it?' she said. 'I used to think it was connected to the sea somehow. A tunnel underground that brought everything up to Dad, all the carvings and mirrors and things. Anything he wanted.'

And Lottie understood why she was going to stay at The Dolphin, why Joanie had returned, why it was built in the first place. She walked down the garden to the compost heap. Dan's snowdrops were coming up, hundreds of green shoots reaching from under the earth, some of them already in bloom.

Acknowledgements

The Dolphin has been a long time in the making and there are many people to thank.

Lynn Michell – for having faith in this book and making it happen.

Linda Lee Welch for helping to shape The Dolphin and for endless encouragement during its very slow gestation.

Tricia Durdey and Laura Wake for critiques, comments and keeping me going – I so value your friendship.

Noel Williams whose insightful comments I very much miss.

The ZenAzzuri Writers from whom I learned so much over so many years – in particular Elise Valmorbida, Roger Levy, Anne Marie Neary, Steve Mullins and Simon Campbell.

The most enlightened employer, AVN, who enabled me to do my MA, where The Dolphin started – thank you Shane and Jenny Lukas.

And of course, to my family – Lee, Anna, Frances, my mother Sheila and much missed father John, my sister Jane – love you all.